POUNDING ANGEL

POUNDING HEARTS BOOK FIVE

IZZY SWEET

SEAN MORIARTY

DIRTY NOTHINGS PUBLISHING

ABOUT THIS BOOK

Once I was on top of the world. I had the title, fame, and
respect.
Then everything came crashing down.
I lost my title and my best friend.
Unable to cope, I fell into the bottle and never wanted to
come out.
Until Bree walked into my life with her gorgeous eyes
and kissable lips.
She lights a fire inside me I haven't felt in months.
She's awoken the beast that refuses to bow down and takes
what he wants.
With her in my sights, I'm fucking unstoppable.
I'm going to get my title back, kick some ass, and win the
girl.

"Emmett Bailey just tapped! Oh my god, Bailey just tapped out!" Marshawn Anderson yells through my TV speakers.

Pressing rewind, I watch the same fifteen seconds over again.

There, live and in living color, I watch as Jamey Silva tweaks my arm past the point of no return. My shoulder makes a pop that's heard over the screaming fans. I didn't plan on tapping out while he was trying to rip my arm from my body, but the moment I felt all the ligaments tear and the shoulder pop out of socket, I tapped.

I press rewind on the DVR and watch it again.

"Emmett Bailey just tapped! Oh my god, Bailey just tapped out!"

"I can't believe it either, Marshawn. I just can't—" Jack Harper starts to say before Marshawn cuts him off.

"Wait... That doesn't look good, Jack. Bailey isn't getting up."

I watch as my trainer and best friend Tommy Babson rushes into the cage. Jamey Silva is still doing his victory lap.

He does his signature backflip and just about knocks over the doctor who rushed in behind Tommy with his antics.

There's a serious medical emergency in the ring and that douchebag couldn't fucking care less.

I leave the recording playing as the commentators of the match start trying to ease the viewers into the unfolding drama that became my life.

Right there on the mat, I'm aching, trying to sit up. My left arm is dangling uselessly at my side. My face, bloody and sweaty, shows the immense pain I'm going through. I know I should be all manly, ignore the pain and shit, but right then I thought I was about to fucking *die*.

I've suffered losses before, after all an eighteen-to-three record isn't bad by any means, but I'd never been through anything that came close to the hell I was experiencing at that moment. It was both physical and mental.

When I walked into the arena that night, it never even occurred to me that I would be leaving in an ambulance to the hospital, no longer the Welterweight Champion.

I know of loss and pain, I've dealt with it my entire life, but watching as Tommy helps me up, I've never felt so weak before. Ever. So weak and fucking useless.

Setting the remote down on the couch beside me, I lean over to my end table and grab the sweaty bottle of beer off the coaster. Taking a long swig, I continue to watch the TV.

It's the look on my face that tells the world it's all over. That I've officially been beaten. I've lost my belt, lost my sense of self-worth, and lost my job.

It's all fucking over.

Jamey Silva starts dancing around as the ref comes over to stand between us. Then the ref lifts Jamey's hand while mine stays down.

Tommy stands by my injured side, holding me up. Every single fond childhood memory I have has him there in the background, always the fucking cheerleader to my jock lifestyle.

Tears well up on the brim of my eyelids. Yeah, always there for me. He and his parents always there for me when I would catch a beating from my dad. The Babsons took me in when my mom died and kept me fed when my dad was out on another crack-filled bender.

Kept me clothed when my shoes fell off my feet.

In the background, past the cage, I can see both Helen and Bill Babson standing together. Bill has his arm around Helen's shoulders as they anxiously wait for me to exit the cage.

It's fucking crazy watching this video again for the eighth time tonight, but I do. Why shouldn't I watch the beginning of my end?

It's been exactly six months to the day.

After taking a long pull from the bottle, I reach over and set it back down on the table. It clicks against the other empty ones I have stacked there. I'll have to switch to the harder stuff tonight if I want to keep the pain away. I'm not entirely sure when I started running out of all my stocked-up beer, though. Probably last night.

These last couple of months have been kind of fuzzy lately.

Grabbing my phone from the couch cushion next to me, I pull up the screen. I peer at it blearily as I scroll down my messages and pull up the last message from Tommy.

Pushing play, I put it up to my ear.

"Come on, asshole. Pick up the damn phone! That's

why man invented cellphones, so we can get ahold of each other whenever we need to."

Yeah, I don't like answering my phone much. Too many people calling to talk to me about shit I can't deal with.

"Fine," Tommy goes on. "I'll say it here *and* when I get to your house. You need to get off the fucking couch and get into the gym. You got beat, who gives a shit? Shrug this shit off and let's get back to the basics. You remember them, don't you? Before you became a big pussy."

Stupid asshole Tommy always uses the humiliation factor to get me wound up.

I watch the screen as he helps me cradle my injured arm. Damn thing was junk, I could barely move it.

At that moment, I didn't think I could feel any shittier. Then Jamey came up to me in what I thought was a show of good sportsmanship and goodwill. I thought he wanted to check on me or something.

How wrong I was.

The announcers and crowd didn't hear what he said, but Tommy and I sure did.

"You got your faggot boyfriend to help your little bitch ass out of the ring?" Jamey said.

Stunned, I just stared at him. I couldn't quite grasp what the hell he said at first, but Tommy sure as fuck did.

I've never seen Tommy as mad as he was right then. He bolted toward Jamey with a fucking purpose. Bad thing was, though, Tommy wasn't an MMA fighter.

Jamey swiftly gave him a two-punch combo that had Tommy dropping to the mat.

"Holy cow, what in the hell's going on there?" Marshawn yells over the screaming fans. His voice is struggling to be heard over the sudden roar in the arena.

Usually his voice breaks through crazy moments, but not that time. On the screen, the camera shows Tommy laid out flat on his back.

Hitting the power button on the TV, I watch as the screen goes blank. I zoned out while watching that little by-play.

Shaking my head, I hear the end of the voicemail.

"I'll be there soon, brother. We need to get your dumb ass sobered up. You still have a rematch clause in your contract. There's no fucking chance in the world you won't be using that bitch. You need to put Jamey in the fucking ground."

Setting the phone down on the couch, I push the power button on the side and watch it turn itself off. No use in keeping it on.

I really don't want anyone fucking calling me tonight.

How the fuck I ended up out on my back porch is a blur. I don't remember parking my ass out here with a blanket around my shoulders. The almost-finished bottle of rum cradled with my good arm tells me I must have hit the booze harder last night than I planned.

I guess it's not that unusual though, I've done this before.

Yawning in the late morning breeze, my mouth tastes like what I imagine a freshly warmed-up skunk's asshole must taste like.

Pulling the cap off the top of the bottle, I take a long swig of the almost sweet burning liquid. A little bit of the dog that bit me, I guess. I don't really get hungover anymore. I guess I've killed off the body parts that alcohol seems to affect the most.

Shit. Today isn't going to be a fun day. I don't want to face the world, but I can't get a good delivery service for my drinking needs.

It's almost like a punishment. I want to drink to stay out of the world, but I have to go out into the world so I can get the damn drink.

My black Jeep sits in the hot sun, and I can see the heat shimmering off the hood from here. Fuck. I don't want to go out into the heat today. I'd rather just sit in the cold air conditioning of my shitty house and not see people or deal with anything human.

Shit, it's good that I don't have a pet. Given that my entire yard is dead, it's obvious I can't take care of anything besides myself.

And I'm barely doing that.

A fucking headache starts to throb behind my eyes. They've have been plaguing me for the last couple of months. I'm pretty sure I've pickled myself with all the alcohol in my system, but the headaches don't go the fuck away.

They're not the hangover kind, either. Just this incessant pounding behind my eyes. Even when I drink to numb them, I can feel them on the periphery, waiting in the corners to come back in full force.

I drive over to the liquor store and have to keep adjusting my baseball cap and sunglasses. I need food as well, but that can come after I've secured my priorities.

Even shopping is an exercise in caution for me today. Despite growing a beard and getting pudgy, I still have a recognizable face in this city. My ugly mug has been on enough TV screens and billboards that every now and then I get the random fan who wants to talk to me.

Shaking my arm out a bit to remove the tension in my shoulder, I try to just focus on my day and take it one step at a time. I know that shit's from one of them rehab mantras, but it works for us drunks too.

One bottle at a time, one pickled liver away from finishing myself off.

As I'm lifting up a second case of shitty beer to put in my cart, I hear a loud laugh.

"Jesus, it's fucking Emmett. Where the fuck do you get a beer gut that fast?" a gruff voice asks, and it's about all I can do not to toss the case of beer at the fucker's head.

Not bothering to turn my head to respond, I growl out in what I was hoping would sound tough, but comes out more tired than anything else, "Nice to see you too, Brett. It comes from shit food and drinking. Try it out, you'll love it."

Pushing the cart away from the beer racks, I start heading for the liquor shelves a couple of aisles over.

Brett's not a bad guy. He's cocky as a motherfucker, but he's a fighter like me…

Or well, like I was.

The shit that comes out of his mouth is as natural as a sermon is to a preacher. It's only that he's like a fucking rabid dog sometimes. He doesn't know when to leave people the fuck alone.

"Interesting. I tried that when my girl got knocked up but it didn't work out so well," he says as he follows me to the liquor.

Behind me, I hear the thumping of skin on skin. Fucker is probably slapping his fucking washboard abs.

"Great," I say and keep my eyes forward.

I don't need to look into another person's eyes and see the fucking pity I always get.

Pity is what got me to where I am now. Pity for myself and how fucking shitty life can be.

Stopping in front of the rum section, I grab a couple bottles of the cheap shit, along with a good bottle of the expensive stuff. Cheap goes with the rum and cokes, expensive is for when I need to black the fuck out.

Brett bangs his cart off mine while he grabs a bottle whiskey and the squeaky wheels grate on my nerves.

"What have you been up to for the last couple of months, man? I haven't seen you since—" he starts to say before I quickly cut him off.

"Nothing, relaxing and making decisions," I say.

What the fuck? Does he not take a hint?

"What kind of decisions? Like the ones that usually take me the longest are which shirt I need to wear in the morning," he says, and I finally look at him.

"Hey man, I know it's probably a style thing and all, but wearing a hat and sunglasses in this dim and gloomy store is like a cry for… something…" he trails off as I turn away from him.

"Yeah, it's all about fashion, Brett," I grunt out.

"Well, I guess so. Hey, I know that Reaper's been trying to get ahold of you and shit, but he hasn't been able to. So I wanted to show you what's set up for Friday," he says as he pushes a cellphone into my hands.

There, staring back up at me, is a picture of Tommy with a grinning smile. He looks so young and fucking happy.

"Chase has set up a small invitation only tourney for some of the up-and-coming guys at his gym. He's calling it the Tommy Babson Invitational. Wants to do it as an annual memorial for…"

Memorial. Tommy.

Pushing the phone back into Brett's hands, I leave the cart behind me as I walk away.

"It starts Friday at eleven. I'll let Dale know you saw it," Brett calls out after me.

Slamming the door to my Jeep shut, I have sit for a few moments before my hands are steady enough to put the key in the ignition.

Whether it's from the lack of alcohol in my system, or the steady stream of pictures showing the aftermath of a semi-truck crossing the median while the driver was asleep at the wheel, destroying a little foreign-made car, I'm not sure.

But I can't catch my breath.

I feel my lungs rasping deeply.

Shit.

I think I'm having a heart attack.

Right here in the middle of a liquor store parking lot.

Thump.

Thump. Thump.

No matter how loud I turn the radio up, I can't get the sound of the bed thumping against the wall out of my head.

Thump.

Thump. Thump.

Like a cursed melody, it haunts me, chasing me across the desert.

Blindly reaching for the dial, I crank it over to a rock station. Heavy bass begins to rattle my car, and as the singer begins to shriek like a demented banshee, my head begins to ache so bad I can no longer hear the rhythmic banging of headboard meeting plaster.

The relief is only short-lived though. I can't even make it to the end of the song before I'm forced to turn the radio off so my throbbing head doesn't explode.

Silence fills the car and I focus all my attention on the road stretching before me, urging the memory to stay back.

To give me a few minutes of peace.

Please.

But my asshole brain drudges up the scene, forcing me to watch it all again. To face it. To process it.

To experience the consequences of my choices all over again.

Thump.

Thump. Thump.

There's a mirage on the horizon, wavering in front of me. But instead of an oasis beckoning me, I'm watching myself open the door to my apartment.

At first, I was completely oblivious, focused on grabbing the bag I forgot.

But then that thumping drew my curiosity.

Part of me knew what it was… what it meant… It was something straight up out of a bad movie, but I had to see it with my own eyes.

I doubt I'll ever forget the feeling I had when I opened the door to my bedroom.

Or the sight of Tristan's bright white ass clenching as he pounded himself into my best friend Ashley.

I should have been upset… angry… hurt… devastated…

But all I felt was *relief.*

Relief that it was all finally over. The house of cards I've been struggling to hold up for so long was finally crashing down.

The truth was finally coming out into the light, overshadowing all the lies.

I tried to sneak away before they could see me. To make a clean break.

But then Ashley had to screech in surprise, and that… that fucker had to notice me.

I tried to get away. I tried to run, but damn, even naked, balls deep in a girl, Tristan is a prime athlete.

He caught me before I made it out the front door.

My shoulders still ache from being shoved hard into the wall. The pain is so bothersome, I try to focus on rolling the tension out without jerking around the steering wheel.

But like a punch in the gut, his declaration hits me.

"If you weren't such a stone-cold fucking ice queen, I wouldn't have to fuck all your friends."

I laughed. At least I think I did before he grabbed me by the shoulders and shoved me into the wall again.

For a moment, the memory becomes all too real and I can smell his breath from when he leaned into me.

It smelled of him and Ashley.

"You think this changes anything? It changes nothing. You still belong to me, Bree."

Thank god there's no one on the road behind me. Jerking the steering wheel to the right, I pull over and manage to jump out before my stomach revolts.

With the sun beating down on me, I slap my hand against the side of my car, bend over, and puke my guts up.

With each clench of my stomach, I purge a little more of the last four years up.

All the choices I've made.

All my fuck ups and mistakes.

If it wasn't for the hot metal searing into the tender skin of my palm, I'd wonder if this was a bad dream. But no, this isn't a dream, this is my life. A life that's so twisted and fucked up by others, I don't even know who I am anymore.

Once my stomach stops clenching, I straighten and wipe my mouth off with my arm.

But I keep my palm pressed against the hot metal.

The pain… it's nothing compared to what I'm feeling inside, but it keeps me here.

It keeps me in this moment.

And I desperately want to stay in this moment.

I'd rather be stuck out here in this scorching heat, puking my guts up, than reliving what happened this morning all over again.

I rather be stuck out here in this wasteland, alone and completely isolated, than return to my gilded cage back in California.

I can only stand the pain for so long though before I have no choice but to yank my hand back.

And as soon as the pain begins to fade away, before I can even catch my breath, the memory delivers one last brutal slap.

"There's no point in telling your father, he knows. He's always known, so save your fucking breath."

The road blurs, the yellow and white lines thinning until they look as if they were painted on with highlighters. I've been staring at the asphalt for so long my damn eyes are starting to feel gritty and my ass is numb.

After my little stop on the side of the road, I've been driving for eight hours, nonstop. Running away from the mess I left behind me.

Afraid it will catch up to me if I stop.

My shoulders tense and my hands tighten around the

steering wheel as my stepfather's house comes into view through my windshield.

After spending so many hours on the road to get here, I should feel relieved. I finally made it. I'm safe. I'm free.

But all I feel is more anxiety and worry.

What the fuck am I bringing here? What shit am I dropping on their doorstep?

Would everyone be better off if I just disappear?

I follow the driveway as it curves around the front of the house then force my foot to the brake. What I really want to do is slam on the gas and peel out of here, to keep running.

But my mom is already standing at the bottom of the front steps, waiting for me.

Killing the engine, I take a moment to get my anxiety under control before I have to act like I'm normal and not about to have a nervous breakdown.

Deep breath in, deep breath out.

This isn't the first time I've had to pretend everything is okay while my world is crashing down.

You've got this, Bree.

No more puking.

Pull those big girl panties up.

"Aubrey!" my mom calls out as soon as I pop my door open.

I manage to get one foot out the door before my mom pounces on me. She pulls me into a hug that's so tight my lungs compress against my ribs.

Fuck, when did she get so strong?

"Mom, can't breathe," I find myself gasping.

"Oh, sorry!" She laughs and relaxes her arms. Her smile is so warm it flashes in front of my eyes like a beam of light. "I'm just so happy to see you, honey."

She gives me one more squeeze then takes a step back, her eyes drinking me in as if it's been years since we've seen each other and not a few months.

"I missed you too, Mom," I wheeze out and let my own eyes drink her in before I remember myself.

Shaking my head, I smile and ask, "Wow, where'd you get the guns?"

I haven't seen her since spring break, but she looks younger. Rejuvenated even. There's a sparkle in her eyes and a glow about her that wasn't there before she met and moved in with my stepfather.

"Guns?" My mom blinks in confusion and looks around her as if she's really looking for them. "I don't have any guns…"

"She means your arms, Olivia," my stepfather chuckles as he comes up behind her and wraps an arm around her waist.

He does it so casually, so naturally, I doubt either of them are even aware that he's pretty much staking his claim right in front of me.

It would be annoying if it wasn't so damn cute.

In fact, everything about them is so cute that if I didn't love them both so much it would probably make me puke again.

My stepfather, Logan, towers over my mother by at least a foot. He's a big, burly, dark-haired guy with a deep, booming voice that was intimidating as hell the first time I met him, but he treats my mom with the gentleness of a teddy bear.

My mom on the other hand is a petite blonde with a slender frame who looks like she could get blown away by the wind at any moment. Even with the muscle she's packed on it doesn't look like it would take much to knock her over.

We Mckenzie women run small. Hell, I'm lucky I managed to grow a couple of inches above five feet in eighth grade.

I'm officially the tallest girl ever born in our family.

"Oh." My mom tips her head up to smile at Logan before she turns that smile to me. "I've been working out with Logan and Chase at his gym."

"Seriously?" I ask, and Logan nods his head with pride. I let out a low whistle between my teeth and start to move around them. "That's impressive."

Chase, Logan's son and technically my stepbrother, is a former heavyweight MMA champion who retired from the fighting scene after he met his wife, Avery. He owns and runs a prestigious training gym now. He's even bigger than his dad and more intimidating. I can't even picture my little mom training with the two of them.

"You're welcome to join us, if you like," Logan offers, and I sense his tall, towering frame coming up behind me as I pop my trunk open. "We start at six."

I reach into the trunk to grab my bag and the tips of my fingers brush against the handle a split second before Logan grabs it out of my hand.

Who says chivalry is dead?

Logan grabs my other bag, hauling them both up easily in his big mitts. There are handles and wheels he could use, but I doubt he's even considered it.

I close my trunk then click my clicker, locking up my Audi after taking a second to suck in a calming breath. "In the evening?"

Logan's eyes glitter with amusement under his bushy brows. "In the morning."

I make a face and Logan chuckles. "No thanks. That's way too early for me."

"You do look tired. Are you getting enough sleep?" my mom remarks with sudden concern, giving me another once-over as we all head up the front steps.

When I called this place a house earlier, I was downplaying it a bit. Really, the place is a mansion with a sprawling artificial lawn nestled within a copse of trees. The interior itself features six bedrooms, five baths, and a kitchen as big as my apartment back in California.

"It's been a hard semester," I reassure her with a tight smile then quickly change the subject.

I'm in my role now and it's everything I can do to maintain it. My energy is running on empty. What I really want to do is hole myself up in a room somewhere and sleep until I forget the past twenty-four hours.

But I can't do that yet.

I don't want my mom to get one whiff of the crap I've been dealing with. I want to keep her as far as possible away from it, so I have to pretend that nothing's wrong and everything is fine for a little longer.

"Wow, Mom," I find myself saying as we pass through the double front doors. "I love what you've done with the place."

With just a glance, I can see her touches everywhere.

My mom beams with pride and begins to flutter around the huge living area, pointing out and explaining all the changes she's made since she moved in.

She's an interior designer who lives and breathes color, textures, and fabric. Me? I could care less what my surroundings look like as long as I have food, a bed, and the internet.

My eyes start to glaze over as my mom finishes up

describing how she rearranged all the furniture to increase the flow of the room and moves on to describing all the projects she's working on with Logan.

That's how the two of them met. Logan is this huge real estate mogul here in Nevada and my mom is one of the best interior designers in this part of the nation.

"I've put your bags in your room," Logan's deep rumbling voice jolts me back to reality.

I shoot him a grateful, though tired, smile as he thumps down the winding staircase that leads to the second floor. "Thank you."

"You're welcome, runt," Logan chuckles and rubs my head like I'm a small child as he walks past me.

I huff out a breath, blowing the hair that's now in front of my eyes out of my face.

I don't know why I'm the runt when my mom's shorter than me, but it's been Logan's nickname for me since I've met them.

"Do you want some lunch, Bree? I can prepare some sandwiches," my mom offers, but I immediately shake my head at her.

I can't even remember the last time I ate, but I don't think my stomach could handle it right now.

"No, thank you. I think I'm going to lay down for a bit and nap. It was a long drive…"

My mom smiles and nods her head, but she can't keep the disappointment out of her eyes. "That's probably a good idea. You should get some rest. Chase, Avery, and the kiddos will be here for dinner in a couple of hours."

Oh, that's right. Damn. I forgot. It looks like I'll be trying to keep my shit together all night.

"Alright, I'll see you in a couple of hours," I say,

suddenly feeling anxious to escape their unwavering attention and this role I'm playing.

Before anything else can come up and delay me, I head for the staircase.

I make it up two stairs before my mom suddenly calls out and stops me.

There's a strange softness to her voice, almost like she's self-conscious as she says, "Aubrey?"

Before my brain even processes my name, my feet are stopping.

"Yeah?" I ask, unable to keep the exhaustion out of my voice as I turn back to her.

The smile is gone from my mom's face and that glow she had about her earlier has dimmed with a touch of sadness.

Wringing her hands in front of her, her eyes lock on mine as she says, "I'm glad you're here. I missed you, honey."

Staring at her, into her warm, loving eyes, that chasm that's grown between us over the past couple of years yawns wide inside me, full of my regret.

Regret that the choices I've made have created this distance between us that was never there before.

We used to be so close… so damn close. But I chose a path that took me away from her.

I let myself be lured away from my pillar of love and strength…

I let myself be lured away for the promise of money, power, and popularity.

All the things my life lacked.

I willingly took the path my father laid before me and didn't even look back at her.

I've done shitty things and sold my soul all for the sake

of a different life than what she could provide for me at the time.

And I know I've hurt her.

Hurt her in ways I didn't mean to, but hurt her nevertheless.

But if that love glowing in her eyes means anything, maybe it's not too late for me. Maybe I'm still redeemable.

Maybe I can fix all these mistakes.

Maybe I can be *me* for once.

My throat closing up on me, I manage to choke out, "Me too, mom."

Then I haul my ass upstairs before I burst into tears and completely fall apart in front of them.

Someone pounds on my front door and it's so fucking loud it sounds like they're trying to use a battering ram to break it down.

"Go the fuck away!" I shout at the door from the couch I was so recently passed out on.

I check the time on my phone and it's fucking nine in the damn morning.

Just like my fucking headache, the pounding doesn't stop. It only continues at a steady fucking pace.

Boom. Boom. Boom.

Like a goddamn sledgehammer.

Dropping my phone to the ground with my shaky morning fingers, I shout out, "Fuck off unless you have a fucking warrant!"

There's a loud noise outside that sounds like a foot hitting the door, and I groan.

What the fuck did I do last night? What in the hell did I do? As far as I know, I blacked out here on my couch from the rum I was slamming back.

Fuck. Last night was a bad one. I must have listened to

the message from Tommy a couple of dozen times. Each time he said goodbye, I'd take another drink. It was like I was playing my own little drinking game.

Goodbye. Drink. Goodbye. Drink.

Pound. Boom. Pound. Boom.

The beating on the door continues. I'd be better off going and sleeping in my fucking bed. But whoever the fuck is trying to beat my fucking door down is gonna catch a beating first.

Thankfully the world doesn't spin in circles as I stand up from the couch. And fuck me if I'm not lucky, I still have my damn pants on and they're dry.

Goodass luck.

"Whoever the fuck you are pounding on my fucking door, you need to fucking stop right the fuck now!" I shout out as I move to the door.

Unlocking the door, I yank it open only to see a massive chest standing there in a black fucking shirt.

"You big, fucking asshole! What the fuck do you think you're doing shit like that for?" I ask as I look up and see Chase's face.

"I wanted to make sure you heard me."

He laughs as he steps to the side so I can see who else is laughing.

"Fuck off the two of you," I snarl at Dale as he steps into view.

Chase grins. "That's not very polite of you."

"It wasn't polite of your mom to birth you into this world," I snap as I start closing the door.

"That wasn't a very nice thing to say, Emmett," Dale says with a chuckle.

They both just stand there as the door closes until a giant shoe pushes its way between the door and the frame.

Fucking dicks.

Pulling it back open, I ask, "What do you want? Tell me now so I can say no and go back to bed."

Dale pushes past me and takes a long look at the fucked-up living room. Chase follows after him and looks around as well.

Both of their faces pinch as they turn back to face me.

"What the fuck are you doing? Trying to open a distillery in your liver?" Dale asks.

"Yeah, I figured it would be worth something when I die," I grumble as I head out of the living room.

"Well, get showered up. You need to be ready in fifteen," Chase grunts as he starts pushing empty bottles out of his way to sit on the couch.

"Jesus, it smells like you were taking a bath in those bottles," Dale grouches, following behind me as I make my way to the kitchen.

"Where the fuck are you going?" I ask as he pushes past me and stands in front of the kitchen entrance.

"Shower's that way, dickhead." He points to the opposite direction of where I want to go.

"Shower for what? And get the fuck out of my house. I need to call the cops or something," I say as I try to squeeze past him.

Arm pushing on my chest, he shakes his head. "Wrong way again, Emmett."

"No, this is the right way. That's where all my drinks are," I growl out in irritation.

I'm really starting to get pissed off that these fuckers are acting like they know what I need to be doing.

"Chase, come here a moment. We need to have a talk with Emmett," Dale shouts out.

"Fuck Chase, the big, stupid ass pussy. Get the hell out

of my way!" I shout as I try to manhandle Dale out of the way.

And fuck…

A big meaty arm wraps around my throat as Dale smirks at me.

"Big what?" Chase asks as he starts to drag me away from the kitchen.

"Pussy!" I warble out as I try to pry his arms away from my breathing passage.

"Nah, brother, that's not the right word for the day. I think *friend* would be a better name to call me."

"Let me the fuck go," I shout and try to slam the heel of my foot into his shoe, but since the asshole is wearing some thick-ass shoes it doesn't have the desired effect.

"Now, now, Emmett, there's two ways to do this. You either get into the shower and clean your fucking shit up or I have Dale run you a bath."

It's amazing to me that for all the my struggling and fighting, I'm still being slowly dragged back toward my bathroom.

"Why the fuck would he run me a bath?"

"Because I sure as shit ain't standing in the shower when I scrub the fucking alcohol off your fucking body."

Chase grunts as I slam an elbow into his ribs.

Finally achieving the desired effect, I drop beneath his arms and move toward Dale. The only problem is Dale's grin has gotten even bigger.

Shit, that's probably not good. Especially since I don't hear Chase coming after me.

Watching Dale step out of my way with a malicious grin, I turn around the corner only to come face to face with Bear.

"Motherfucker," I groan.

Silent as ever, Bear just crosses his arms and nods his head.

Turning around, I look at Dale. "What the fuck is this all about?"

"We've got a tournament starting up this morning for —" he says, but I don't hear anything else after that.

It's like a static sound is filling my brain as I lean into the wall. I watch Bear's lips move, but I don't hear anything.

When he finally finishes speaking, I wait a few moments for my head to clear as he just stares at me.

"Casey. Tommy's parents are bringing him to the gym. They've been having a rough time with him," he says, his voice finally breaking through, and I can feel all the air in my chest crushing out.

It's like Chase is bear hugging me. No air, just a reeling feeling.

"What do you mean a rough time?" I ask.

Tommy's shining light in the world was his son. He loved the child more than any other parent I've seen love a child. Casey was Tommy's very reason for being. He was also one cool ass kid, a little diamond of awesome.

"He's twelve, Emmett. He's lost his father. He's drowning in depression and as lost as you are," Dale says with a voice filled with sadness. "He ain't the same kid. I know that is to be expected, but he's now just a shell."

"Yeah man, we've been trying to get through the walls he's got surrounding him… But it ain't working," Bear says quietly.

Looking to the three men who surround me, I feel trapped. Trapped by my own grief, rage, and shame. "What the fuck do you think I can do?"

"Something besides being a fucking waste," Dale shouts as he pushes on my chest.

A waste. That's all I am. A waste. I don't need to be near someone as fucked up as me. I'd just ruin them.

Edging up into my personal bubble, Dale puts his nose right up against my own. "Be a fucking stand-up person for fucking Tommy. His son is dying from the inside out and you can't be fucking bothered to even pick up a fucking phone when his grandparents call you!"

He's right. Every time the phone rings, I push it to my message box. Which, besides the one from Tommy, have all gone unheard. I'm pretty sure the box is full by now, especially since the phone never rings anymore.

Or maybe it isn't full… maybe everyone has given up on me. They probably should.

"Fuck it!" Dale roars into my face when I don't respond back. "Let's go guys, fuck this shit. We'll figure something else out."

Shaking his massive head, Bear just looks from me to Dale. "Nah, I'll get a ride back on my own."

Fuck.

Watching Dale and Chase leave the house gives me more dread than I'd like to admit.

Dread, lots of it. Dread that this is the last chance I have of stopping what's surely going to be an early death. Dread that Bear is standing silently behind me, the complete lack of judgement searing into my body. Maybe I'd be happier if he was judging me, like Chase and Dale surely are right now.

Turning to face him, I say tiredly, "You don't want to stay around here, it's only going to get worse."

"You planning on drinking till you pass out?" he asks just as quietly.

There's no judgement in his features and it hurts me even more. Why, I can't figure out, but it does.

"More than likely," I say and walk past him.

I can't look him in the face anymore.

Heading for the kitchen, I hear and feel him walking behind me. Whatever. I need a drink.

Pulling an unopened bottle of rum out of the cabinet, I watch as Bear walks over to another cabinet and pulls two glasses down.

"You ever drink like a civilized person?" he asks as he walks past me to the living room.

"What the hell are you doing?" I ask loudly, following him out to see him already making himself at home on the couch.

"I'm drinking with you," he says.

"Aren't you supposed to be on restriction?" I ask, eyeing him.

"Nah, that was last month," he answers. "I'm taking off for a couple of months. Grace is pregnant again and it's getting closer to the due date. I figure I shouldn't make Hope do so much work with her mama and little sister, then add another one."

"The fuck? You trying to field your own cheerleading squad?" I ask with a laugh.

Jesus, three fucking daughters?

Snorting with laughter, he shakes his head. "Not my little Hope. She's already tearing through her striking and grappling classes. She wants nothing to do with all that girly stuff. She's going to be a fighter like her dad."

Thank god she doesn't look like him. I can't imagine a female version of Bear walking around.

"You gonna pour me some of that?" He motions to the bottle I'm holding.

"You planning on drinking with me the whole day?" I ask.

"Nah, just till you pass out," he says.

"That's not gonna be anytime soon," I say and crack open the seal on the bottle.

"Rehab centers take drop-ins at all hours. I'm sure they won't mind me bringing you to them in the middle of the night," he says with a shrug of his massive shoulders.

"What the fuck?" I growl out.

I can feel the blood pounding behind my eyes as the headache slams back full force into the front of my skull.

"You've got two choices, as I see it," he says as he leans forward, his eyes suddenly becoming more intense than I've ever seen them before.

"I've got a feeling you're not going to say something I want to hear," I say and roll my eyes.

"Yep. Two choices," he repeats. "Choice number one: We drink till you pass out. Then I toss you over my shoulder and take you to a nice rehab on a seventy-two-hour wellness hold. Involuntary more than likely. But me and the guys at the gym know a couple people who will help keep you in for the full seventy-two."

The bottle isn't even fully opened and I get that sick drop in my stomach at the thought of going through what he just said. I'd be able to get out of the rehab after the hold, but he's right, they've all got connections throughout the city. I'd stay every single fucking hour of that hold.

Sober. Completely fucking sober.

"Option two?" I croak out.

"You leave the bottle on the end table there, go take your shower, and come with me," he says.

"That's…" I try to think of something to say, but suddenly my tongue is thick and dry in my mouth.

"It's pretty simple. Two choices," he says and leans back against the couch.

"It's not that simple, Max," I say to him, calling him by his real name and not his ring name.

"Actually, it is, Emmett. You have two options. You choose one and everything else follows after. You just need to figure out which way this is going to work. Each one will be a fight for you, but drinking yourself into an early grave or putting a bullet through your skull isn't an option."

For the last two months, I've debated those two things. Debated how I'd like to go out. Something inside of my brain doesn't do what I expect though. I watch my hand shakily move the bottle to the end table.

"No promises beyond today," I say as I stand up and avoid looking at him.

Bear nods. "I can get behind that for now."

CHAPTER FOUR

BREE

S lowly awakening from my nap, I linger in that place somewhere between sleep and awareness, enjoying the sweet oblivion.

Here, there are no worries, no problems, and most of all, no cheating ex-boyfriends and backstabbing best friends.

There's only the warm blanket wrapped around me, the soft pillow beneath my head, and this wonderful feeling of weightlessness.

In a way it reminds me of when I was younger. When my little brain couldn't even comprehend that the monsters in the world aren't imaginary, they're other human beings.

I try to hold on to this feeling for as long as I can, but it seems the harder I try to hold on to it the quicker it leaves me.

It's completely gone by the time there's a light knock on my bedroom door followed by my mom's voice.

"Aubrey? Are you awake? Chase and Avery are here."

My brain begins to wind up, and even though the gears

aren't fully spinning yet, I can sense the shitstorm waiting for me at the edge of my consciousness.

"Yeah… I'll be down in a minute," I grumble out and blink my eyes open.

I'm not ready to face the shitstorm yet.

"Okay, honey," my mom says cheerfully.

I listen as her footsteps trail down the hall then reach out beside me, blindly grabbing my phone.

Out of habit, I check my messages, and instantly regret it.

The first text that pops up on my screen is from Tristan, telling me to text him as soon as I get in.

The fucking nerve of him…

I almost throw my phone across my room, but then my eyes land on the other messages.

There's about a hundred texts from Ashley, all of them apologizing and begging me to forgive her.

Shit.

I don't want to deal with this right now, but there it is.

Closing my eyes, I plop back on my pillow and squeeze my phone so hard I'm surprised it doesn't crack in my fist.

So this is the game they want to play?

But to what end?

I can easily guess what Tristan wants. He's made it clear he doesn't expect his infidelity to change anything. He's simply trying to maintain the status quo.

But what does Ashley get out of this?

I doubt she's feeling guilty for what's she's done.

Maybe she's simply saving face?

Even then…

My curiosity getting the better of me, I pull up my Instagram. If she made a public apology, I'll be shocked shitless.

I only have to scroll two pictures down to see Tristan's latest post.

It's a fucking picture of the two of us together.

In the picture we're snuggled close on a couch. His arm is wrapped around my shoulders and we're both beaming for the camera. I've taken so many damn selfies with him, I can't even remember when this one was taken.

Below the picture, he's captioned: Missing my girl already. Hurry back home Bree baby. #futurewifey #lonelywithoutmybaby #missingyoucrazy #wakemewhensummerisover

I shouldn't be surprised... I shouldn't. But the sheer, arrogant audacity of it causes my blood to boil and I can't think straight for a minute.

Once I'm no longer seeing red, I look at the post again. Really look at it.

He didn't make that post out of stupidity. No, as much as I dislike Tristan, he's not just a pretty face, he's also as cunning as a fucking fox.

Still, even knowing that, something about it really bothers me. The only way he'd have the balls to make that post is if he's supremely confident that I won't be able to dump his ass.

Has he already spoken to my father? Dammit.

The post is up to a few thousand likes and there's a few dozen comments from our circle of friends.

Even Ashley commented how much she's going to miss me.

Bitch.

Scrolling down, I rush past the photos of everyone's lunch and vacations until I reach Ashley's post.

Copying Tristan, she's posted a picture of the two of us, like we're still best friends.

I click off my phone, not bothering to read the comments. If I do, I just might have a rage aneurism.

But I'm not mad that she slept with my boyfriend. No, that's just her nature. I can't blame her for that any more than I could blame a cat for eating a canary or a lion for hunting the gazelle.

What I'm mad about is that she betrayed me and won't let me go, just like Tristan. For whatever reason, she's joining him in trying to keep me tied to their existence.

Every vengeful, wrathful bone in my body wants me to make a post calling them out. To scream from the rooftops what happened.

To show the world their true faces.

But would the effort, energy, and fallout be worth it?

Knowing my circle of 'friends', they've probably known about this for a while now. Given that I'm only now finding this out, there's no doubt that Tristan and Ashley have had help to carry on behind my back.

If I make a peep of this, I'll only look sad and pathetic. I know because I've seen this kind of thing go down before.

Four years ago it came out that one of the guys in our group of friends, Spencer, was cheating on his girlfriend. I can't even remember her name, but I remember the sympathy I felt for her when she came to confront him with mascara tears running down her face at one of the basketball team's after-parties.

I also remember the jab Ashley gave me in the ribs to keep me from standing up and comforting her as she sobbed her heart out.

She was the wronged party, but to the group it didn't matter. She instantly became the one in the wrong for making a fuss and creating drama. Everyone stood by

Spencer and ostracized her to the point that she ended up transferring schools.

Even now I feel guilty for not reaching out to her. At the time, though, my position in the circle was still new, and I was so afraid of losing the friends I had finally made.

Perhaps it's karma that I'm now going through exactly the same thing.

And I deserve it.

If I would have stood up for her, I probably would have been kicked out of the group and been saved from this massive headache.

But then again, our situations aren't exactly the same…

After all, I'm not heartbroken over Tristan. No, I now realize that I fell out of love with him a long time ago. I think the only reason I was still with him was because it was *expected*.

Expected by my father and our social circle.

Now, all I care about is getting stuck with him.

Staring at the black surface of my phone, I try to think of what I could possibly do to keep a small shred of my dignity and send them a message in the process.

Then it suddenly hits me.

Silence speaks volumes. Especially to people like Tristan and Ashley. They thrive on attention. They need it like the rest of us need to breathe.

After a quick web search, I log back into Instagram and disable my account. Then I block their numbers in my contacts.

There… Let everyone make of that what they will.

Because I'm done. Done with caring about people who don't care about me.

Done trying to be what they want me to be.

Having put this little family reunion off for long enough, I quickly change out of dirty my clothes and try my best to clean myself up. As much as I would love a shower, I don't think I have the time for it. It would take me at least another twenty minutes to get clean and dry my hair, and the last thing I want my new stepbrother and his wife to think is that I'm a high-maintenance, spoiled princess.

Something I've been accused of being one too many times.

People look at me, at my family, and the things I have, and they assume I've always lived this way. Too many assholes assume I've grown up with a silver spoon in my mouth and take everything I have for granted.

But it couldn't be further from the truth.

Before my mother achieved success as an interior designer, we were living in studio apartments, paycheck to paycheck, barely making ends meet. I know what it's like to go without. Up until starting high school, that was my life.

Without.

Without time with my mom because she was working two jobs while putting herself through school for her degree.

Without an extra penny to spend on anything that wasn't a necessity, and sometimes without the money to buy the necessities.

Without a father who gave a shit about me.

Shaking those thoughts out of my head, I do a quick sniff test of my pits. Yeah, I definitely smell like I've been stuck in a car for eight hours.

After spraying on half a can of deodorant, I brush my teeth and gargle some mouthwash.

Then I say a little prayer and make my way down the staircase.

I've only met my new family once, when I came back to Nevada from school for my mom's wedding. While everyone was nice to me, especially Logan, it felt like we were polite because we were afraid of ruining the happy couple's moment. With everything going on, the family dinners, the rehearsal dinners, there just wasn't enough time to really get to know each other.

Well, we'll certainly get to know each other now because I'll be here all summer.

That thought alone causes my stomach to clench with a touch of apprehension.

It's been so long since my mom was happy, and I don't want to ruin this for her. Out of all the people in the world, I personally believe she deserves it the most.

Before I make it completely across the foyer, the tinkling, musical sound of children giggling reaches my ears.

It's weird but I swear a little jolt of warmth courses through body.

Funny, I didn't even realize I was cold. Especially in this dry, desert heat…

Confused but drawn to the pull of the sound, my footsteps quicken, carrying me across the lavish foyer until I'm standing in the dining room doorway.

All at once my feet stop, planting me on the spot, as I peek in and take in the scene.

It's all a little chaotic but reminds me of something straight out of a Hallmark movie.

Two little girls with dark pigtails run around the dining

room table, giggling and carrying-on while the adults attempt to eat dinner.

Everyone looks so happy, so relaxed and at ease with each other, I can't help but be a little disturbed by it.

Yeah, I guess I'm really fucked up if the sight of a happy family seems strange to me. It's so foreign to me, I might as well be watching aliens.

Aliens who seem to be happy just being in each other's company.

Standing here in the doorway, I've never felt more like an outsider.

Where do I even fit in here?

I don't know how to act like them… to be like them. Not with all this shit I've got up in my head.

My eyes drift over to my mom sitting beside Logan. He has his big, hairy arm wrapped around her waist and she's leaning into his side with a smile on her face.

She's always been my anchor, my place in the world. The only other person like me. But, even seated across from Chase and Avery, she looks like she belongs here. That she's always belonged here, with her family.

The urge to flee, to escape, suddenly hits me. I'm an intruder, an interloper, and I should have never come here.

But before I can act on the urge, Logan's deep, booming voice calls out to me.

"'Bout time you joined us, Ms. Sleepyhead."

Panic grips me, and for a moment I can't breathe.

I don't want to ruin my mom's happiness, but now that I've been spotted I can't run away.

What the fuck do I do? I don't want to taint this happy family with all my shit.

"Aubrey!" my mom exclaims and stands up from her chair.

I thought she looked happy before, but as soon as her bright gaze lands on me, her entire face lights up with unrepressed joy.

It's enough, just enough to shatter all these insecurities that have suddenly consumed me.

I start to take a step toward her so she doesn't have to leave her place when two little bodies suddenly slam into me.

"Aunt Bree!" two little voices squeal as they wrap themselves around my legs.

"Emma, Emily, let Bree go!" Avery says in her stern, mommy voice.

Ignoring their mother, Emma and Emily tip their identical little faces up to peer at me.

"We missed you!" one gushes with pure, childlike honesty while the other frowns, her eyes darkening with reproach.

"Yeah, why haven't you visited us?"

I open my mouth, at a loss because I wasn't expecting to get scolded by a five-year-old. Especially a five-year-old I've only met once before.

Yeah, I played with them off and on during the wedding to help keep them busy because there were points when they seemed to be getting antsy and bored, but I definitely didn't expect them to remember me.

Stepping in to save me, Avery says, "Emily, don't give Aunt Bree a hard time. You know she was at school and school is important."

"Is that true?" Emily asks with a look of doubt that makes her look twice her age.

It's mostly true, so I swallow down the sudden, unexplainable sense of guilt I'm experiencing and answer, "Yes, it's true. You know I go to school in California…"

Emily purses her lips for a second, as if she's digesting that information. Then, as if her reproach never existed, she beams at me.

"Okay! Want to play with us? Daddy let us bring our Barbies."

"Girls…" Chase says, his tone firm but his eyes sparkling with mirth. "Let Bree eat first then ask if she wants to play with you."

Both girls purse their lips into adorable, most likely practiced, pouts and say at the same time, "Yes, Daddy."

Avery shoots Chase an exasperated look and I watch him smirk back at her.

Shaking her head, Avery mutters something about the girls only listening to him.

Chase tips his head back and laughs.

"Aubrey," my mom says over Chase's laughter to get my attention, "I've saved a plate for you."

Tearing my eyes away from the couple, I make my way around the long, elegant dining table to take the seat beside her.

Plopping down on the cream-colored padded dining chair, I grab the metal lid that's been placed over my plate to keep it warm and whip it off.

"She made your favorite," Logan says with a touch of pride.

My throat starts to close up as I stare down at a plate of my mom's homemade lasagna.

I must stare a little too long, though, because my mom asks tentatively, "Is it okay? I can make you something else if you would prefer—"

"No, mom. It's great. It's perfect," I say quickly and force my lips into a smile as I look up at her. "Thank you. It's exactly what I want."

And didn't know I need.

My mom's shoulders relax and she smiles with relief. "You're welcome, honey."

Picking up my fork, I take a bite and have to swallow down a moan of joy.

It tastes like all my happy memories.

My mom's lasagna is delicious, but it's more than that. It's something special she could only do on those rare days when she had the time. And it takes so long to prepare, she could rarely find the time.

But she always tried.

It takes every ounce of willpower I have inside me to keep myself from gobbling down the whole thing and licking the plate clean.

As I'm savoring my fourth bite, one of the twins suddenly plops down in the chair beside me and declares, "Grandma's lasagna is better than Mommy's."

My mom gasps and I widen my eyes as I stare at the little girl smiling up at me.

"Emma Marie, that's not very polite," my mom chastises her, clearly upset that she's being rude and perhaps afraid of offending Avery.

But what's got me is that she called my mom *Grandma*.

Somehow that title completely slipped my mind.

"It's true." Avery laughs, seemingly not the least bit offended. "But Grandma is right, it's rude, Emma, and you should be careful about what you say. You don't want to hurt someone's feelings."

As the grownups try to explain to Emma what she did wrong, I finish my lasagna with the realization that my mom is now a grandma running through my mind.

I don't know if I love it, hate it, or even care.

Unable to decide, I scrape up every last drop of sauce and push my plate away.

"So… Bree…" Avery smiles at me from across the table. "It's been awhile. How have you been? How's school going?"

I know Avery is only being nice and trying to make small talk, but with everything going on, her questions immediately put me on edge.

"Good," I answer and smile, hoping to leave it just at that.

"She just earned her associate's," my mom chimes in for me.

"Oh?" Avery asks, perking up with interest as I cringe inside. "What program did you take?"

I pick up my glass of water and say quickly, "Liberal Arts," before taking a deep drink.

Undeterred, or perhaps truly interested, Avery starts to ask, "Are you planning on—"

Only to be cut off by the sound of a baby crying.

"Oh, Lane must be up from his nap," Avery says as she picks up a baby monitor I didn't even notice until now off the table and switches it off.

She shoots me an apologetic smile as she stands from her chair. "Sorry, excuse me. He's usually cranky when he wakes up from his naps and wants his mommy."

"No problem," I smile back at her, relieved I've escaped her questioning.

Once Avery leaves the room, I lean back in my chair and start to relax. I'm so full of lasagna, I'm beginning to feel sleepy.

Chase suddenly says, the deep, commanding tone of his voice jerking me awake, "Do you have any plans this summer, Bree?"

I blink at him in surprise, my heart stuttering. "No… not really."

The full, penetrating force of his gaze hits me and I almost squirm in my seat. Damn, just his eyes alone are intimidating as hell. No wonder he was undefeated in the cage. Between that look and his sheer size, I have no doubt with one look he could make grown men cry.

"Really?" he questions as if he doesn't quite believe me while arching his brow. "You don't have anything planned?"

Fuck. Does he know something?

"Well…" I stammer, actually squirming this time, "I thought I'd tan by the pool…"

Chase continues to just stare at me, and I'm about to start apologizing for everything I've ever done in my life when he asks, "How would you like a job?"

"A job?" I repeat dumbly.

What the hell is going on here? Is he messing with me? Or testing me?

"Yeah, a job," he drawls out and then his lips quirk up with a smirk. "You know, those things you do for money."

Fuck. I bet he is testing me. Testing to find out if I'm a spoiled brat who won't earn her keep.

"Oh, one of those," I smirk back at him and roll my eyes. If he thinks I'll balk at the thought of a job, he's got another thing coming. "Sure, I could use a job. Do you have something in mind?"

I must have passed his little test because Chase's smirk softens into something that's close to a smile. "I could use some help around the gym now that Avery is busy with the kids."

"What kind of help?" I ask, curious but also a little apprehensive.

I'm not in the best of shape. Working out has never been my thing. I've tried some yoga and Pilates, but never stuck with it. If he needs someone who's into fitness, I'm going to have a hard time.

Perhaps sensing my apprehension, Chase reassures me, "Just some help around the office with the administrative stuff. Dealing with memberships and such. It would only be a couple of days a week."

"Oh, okay… I could do that," I smile, relieved. "No problem."

Anything for family, right?

"Great," Chase says, his smile stretching into a full grin. "Can you come in tomorrow? We've got a big event going on."

"Sure," I answer automatically.

Why not? I don't have anything else going on, and it would be cool to see his gym.

"What time do you need me to come in?" I ask, relaxing again in my seat.

Logan starts to chuckle beside me, and I don't understand why he's doing it until Chase answers, with his eyes gleaming, "I'll need you to help me open at six in the morning."

Having Bear, the big, hulking motherfucker, beside me, breathing quietly and not saying a word, is unnerving as hell right now.

I haven't had a drink since last night, and I can feel the nerve endings in my shoulder just fucking buzzing with the tingles. There's also a headache threatening to encompass my entire head.

The tingles, though, are supposed to be more of a psychosomatic thing, at least that's what the doctor said before I stopped seeing him.

He kept giving me too many warnings about how I was going to kill myself drinking.

"You going to fucking say anything or is this one of those silent gigs?" I ask as I pull up to a red light.

Still with the fucking silence. Nothing out of him beyond a grunt.

"Big, motherfucking, bear," I grumble and push down on the pedal as soon as the light turns green.

It's not like I really need his ass acting like a babysitter or anything. Though, if I had it my way, I'd still be passed out in my living room, or maybe awake with a good ice cold beer in my hand.

I don't need this shit today.

"You planning on taking the longest way possible?" Bear asks in that deep, quiet rumble of his.

"No…" I say, and then turn off my blinker.

For some damn reason my mind was trying to turn away from the gym and head toward the interstate.

Subconsciously, I was absolutely going to go the other way.

"Then let's skip the long way around and just get it over with. You've got obligations at the gym today, and like you said, no promises past today," he says.

Nodding my head, I refocus on the drive to the gym. Not that I really need to remember how to get there. Before everything that happened, I practically lived there. Tommy and I were there almost every day and night.

Shit, even his son was a fixture.

Casey started getting involved with the youth MMA group Chase was running. He worked as hard as we did a lot of the time, and fuck… I haven't seen him since the funeral. I tried listening to the messages Tommy's parents left me, but I just couldn't do it.

I couldn't bear the thought of letting all those old fucking wounds open up.

"Bear," I say quietly, "I… I'm not exactly sure I can do this."

"Why not?" he asks, and I expect to hear judgement in his tone or maybe even anger.

Instead, he sounds so calm and interested in what I have to say it hurts my stomach.

"Because I… I should have swallowed that bullet," I gulp out and my eyes start going fucking hazy on me.

Silence again reigns supreme.

Silence is not always golden.

Fuck.

I actually meant what I just said, and it scares the living fuck out of me. I meant that I might be better off putting a bullet through my thick skull. Getting rid of all the bullshit I've turned into.

Putting myself out of everyone's misery, including my own.

"Emmett, when you're past this point in your life and the alcohol and self-doubt are gone, you'll realize just how selfish of a thought that truly is. And how extremely cruel it is to every single person around you," Bear says as he shifts in his seat to face me.

"Fuck man, I mean…" I try to say, but he cuts me off.

"I know what you mean, we've all had those moments in our life. Everyone has. But it's only a moment. You see your life as over. You lost your best friend and you don't have any family." He stops and pauses but only for a moment. "But like I said, you've got obligations."

"Which are?" I ask with all the weariness I feel.

Not answering me, he asks a question instead, "Who else is suffering with this in their life?"

I'm not up for games, but I try to think outside of my own little corner of hell for just a moment.

And I don't like any of the answers I come up with.

"Yeah, I can see it on your face, you thought of who pretty quickly," Bear says.

"What am I supposed to do, man? I don't have the answers he needs."

"I got a feeling it's not about the answers, Emmett."

~

The rest of the drive is at moments uncomfortably silent and then at others absurdly silent. I'm not the type that likes to talk anyone's ear off, but right now I can't think of a single thing to say.

The big fuck beside me doesn't bother talking either, and I almost wish he would lay into me just so I could get out of my own head.

But that doesn't happen. No, I'm stuck with my own sober thoughts, and it just reminds me that I'm a fucking deadbeat drunk.

With a bit of shakiness, I turn off the engine and sit here, letting the sun bake us inside my Jeep. I don't really want to get out of the car, but I sure as fuck don't want to die in here either, suffocating with Bear beside me.

Being completely honest with myself, I'd rather live than die with his big ass beside me.

"Want some advice?" Bear asks as I make no move to exit.

"Sure," I grunt to him.

"Leave everything in this Jeep, all the emotions and all the baggage. Get out of the car, don't stare at the ground, and keep moving. Shit's going to get real, soon, and you need to get your brain out of the stupor you've let it stew in all these months," he says before opening the door and climbing out.

Fuck, that asshole is big. The fucking Jeep rocked when his weight left it.

Snickering to myself, I open my door and try to shake away the headache I feel coming on. It's going to be a long day one way or the other.

"Something funny?" Bear asks with a tilt of his head.

"Only to me, big guy," I grin, and for the first time it doesn't feel fake to me.

"Let's get in there, we've got a bunch of young up-and-comers doing some exhibition bouts today. We need to see who's got that little spark of fire," Bear says and heads into the gym.

Thank fuck it's not me fighting today. Looking down at my body, I feel ashamed of how I've let myself go.

Only today, I promise myself again, *I just have to make it through today.*

Bear enters the glass front doors and stands there holding them open for me. I know it looks like he's being polite, but I see it his eyes. He's not letting me get away from him.

It's not like I'm going to run now, it would cause way too much of a scene. And I don't like fucking scenes. I don't like negative attention on me. I'm a confrontational prick in the cage... or was, but in public I like issues settled quietly.

Walking past him, I get hit with a wave of emotions and memories. This place was a home for me, where I learned who I was and what I could do. Learned to be a man practically, me and Tommy both.

Walking up to the desk, I look all around me, at all the familiar faces and strangers. Anyone who knows me and takes notice just nods or smiles. No looks of incrimination or disgust, no awkward glares. Just as if I never left, everything is business as usual.

It's as fucking jarring as it is comforting.

I see Chase standing behind the main counter of the gym, talking to Avery and a petite blonde chick who looks like she could be a model on some runway if she wasn't so short. She's not even that short really, but everyone who ever ends up next to Chase always ends up looking like fucking munchkins.

"Emmett!" Avery beams at me as she rushes around the counter and wraps me up in a quick hug.

Fuck. I hate hugging people. I never know how long to return it or if I even should. It's always creeped me out actually. But with Chase's dark fucking eyes daring me to be a dick to his wife, I give in and give her a quick hug back.

"Hey Avery," I say with a smile, "nice to see you."

"It's good for you to be seen here in our lowly establishment." She smirks at me. "I was beginning to think you forgot where you're supposed to be."

There's a couple of smartass answers I could give her, but even if Chase wasn't around, I don't feel like bothering.

Avery's one of those pure people. She doesn't harbor bad thoughts and shit, she cares and loves everyone. She's genuinely a warm, kindhearted soul.

She takes in all the kids in the gym and is like a mother to them all. This gym used to be only about MMA fighters and their training, but Chase and Avery have made it so much more. They actively recruit kids from the bad neighborhoods, and they give shelter and food to those in need.

Being a dick to her isn't in the cards.

"Yeah," I say as I rub the back of my neck, "been awhile."

"Don't worry, everything's the same. Everything except for our new administrator, Bree." Avery smiles as she leads me over to the front desk.

"Bree, this is Emmett. Emmett, Bree," Avery says, introducing us, and gives me a nudge to extend my hand.

Fuck what I said about being model material, this chick is straight up insanely hot.

Taking her petite hand in mine, I give it a quick shake

before letting go. I don't need to get my dirty fucking mitts all over hers.

"Nice to meet you," I mumble out.

"You too," she says with questioning smile to Avery. "Are you in the tournament today?"

Fuck no, I shout in my head. My out-of-shape ass would get pounded in front of her, which would suck big fucking balls.

"Nah, he isn't ready for fighting just yet, Bree," Dale's cantankerous ass says from behind me.

And just like that, all thoughts of the blonde angel standing in front of me are wiped completely from my head.

Fucking Dale.

Turning to the shitbird, I'm tempted to give him the finger, but I just shake my head and start walking after him instead.

"It was nice meeting you…" I hear Bree say from behind me, and again I feel like an ass.

Turning to face her, I see there's a faint blush on her cheeks, but she gives me a warm smile.

"You too, Bree," I say, and then turn to face the shitstorm my life is about to become.

"Now that you're done fucking around with the staff, we've got things to do today," Dale growls at me in his usual fucking manner.

"What the fuck are you expecting me to do?" I ask as I look around the gym.

All the guys around us are going about their business, either training or prepping for the fights today. Chase has two rings set up, and the billboard set up between them shows that there's eight fights scheduled for today and four tomorrow.

"Casey," he says without any further words.

Like that's supposed to give me any clue of what the fuck I can do.

Damn, this isn't going to be easy. It's going to be a fucking ordeal no matter what I do, and I deserve it to be horrible. Even in my drunken haze these last few months, I knew I was neglecting the outside world, and I knew there would be consequences for doing it too.

Especially if I didn't drink myself to death beforehand.

"Where's Casey?" I ask, trying to ignore the deep sour feeling come up from my stomach.

"He's going to be here in about half an hour. His grandparents are having a rough time getting him to do just about anything," Dale says quietly, and then turns to give me a look that I know I deserve. "It hasn't been easy on them. Losing their only kid and having their grandkid fall into a well of depression and misery. No one should ever have to bury their own child."

If Chase and Bear were to both hit me as hard as they could, I don't think it would feel as bad as what Dale just said to me.

"I..." I start to say, but don't even bother finishing.

Dale's heard all of my excuses. He and I both don't need any more of them.

"Tommy's dad is in the hospital too. He's not doing too good. So everything is now on his mom. She had to bury her child, her husband's health is in the shitter, and her grandson is fucking falling apart at the seams," Dale says to me as he stops to look out across the gym.

"I'm fucking here, Dale," I growl at him quietly. "I get the fucking message."

"I'm not sure you really do."

Dale turns to me. The usual piss and vinegar is gone

from his face. He's not giving me any blustering or the usual callousness.

No, he's looking at me with genuine anger.

"I'm here. I've got no fucking clue what to do, but I'm here," I say.

"Good enough, I guess. I mean it's not like someone's future is on the line. Some kid's who's lost everything and everyone," Dale says before he turns toward the sign hanging in the back.

On the sign are the names of fighters and who they'll be up against.

God, what I wouldn't do for a drink right now. Just a sip of rum or bourbon. Maybe a quick visit to the Jeep would be a good way to calm the nerves…

"Go look over Mia Collins and Blake Gorlewski. I need to see them with a fighter's eyes. They're new and I want to know if they have any raw talent," Dale says in a much more normal voice.

"I've never done anything like that—" I stop for a moment, trying to figure out what good I'll be looking at someone.

"You've fought enough to have eyes on a fighter. Look for the little things. We've got some raw talent in here and I want to see who will be going on to bigger things," Dale says.

"Um, I don't know anything about girls, Dale," I mutter quietly.

"I didn't either, but they're just like us, except meaner," Dale says with a loud laugh.

Fucking dick. He's going to enjoy watching my discomfort.

Turning away from him, I look up at the board and see the two names. Blake is in the Middleweight class and

Mia's a Bantamweight.

"Where are they at?" I ask as I look around the gym.

"I saw Mia running to the locker room with a hand over her mouth, and Blake is over there working on the bags," he says as he nods toward a guy who doesn't look much older than eighteen.

Looking back to Dale, I ask, "Was she puking because of you or nerves?"

An evil grin spreads across his face as he says, "Probably both. I'll have Casey come over when he gets here. If Puking Beauty makes it out of the bathroom, I'll send her over to the bags to get warmed up."

"Fucking dick," I laugh as I walk away from him.

Dale doesn't feel like he's doing his job unless someone pukes. He loves to make the fighters work and work *hard*.

"Just because you guys aren't working out today doesn't mean you get to sit and play grab ass. You, Bear, Brett, and the others will be working," Dale says to my back before I hear him start to yell at some poor soul.

We're not working out today? I'm not planning on working out anytime in the near fucking future either. This is a one-time fucking gig.

Heading for the fighters, I have to pass by Bree.

Shit.

With the fucking whirlwind of pain and emotions this place brings, her damn smile keeps entering my head, making me feel like I'm getting slugged in the lower part of my gut.

And it's not in a bad way.

Fuck. This is probably what a lack of alcohol is going to do to me. Reduce me to a drooling idiot.

But one look at her and I don't know if I mind it.

She's fucking beautiful, and not in the typical way I've

come to see in the women around Vegas. She's naturally sexy and doesn't look she's had any fucking work done on her. Her makeup is minimal, and her clothes are for comfort, not show. Her pale blonde hair and vibrant blue eyes are showstoppers, and those plush fucking pink lips look so damn kissable.

How the fuck did Chase get her to work here? I mean, this place is definitely on the map as a world class gym/MMA facility, but she's a cut above every woman I've ever seen. She's also noticeably not a gym monkey, she's not all lean and hard. No, she's got the curves of a woman who takes care of herself but doesn't break herself to do it.

And now she's looking at me as I walk past.

Fuck.

"Hey, how's the front desk treating you?" I ask as I slow down.

"Good, at least for my first day. It's been… interesting," she says with a quirk of those damnable lips.

Kissing her is surely a sin.

Nodding my head, I ask, "Everyone treating you okay?"

Laughing quietly, she nods her head. "I'm pretty sure Chase petrifies everyone enough to keep them from being mean."

"Eh, he's a big pussy cat," I say with a grin.

Shaking her head, her smile widens to show her teeth, and damn if it doesn't make her even more intoxicating.

"Pussy cat, huh?" Brett, the fucker, says from behind me.

Sighing and putting my head down for a moment so I don't show my lack of timing, I turn to look at Brett.

He's wearing a bright pink shirt that matches his wife Mandy's.

His says: I Bring The Pain. And hers says: I'm A Pain.

"What's going on, Brett?" I ask.

"Not much. Was wanting to introduce Mandy to the Pussy Cat's sister, Bree," Brett says.

When the couple walks past me, Brett turns for the briefest of moments to give me a wink and smirk.

Yep, he just let me know how fucked I really am.

Waving my hand at Bree, I smile and keep my mouth shut for the time being as I walk off. No need to stir up a hornet nest when I need to focus on the two fighters Dale has me looking over.

Watching first Blake and then a very pale looking Mia work over the bags gets my legs twitching. My arms almost start raising up to make the same motions.

It's unnerving to feel just how quickly my body wants to fall back into the rhythm of pounding the bags.

It was the first thing I discovered I was good at, that I was actually talented at, and that I could do for myself. I could see the results in the mirrors, and I could see the results on score cards. Most of all, I could see the results when I looked down at my opponent on the mat.

It's like some zen-like tranquility flows over me as I give pointers and little instructions on how to improve. I don't notice the time during this and I don't notice the world outside of this little corner of the gym.

I notice nothing but the way to work and improve, that is until the sound of the front doors banging open brings me back to the here and now.

Turning to look back, I see it's only members of the gym, not Casey.

And fuck, I have no clue what to do.

Signaling to both Mia and Blake that they need to take a rest, I look around to see what else is happening. When I spot Dale, I head over to him.

"How do they look?" he asks.

"They're not too bad. Blake, he's…" I pause for a moment, thinking on what I saw. "He's got a mean kick if he can keep it on target. And Mia, she's going to be a killer if you can get her core muscles up to snuff. Both are resting up for the fight."

"What about Blake? That was a long pause," Dale asks.

"He's good for fighting, but he won't ever be a top contender. At least not right now. He doesn't have that look in his eyes. He seems more…" I trail off as I watch Dale nodding at me.

"Yeah, I noticed that too. Great kicks and punches, but he isn't catching the reasons why he needs to do certain things. Even after we've tried talking and showing him the reasons. He'll probably drop out after he figures out being an MMA fighter isn't easy," Dale says quietly.

"You knew that before I went to take a look at him?" I ask.

"Yeah, Chase and I both have worked hard with him. He seems more interested in strutting around the gym than actually being a fighter," Dale says with a shrug.

I grunt at him.

Fuck, I never wanted anything more than to be a fighter.

Soft feminine giggling suddenly floats over from the front desk and I turn my head to see Bree laughing with Avery.

Damn… if that doesn't make me feel something I haven't felt in a long, long fucking time…

An elbow in my ribs reminds me none too gently that I'm not here to ogle the boss's sister.

"Eyes front, asshole," Dale growls at me.

That's easier said than done. My eyes don't want to focus on anything but the way she smiles.

Turning back to the fighters, I force myself to keep watching with Dale when all I really-want to do is watch Bree.

I check my watch then look to the front doors of the gym. I keep expecting Casey to show up and for Bree to walk back in from her break.

Both thoughts are warring through my chest.

Casey is dread and Bree is maybe a spot of sunlight in this miserable day. Man, I feel like a dick though, thinking of her smile to get through the dread of seeing a living reminder of Tommy.

It's strange how my fucked-up head is spinning in circles.

Casey's long overdue and it's causing me to have heart palpitations every time I hear a door open.

"Emmett!" Bear shouts at me from the front of the gym when I've finally given in to ignoring the door like a boiling pot of water.

Eventually the fucker's going to boil.

Bear ushers Casey a couple of feet toward me before he pulls back to stand next to Tommy's mother, Helen.

Dammit. I'm fucking craving a shot of rum so bad right now that it's good Bear is standing next to Casey's grandmother. He's positioned both her and himself between me and the doors out of here.

Time and again Tommy would jokingly say to me Casey got his good looks from his mom, and he was right. Casey looks a lot like her… everywhere except the eyes.

Casey has Tommy's eyes.

Those stormy dark blue eyes that show the whole world what he's feeling stare at me with unrestrained anger and contempt.

He looks so much like Tommy, all the alcohol I had last night wants to come back up.

Sweat beads across my forehead and down my spine when I see the anger on Casey's face. He's mad and he's looking at me like the piece of shit I am.

He's grown bigger since the last time I saw him, but just like his dad, he's on the smaller side for his age.

Jesus, my fucking heart feels like it's skipping beats as I slow to a stop before him. There's a huge fucking ache behind my ribs.

Fuck, am I having a heart attack right here, right now?

"I'm here," he grunts at me.

He's looking up at me with those damn eyes and I feel like I'm slowly falling into the deep black as I stare at him.

My throat catches before I can speak, and I have to take a breath before I say, "Me too."

Dropping to the floor, I kneel before him and look into his eyes. "I'm so fucking sorry."

The fist comes out of nowhere, and I'll be damned if my head doesn't rock back and then to the side.

Looking up, I see his loathing, his pain and suffering. But most of all, it's his broken heart that makes me feel every bad emotion I can think of. He doesn't say another word before he breaks away from me and runs out the front doors of the gym.

"Fuck," I hiss as I stand up from the floor.

"That could have been worse, I guess," Dale mutters as he grabs my arm to keep me from following. "Give him a few minutes before you go chasing him down."

A few minutes of hell. Now I'm straight up the center of attention in this crowded gym. Center of attention and I feel like I'm going to puke.

I'm going to go on one hell of a bender tonight, I can feel it.

CHAPTER SIX
BREE

Waking up at five in the morning is rough, especially for a natural night owl like me. So when Chase lets me know it's time for my second break of the day, I nearly fall over with relief.

It's been a long day. A satisfying, eye-opening day, but a long day regardless.

Feet dragging, I hear Chase chuckling behind me as I somehow manage to haul my ass over to the office to grab what remains of this morning's coffee. After gulping down a few mouthfuls out of a mug, I pour it into a paper cup to take outside with me.

I've been cooped up inside all day, and I'm hoping some sunlight will rejuvenate me.

Walking back through the gym, heading for the doors, I take one last peek around, soaking in everything around me.

Honestly, I don't know what I was expecting when I first walked into the gym this morning, but it certainly wasn't to be embraced by this… family.

Everyone, from Brett and his wife Mandy, to the big,

hairy guy they call Bear, has been friendly and welcoming. So welcoming, I almost feel uneasy.

I'm not used to people being so nice to me. In the circle I've been running with, people aren't nice unless they want something.

That mental shit, though, is completely on me. No one has given me any reason to believe that they're being anything but sincere. And I know I can't live the rest of my life suspicious of everyone's motives, so I try to push the uneasy feeling away.

Sighing at myself, I take another deep gulp of my coffee and then nearly choke on it when my gaze happens to land on the guy everyone has been whispering about today—Emmett.

Our eyes meet as if drawn to each other like magnets, and just like it happened when we first met, I feel this strange and unwelcome jolt coursing through my body.

And just like earlier, I find myself smiling nervously.

Emmett smiles right back.

My heartbeat starts to beat in this quick pitter-patter at the sight of his teeth, and I seriously have to wonder what the fuck is wrong with me.

The last thing I need right now is to be getting all boy crazy over some guy. For fuck's sake, I caught my boyfriend cheating on me *yesterday*.

But no matter how much I urge the beat of my heart to slow down, it always seems to pick up when he's around, and it's annoying the hell out of me.

What the hell is it about this guy?

Yeah, he's hot… with that smile… and those muscles… and those dark, soulful eyes… but so are most of the guys strutting around this place, and not a single one of them has had this affect on me.

In fact, compared to a lot of the other guys, he seems kind of… broken in a way.

Everyone's been talking about him today, and the things they're saying aren't exactly great. Apparently, he's been drowning himself in the bottom of bottle since his best friend passed away.

And I have no doubt that what they're saying is true because I swear I got the faintest whiff of alcohol off of him when he introduced himself to me.

Even Chase has gone the big brother route and warned me away in his own way.

But my stupid body and heart don't seem to be listening. He's the last thing I need… Hell, with all the shit I have going on, *I'm* the last thing he needs.

Forcing myself to tear my gaze away, I push through the front doors and out into the near-blinding sunlight.

And nearly crash into an old lady and a little boy.

"Sorry," I mumble and quickly grab the door, holding it open for them.

"It's okay, dear," the lady smiles at me, but the little boy just glares and stomps on past me.

Damn, if looks could kill…

And double damn, if he doesn't look a little young to be so angry. He can't be more than ten… or twelve…

Fuck, I don't know.

Gaze trailing after the two of them, I realize I'm staring and shake my head. Letting go of the door, I make my way down the side of the building, searching out a bit of shade.

Then I do the one thing I've been dreading to do all day, I pull out my phone.

A sigh of relief slips out of me once I see I don't have any new messages on my screen. It might be wishful thinking, but I can't help but hope that Tristan has given up on me.

For the life of me, I still can't understand why he would even want to still be with me. If anything, you'd think he'd be happy to be rid of me.

Before I can get too hopeful though I realize it's a little strange that my father hasn't been in touch, and the fact that he hasn't is worrying.

Maybe he hasn't heard the news yet?

I double-check to make sure I didn't accidentally block him when I blocked Tristan and Ashley. But no, he's still there, unblocked and at the top of my contacts.

Perhaps he doesn't give a shit that I broke up with the son of his biggest campaign donor…

Fuck, who am I kidding? I'll be lucky if he doesn't disown me.

The worry growing inside me until it's a basketball of pure dread, I gulp down some more coffee and seriously consider giving him a call to get the fallout over with.

Maybe if he hears it from my lips, he won't be quite as angry.

Thumb hovering over my screen, I'm just about to hit the call button when I hear a car door slam and someone calling my name behind me.

"Bree?"

Every tiny, microscopic hair on my body stands on end at the sound of that voice.

How the hell did he find me?

Pulse racing and breath quickening, I don't turn around, hoping that my head is so messed up I'm only hearing things.

Best case scenario, I've finally gone completely batshit crazy.

But no, my name hits my ears again, closer this time. "Bree!"

Whipping around, I stare in horrified shock as Tristan walks toward me from the parking lot.

"What the fuck are you doing here?!" I blurt out in panic.

Seriously, how the fuck did he find me? I blocked him on everything.

Another car door slams and my eyes are instantly drawn to the sound. Tristan's best friend, Spencer, leans against the side of his black BMW and gives me a snarky grin and wave.

Fuck. Fuck my life.

I may have blocked Tristan and Ashley, but my dumbass forgot to block everyone else to be safe.

Striding across the parking lot with purpose, Tristan's eyes burn into me as his long legs easily eat up the pavement between us.

"Why did you block my number?" he asks, a look of anger and hurt flashing across his face.

Glancing behind me, I look desperately for an escape. Unfortunately, I'm in the middle of the wall on the side of the building. I have no idea if there's anything at the back of the building, and there's no way I can get past Tristan to make it to the doors near the front.

An All-State track star, he's too damn fast and athletic for me.

"Why did you block me, Bree? Why are you hiding? Are you cheating on me?" Tristan asks, his voice growing more and more heated the closer he gets to me.

Goddammit, he's literally got me trapped between a rock and hard place, and something about it just pisses me off. It fills me with so much anger, I'm seeing red.

What right does he have to do this shit to me?

"Because we're over, Tristan," I say angrily, and lift my chin.

I'm feeling far too much like a trapped animal right now, and after what he did to me yesterday, I might bite if he pushes me.

"The fuck we are," he growls out as he reaches me. "I told you yesterday, it doesn't change anything. You're still *mine*, Bree."

"Doesn't change anything?" I repeat incredulously. "Doesn't change anything?! I caught you balls deep in Ashley. It changes *everything*. We're done, we're over. I don't care what you do, but stay the hell away from me."

Tristan steps into me, forcing me to press my spine into the brick wall to keep some space between us. There's barely an inch between his chest and mine, and I have no choice but to arch my neck back if I don't want to be stuck glaring at his neck.

Bastard. I know he's purposely using his bigger size to try and intimidate me.

His voice drops to an angry hiss as he tries to explain, "It didn't mean anything. She's a stupid bitch and she means nothing to me. You're the only one who matters to me."

I don't even know why I'm trying to argue with him on this. It's obvious his logic and my logic do not mesh. I know I should press my lips together and give him the silent treatment. Freezing him out would probably be the best course of action.

But I just can't stop myself from saying, my voice dripping with venom, "Oh, and that's supposed to make it all better? I'm supposed to be okay with you fucking other girls because you really don't give a shit about them? Fucking spare me."

Tristan's face flushes an angry red and he slams his hands against the brick wall, each barely missing me.

I find myself flinching and then becoming even angrier.

Yesterday, he used his size and strength to bully me. To make me feel afraid and powerless. And I've been carrying that scared, helpless feeling around inside me ever since.

It's been festering.

Festering from fear to anger. And I'm so not putting up with it today.

He opens up his mouth, probably ready to spout some more convoluted bullshit at me, but I don't give him a chance to get the words past lips.

"Go away, Tristan. Get the fuck away from me," I warn.

I'm so upset, so angry, I'm starting to shake with it.

He leans down, pushing his face into my face. "No, I'm not going away, Bree. You're coming back to California with me, even if I have to drag your ass back."

The look he gives me causes the true weight of my current situation to slowly sink in like a cold finger dragging up my spine.

Staring into his eyes, into his sick, twisted determination, it finally dawns on me that I'm not dealing with a rational man. He's completely irrational, and if I don't get myself out of this situation, things are only going to get worse.

He might seriously hurt me.

"Fine," I huff, my emotions doing a complete one-eighty. The sudden, instinctive need to flee, to escape, is nearly overwhelming me. "Then I'll leave."

I try to duck under his arm, hoping to slip quickly past him before he can stop me. But when I'm about to pop back up on the other side, his hand comes down heavy on my shoulder.

"Don't you dare try to run away from me," he bellows in my face as he shoves me back into the wall.

My shoulders connect first with the hard brick, followed by the back of my head, and I cry out against the sharp bite of pain.

"You don't get to leave until I say you can leave!" he continues to yell at me.

I'm so freaked out by his sudden aggression, I try to make myself as small as possible.

Chest heaving and huffing with his anger, Tristan watches me wrap my arms around myself and gives me a look full of disgust. "And fuck, don't you dare look at me like that. Don't fucking flinch, I barely touched you."

I don't even know how to respond to that, but thankfully before I have to, someone calls out, "Hey! Get away from her!"

Tristan doesn't tear his gaze away from me as he shouts back, "Fuck off, this is between her and me."

I want to see who called out, but as soon as I try to lean around Tristan, he pushes his body back into me.

Tristan leans down, following me as I shrink in on myself.

Grabbing me by the chin, his fingers pinch into my jaw bone as his voice drops to a hiss. "Don't look at them, look at me. We're not finished."

"I said get away from her!" someone screams, and then suddenly Tristan is no longer in front of me.

It happened so damn fast it takes me two full blinks to realize Tristan is now sprawled out on the cement in front of me.

It takes me another two full blinks to see the angry boy

who stomped by me earlier pushing himself off the ground.

Getting to his feet first, the boy clenches his hands into fists and looms over Tristan.

Chest heaving, the boy says, "Only pussies pick on girls!"

"You little fucking shit," Tristan snarls as he starts to get to his feet.

Shock keeps me rooted to the spot, unable to move, a silent witness to the craziness that's playing out in front of me. My mind just can't seem to wrap around it until Tristan gets to his feet and I see the size difference between him and the boy.

There's at least a foot and a half, if not more, of height difference between them.

I have no clue how old the boy is, my experience with kids is very limited, but I'd bet he can't be older than twelve.

And I'm pretty sure the only reason he got the jump on Tristan was out of sheer surprise. Tristan wasn't expecting it. Hell, I wasn't expecting it.

But seeing the two of them square up on each other utterly terrifies me.

The boy doesn't stand a chance.

As Tristan lunges for the boy, I react on pure, protective instinct. Jumping forward, I push my way between them.

"Tristan, no!" I scream, throwing my arms out to protect the boy.

Tristan either doesn't want to stop himself or can't stop himself because he barrels right into me.

Taking me down to the ground, the most horrible pain I've ever experienced in my life crashes into me as all the air whooshes out of my lungs.

"What the fuck is going on here?!" a new voice roars as I stare up at the sky, gasping for air.

Even as I struggle to cope with the pain, the voice is so strong, so thunderous, it seems to vibrate through my body.

"Are you okay?" someone asks from close by.

I think it's the boy.

Wrapping my arm around my aching chest, I try to sit up and remember how to breathe at the same time.

"Here, let me help you…"

"Fuck," I hear Tristan mutter as I finally get myself into a sitting position with the help of a hand on my back. "Fuck this shit."

"Did you fucking hurt her?!" the roaring voice from earlier thunders out at the same time the boy tells me to relax, my air will come back.

I'm so focused on trying to fucking *breathe,* I can't focus on what's going on around me.

I have no clue who's roaring, and I can't bring myself to try and twist around to look, but part of me hopes it's Chase.

Chase will protect us.

I don't know why I believe that fact with every fiber of my being after only knowing him for a few days, but I do.

Footsteps pound against the pavement behind me just as I manage to drag in my first breath. The breath is almost blissful because I know now that I'm not going to suffocate to death, but at the same time it hurts like a bitch.

As I suck in the air though, I can't relax like the boy is telling me to because I'm too aware of the precarious situation we're still both in. Unfortunately, I can't see much from down here on the ground, only Tristan's legs.

And he's too close, too fucking close… until suddenly he's not.

The footsteps hitting the pavement behind us grow louder and louder.

And then suddenly Tristan's legs are pumping as he takes off, running away from us.

It seems like only seconds later car doors are slamming and tires are squealing as someone peels out of the parking lot.

"Fuck you, you pussy! Get your ass back here and face me like a *man!*" the newcomer roars even louder than before.

The last word is so forceful and guttural it lingers like an echo in my head, repeating over and over again.

"Are you okay now?" the boy asks, his face appearing in front of my face.

There's so much fear and worry in his expression, it makes him look young. So young a cold chill flows through me.

Goddammit, this boy, this child, tried to go up against Tristan to protect me.

"Yeah," I croak out and try not to grimace as he continues to peer at me like he's afraid I'm going to suddenly drop dead at any second. "I'm fine," I force my lungs to add with a gasp. "Thank you for saving me."

I try to will my lips to curve into a smile too, but they don't quite manage it.

The boy's brows scrunch together as if he doesn't believe me, but he gives me a nod of his head.

Dammit, I don't want him to worry about me. Yeah, my head is starting to throb with the beginning of a killer migraine, and my lungs ache like I breathed in a bunch of water… But fuck, I don't want him to be traumatized by this shit.

Especially because it's *my* shit.

As a wave of guilt washes over me, I strain my throbbing brain for a way to somehow fix this whole mess.

Is there even a way to fix it, though? I let everything spiral out of control for so long, it's come to this…

"You're my hero," I decide to say before finally forcing my lips to obey me. "And yet I don't even know your name…"

The boy begins to smile back at me until a shadow slides over us.

"Casey," someone says from above.

Someone with a deep voice that's a little hoarse from roaring.

I watch Casey's smile slide off his face as he glances up.

I peer up too, my eyes squinting against the sunlight. It takes me a moment to make out the face silhouetted against the bright light, but when I do my stomach drops to my damn feet.

"Are you okay?" Emmett asks, his features tight with concern.

"Yeah… I'm fine," Casey answers and then glances to me.

"Bree," Emmett practically breathes as he turns that concerned look to me.

Our eyes meet and it feels like the air just got knocked out of me all over again.

Of course, out of all the big, strong guys in the gym who could have come to our rescue, it had to be him…

It had to be him to witness the worst of me.

I don't even know why I care, but I do. I don't want

him to see me this way, especially with that damn look on his face.

Looming over me and staring me down, there's this strange intensity in his gaze. A feral intensity that both terrifies me and excites me at the same time.

As I take in his heaving chest and the sweat glistening on his skin, I don't know if I should throw myself at him or run away, screaming.

Before I can make up my mind, somehow my hand ends up in his hand and he pulls me up to my feet.

Grabbing me by my hips to help steady me, his eyes continue to bore into mine, never deviating, as he asks, "Are you okay? I saw that fucker take you down…"

His voice drops back down to an angry growl and I find myself shivering. What the hell? Is he half beast?

And why the hell do I find the sound of him growling so damn satisfying?

Still trapped in his eyes, at first words fail me. But as his gaze grows darker and darker, I finally manage to tear my attention away.

"I'm okay," I offer softly.

Honestly, now that Tristan is gone and Casey is safe, I wish this whole thing would just go away.

I sure as fuck don't want to have to explain it in any way.

"Are you sure?" Emmett's hands leave my hips and then his warm palms are cupping my cheeks. Gently turning my face back to his face, his eyes dart all over me, searching. "You hit your head pretty hard."

God help me, the way he's touching me feels too damn good. It's only his palms on my cheeks, but there's something about the sensation of his skin against my skin that's totally fucking with me.

Yet again, I don't know what the hell is wrong with me. Now is so not the time for this. After getting knocked around, I shouldn't be getting all weak in the knees over this guy.

I open my mouth with the intention of downplaying what happened so I can make my escape, but Casey decides now is the best time to chime in with, "He also shoved her into a wall before I took him down. She's hit her head twice."

I start to scowl, but then Emmett's face darkens. There's so much anger, so much pure rage in his eyes, it's almost awe-inspiring.

Like staring at a painting that moves you and disturbs you at the same time.

"I'll fucking kill him," Emmett snarls.

And I don't doubt for a second that he won't do exactly that. Shit. Before I can even come up with an argument about why that's a bad idea, a very bad idea, Casey says, "Me too."

Fuck my life.

The last thing I need is these two getting involved in all the drama surrounding me.

Especially Casey.

Emmett must realize this too because he gives a little shake of his head as if he just realized what Casey said, then he asks with a bit of awe, "You took him down?"

"Yeah," Casey says, puffing his chest up with pride.

Emmett grins. "That's my boy."

My ears must be deceiving me, and I must have hit my head harder than I thought because there's no way he's encouraging that little boy toward violence....

But fuck me if the two of them don't seem to share a moment. Like they're truly bonding or something.

And I'm so damn disturbed by what I'm seeing, I start to unconsciously pull away from Emmett.

Only to have his arms lock around me and pull me back.

"Two hits, huh?" he asks, his face growing serious once again as his attention returns to me. "Should we call the doc?"

That's the last thing I need. A doctor and probably a police report that will make the headlines.

"No," I blurt out a little too forcefully and then take a second to suck in a deep breath as Emmett's brows shoot up with surprise.

"I mean," I say slower and more carefully, "it would be a waste. It looked worse than it was."

Damn it all, now I'm downplaying what Tristan did for the sake of keeping this from blowing up even bigger than it already is.

I just can't stop myself from digging myself deeper and deeper into this hole of shit.

And Emmett doesn't look like he's buying it for one second.

"Honestly, I'm fine," I add, wishing he'd just let me go and drop all of this.

Because the longer I stand here in the safety of his arms, the more tempted I am to stay here and indulge myself in his protection.

What I wouldn't give to have someone standing beside me, fighting my battles with me…

Emmett's expression grows so skeptical I'm almost certain he's going to call my bluff.

But before he can, I hear Chase call out from behind us, "Yo, what are you doing to my sister, Emmett?"

"Yo, what are you doing to my sister, Emmett?" Chase asks loudly from behind me, and I can physically feel the tension in his words.

Tension with a hint of violence, like I'm stepping on his turf or something.

"Checking her for a concussion, meathead," I growl out to Chase without looking over my shoulder to see his reaction.

My hands are still holding the sides of this incomparably beautiful woman standing before me. Bree isn't that tall, and the way she has to look up into my eyes makes my gut clench.

Those fucking eyes, a man could get lost in them and never desire to find a way out.

"Why the fuck are you checking her for a concussion?" he shouts and runs up to us.

Reaching up with her small hands, Bree pulls mine down from the sides of her face. After shaking her blonde locks at me, weariness fills her eyes.

"I'm fine!" she squeaks out. "I only fell on the ground."

Chase grabs tightly onto my shoulder as he asks, "This fucker pushed you down?"

Anger flows through me as I smack his hand away and face him. "I didn't do shit, Lurch."

"Look, guys!" Bree shouts. "It was nothing! Just a misunderstanding!"

Her eyes are now full of pleading as she tries to smooth out her clothes.

Turning to face Chase, she says, "Nothing happened, okay?"

"Then why is the little man here checking your eyes and face for a concussion?" he asks, and I couldn't have said it better myself.

"She tripped, I guess," I say with a small shrug.

If this is how she wants to play it with Chase, far be it from me to stop her. Though she will be answering my questions when I get her alone. No way am I going to let some tall, lanky bitch hurt her and get away with it.

"Then why did I get to knock down some big asshole?" Casey huffs loudly.

Ah, there we go, out of the mouth of babes. Now I won't look like the dickhead who's snitching on her.

All three of us turn to Casey and stare at him with interest. I'm curious about what he did to take down the prick. Pretty sure, though, that Bree and Chase are wanting him to say something entirely different.

"What do you mean?" Chase asks in a growl, glancing at me with disdain and then back Casey.

"I gave a leg kick to the back of his knee. Asshole never felt it coming. Kind of messed up, though, when I didn't stop him from taking her down," Casey says and looks almost sheepishly at Bree. "Sorry about that."

Rolling her eyes with a smile, it's like she forgets that

she's trying to keep whatever happened quiet. "It's okay, you're still my hero."

Chase stands up to his fullest height and stares down at Bree. "We need to have a talk, if you don't mind. Privately."

Privately, my ass, I think, but I can't do anything with her right now. Not with Goliath standing in my way. And not unless I seriously want to get fucked up. I accept that, but it doesn't mean I have to like it.

No, I don't like it one fucking bit.

Wrapping an arm around her shoulder, Chase starts walking Bree as if she's a small child to the front of the building. When they're about halfway to the door, he turns back to give me the biggest stink eye I've ever seen.

"Why is he mad at me?" Casey asks in a huff.

"He's not. We're all proud of you for taking care of that asshole. He's pissed I was touching his sister," I say as I watch them walk into the building.

Bree turns her head to stare at me for a moment, and while I can't even begin to describe the emotions on her face, just looking past those emotions makes me realize that she's the prettiest woman I've ever seen.

Like straight up launch a thousand ships and go to war beautiful.

The worst part about it though is that it just about kills me to see any man, even if it is Chase, touching her.

"She's mine," I say quietly to myself.

"Think she has a sister?" Casey asks.

Rolling my eyes, I shake my head to clear the clouds away and focus on the person beside me. "I'm an asshole, Casey."

"You didn't use to be," he says, and I can feel the hurt in his voice.

Turning to face him, I do the same thing Chase did to Bree, and wrap my arm around his shoulder to slowly walk him to the bumper of my Jeep.

Sitting on it, I say, "I'm also an alcoholic dick, if that explains anything."

"It doesn't. Why didn't you pick up the phone?"

I want to ask about which time, but there's too many to count.

The one that hurts the most is Tommy's last message. I should have picked that one up, maybe he'd still be around if I had.

I can feel the craving for a drink starting to race through my brain, but I know right now it's just me being weak.

Weak and fucking stupid.

In my former, healthier days, I would have caught that little bitch running away from us easily. But looking down at the small spare tire that is starting to show, I wince.

In my former days, I was a lot of things I'm not anymore.

"Because I was scared," I say, and for the first time in what seems like forever it feels like I'm finally telling the truth.

The real truth, not the little truths I've been wallowing in.

"Grandma called you a lot, so did Grandpa... so did I. Didn't you listen to our messages?" he asks, and the pain in his voice squeezes my heart.

Squeezes it with all the fucking guilt and shame I'm feeling.

"I tried to at first, but I couldn't get myself to call anyone back. I was hurting so much that I couldn't... deal with life outside my own little hell," I answer. "I want to say I would have eventually, but it's a lie. Bear, Chase, and Dale forced me to come today."

"Why?"

"Because they gave me two options, grow up or be forced to," I say.

He's quiet for a moment before he points to where the scuffle was. "What's that?"

"It looks like a phone," I say, and I'm hoping it belongs to that fuckhead that ran away.

If it's his, I can use it to get a little payback and get past all these fucking emotions. Because right now these fucking emotions are killing me. Guilt, shame, despair, and fucking blinding rage that some fucking douche canoe touched my girl are overwhelming me.

"I don't know, Little Man, go grab it for me," I say, giving him a small shove on the shoulder.

"Don't," is all that Casey says to me, and instantly I know I've fucked up again.

That was his nickname from Tommy and me. We called him Little Man all the time.

Fuck, I miss Tommy so fucking much right now because this was his bag, his part of our team. He knew how to handle people and shit.

We'd been teased more often than I can count about being practically married.

When Casey came around and his shit of a mother ran off on a never-ending bender, I helped raise the little guy. I bought fucking diapers. I bought him clothes and toys. Fuck, I was the one who went with Tommy to the fire department so they could show us how to properly adjust the car seats.

Casey slides off the bumper and heads for the phone to

pick it up. His walk is so fucking similar to Tommy's it makes my soul die a little in remorse.

I'm a fucking shit just like his mother. His dad dies and I leave him like his mom did when he was just a baby. This kid's got more fucking balls than I do.

I fell into a bottle and he's been trying to cope.

Fuck it. New steps forward from today. I don't have time to fucking drink myself into a damn stupor if I want to help Casey, make Bree mine, and beat the shit out of that fucker that ran from me.

While Casey is walking back to me, I make a quick checklist of the things I need to do. Take care of Casey, knock Bree up, beat the shit out of the douchebag, and maybe murder the fucker who started me on this fucking downward spiral.

"Sup, Little Beast?" I ask Casey when he sits back down on the bumper.

"Little Beast?" he asks with a tilt of his head.

"Yup, only Beast would take down a dude twice his size and stand up for a chick in the face of certain death," I say with a grin.

He's deathly silent for a long time, just looking at me with those eyes of Tommy's. So fucking quiet and intense that it freaks me out a little.

"I'm good with that," he finally says then hands me his phone. "It's hers."

"How do you know?"

He snickers at me. "Press the button and you'll see."

Pushing the button, I look down at the screen and laugh. "Yeah, my dear Holmes, your sleuthing seems to be correct. Somehow I highly doubt that dickhead would have My Little Pony as his home screen."

"Who's Holmes?" Casey asks.

Fuck.

"I'll have to explain it some other time. I think right now we need to take this into her and rescue her from Chase," I say as I try to unlock the phone.

"What are you doing?" Casey asks.

"Being a snoop and marking my territory," I mutter.

It's locked, but I figure I can go for broke and enter the one password that might work.

I push in one, two, three, and four.

"What, are you going to pee on it like our dog does?" Casey asks.

Snorting so hard that my head hurts, I begin to laugh as the screen opens for me.

"Something like that," I say before I quickly text myself from her phone.

"Dude, you're weird," he says and punches me in the shoulder.

"Yeah, I know. I used to hear that a lot from…" I start to say, looking up at him, but freeze.

I want to say Tommy, but the word catches deep in my throat and leaves a solid lump.

"I know, my dad," he says, and punches me in the shoulder again, but harder this time. "It's okay, I'm always slipping up and mentioning him to Grandma."

"That's not a bad thing, though," I say. "It's good to talk about him whenever we can. It hurts, but it helps us keep him alive in our hearts."

Nodding his head, he stands up from the bumper. "Hope you don't mind me talking about him when I'm with you."

"Not one bit." My mouth feels dry at the thought of talking about Tommy, but we have to do it. "Whenever you need to talk, we can."

"I guess we'll be doing that a lot then," he says and starts walking to the door.

Whenever and however much he needs.

I've got to step up. This little human being has lost more in his lifetime than most people I know, and he carries it all on those twelve-year-old shoulders.

Atlas.

He reminds me of Atlas with the world on his shoulders, and no one besides his grandparents to help share the burden.

The gym has a different smell to it this time when I walk through the doors. It smells just like it smelled all those months ago. It's the smell that gets in my nose and wants to stick.

I fucking loved being here so much, it was my place of peace for so long.

Losing the match, and then Tommy, took this place from me.

Took my purpose.

Dammit, I never thought any of this shit would happen when I walked into the arena to fight Jamey, and it feels like the moment I tapped out because of my shoulder I tapped out on life.

Trying to get my bearings, I follow Casey over to his grandmother. I don't know what to do, but I can feel the blood pumping through my veins. It's like that little scuffle outside has set something off inside me that's recharging my batteries for the first time in months.

I want to fight someone right now. I want to feel the roar come out of me.

I want to fight someone and then fuck Bree.

Shit, I'm almost bouncing on my toes as I walk behind Casey to see Helen. That's until I see her face and how tired she looks. Her complexion is a little ashen, and the deep circles under her eyes show the pain and weariness her smile tries to hide.

Coming up to face her, I remember how big of a dick I've been to her and her family in their time of need. How much of a piece of shit I've been even though they took me in and gave me love when I needed it the most as a kid.

She and Bill were the rocks that supported my dreams. God, I've made a royal fucking mess of things.

"Ma'am," I say as I stand in front of her.

Once I would have instantly gone in for a hug and a kiss on the cheek, now I stand here in some horrific parody of what we used to be.

"Don't even start with that stuff." Helen steps forward and wraps her arms around my neck, pulling me down into a tight, almost painful, hug.

Thankfully the gigantic lump in my throat stops me from gasping out the sob that threatens to engulf me.

Snaking my hand out, I grab Casey's sleeve and yank him into the hug. Hugs can heal all wounds. Helen once told me that and I hope she was right.

It takes a long time for Casey to loosen his stiff body, but when he does we all hold on for what seems like an eternity and yet it's only a few microseconds of time.

Pulling back from Casey and me, she smiles a very tired smile. "Bill's not well enough to leave the hospital yet, but he sends his regards."

My words come out stumbled and almost stuttering, but at least they come out. "I'm... I'm sorry I haven't been in touch more, Helen..."

"Well, that will be changing, I suspect. I'm going to need regular updates on you and Casey over the next couple of weeks," she says and then turns to Casey. "Are your bags in the trunk, sweetie?"

"Um, what?" I ask stupidly.

What the hell is she talking about?

"Grandma, I don't think this is such a good idea..." Casey starts to object, and I'm starting to feel like I should too.

"Nonsense, you go get your bags. I need to speak with Emmett privately for a moment," Helen says to Casey.

Casey doesn't move right away. The two of them stare at each other with a tension I've never seen before. Casey's defiance is bordering on rebellion, but whatever the fuck's going on, I can't let him put any more shit on Helen.

She's been through enough to last two lifetimes.

"Little Beast, do what your grandmother is telling you. Don't be a dick," I say only loud enough for him to hear.

He shoots me a look of shock, and I grin. "Hurry up, man. I need my wingman back for today."

Casey looks like he wants to object to me interfering, but the look I give him shuts it down quick. I need to step up and there's no time like the present.

"Whatever, you're not going to like this any more than I do," Casey grunts before walking away.

Shit.

Whatever is in the works, he's probably right.

Turning to face Helen full on, I look at her for a long moment. She's always looked far too young to me to have a child as old as Tommy was, but now those youthful looks have been taken over by exhaustion and grief.

Stepping up close to her, I give her another hug and pull back. "What's going on Helen? And how can I help?"

She looks up into my eyes for a long time, searching for something. She can probably see that I've fallen on the road of depression and self-pity, but I'm hoping she sees whatever it is she's looking for because I desperately need her to see something good inside me.

"Bill's heart isn't doing good, Emmett," she says as she takes my hand and pulls me over to the chairs by the wall.

"Fuck," I say quietly as I sit down next to her.

"Language," she chides me like she used to do when I was kid.

Both of us smile briefly.

"Sorry," I say.

"No, you're not." She smirks at me before continuing. "From what the doctors are saying, it's not a death sentence, but he needs work done to fix a bunch of problems. He also needs rest, from work and stress. Both of which we haven't gotten much of since Tommy passed."

"Helen—" I start to say, but she cuts me off quickly.

"No use putting blame on anything or anyone, the only way is to move forward. That's why I talked to Bear," she says as she looks at me intently.

"He probably doesn't have much good to say," I warn her, "but whatever he's said is the truth, I imagine."

"He said you'd say that." She smiles softly. "He also agrees with me that Casey coming to live with you for a few weeks while I take care of Bill is the best thing for you both."

Well, there goes my fucking mind. Boom. Big fucking brain explosion.

"What?" I ask incredulously.

"Yep, it's high time you got out of the gutter and started putting the pieces back together. And Casey needs someone who can show him the light at the end of the tunnel he's hiding away in."

"But—" I try to say, and she steamrolls right over me.

"It's also high time you start acting like the man I know you are and quit fucking around," she snaps.

Holy fuck, she said *fuck*. That's a first, and I know it's deliberate. She's trying to get through my thick skull.

"Helen, I don't know the first thing about helping Casey, or how to raise a kid… Hell, I don't even know how to raise myself," I say wearily.

"That's probably good for both of you," she says before standing.

Casey comes walking back in the gym with a backpack and a large duffle bag.

"What?" I ask, and I feel like I've said it too many times today, and for way too many fucked up reasons.

"If you did, you wouldn't be able to fix each other."

She motions for me to follow her over to Casey.

My head feels light and kind of fucked up as I follow behind her. She stops in front of Casey and smiles down at him. She's tired and she's got so many heartaches on her heart, but she reaches out and pulls him in like she did all those years ago when she took care of me.

Her voice chokes up a little as pushes him away and holds him at arm's length. "Casey, you can be mad at me and think unkind things, but I do this because I love you more than you'll ever know. You both need each other, and you need to learn that life must go on."

"Grandma, I don't want to live with Emmett," Casey says, sadness staining his cracking voice.

"I know, sweetheart, but you need to do what's best for you both right now and not what's the easiest." She turns to me. "Pick up the phone when I call or I'll send all the guys over again. And next time it's Reaper who comes calling, not Chase."

Fuck. There's a big difference between those two names for the same person. One's a monster, and is the one the boogeyman fears.

"Message received," I say with a chuckle.

Reaching down, I pat my phone in my pocket and hope to hell it's charged.

"Thought so. If it makes any difference, the girls wanted to go the first time with the guys. I said it wasn't necessary," she says with a wink.

Fuck, that probably would have been even worse than what happened with the guys. I've seen the women gang up on the guys when something needs to be done. It's not pretty.

"Just so we're clear, you want Casey living with me for the short term. Not like daycare where you come pick him up at the end of day?" I ask.

"See, I knew you were still smart. Not too many punches to head," Helen teases me before she hugs us both quickly.

"I need to go, I want to get back to Bill."

She walks away, leaving us both standing here in shock.

"Could've warned a guy, Case. Fuck," I growl at him.

"I didn't think she meant it," Casey says quietly.

"Fuck," I grunt.

"Fuck," Casey grunts.

Whapping his shoulder only hard enough to get his attention, I say, "Language."

"Really?" he asks with his eyebrows raised.

"Yeah, if you use half the words I do, she'll rip your tongue out when you see her next," I say with a smirk.

For a couple of minutes, we just stare out the window, wondering what the fuck we're going to do now as we watch Helen leave.

Once she's gone, I shake my head and motion for him to follow me. We both head out to the Jeep. I open up the back and we toss his stuff in before heading back to the gym.

We still need to watch the fights and give Bree her phone back.

~

By the time we make it through the small crowd that's starting to form around the two cages and make it to the front desk, it looks like Chase has interrogated Bree pretty firmly. Well, from the tired expression on her face, I'd say she's been interrogated.

"Hey," I say as we step up to the desk, "how's the head?"

"It's—" she starts to say.

"All good," Chase all but growls at me. "Something you want, runt?"

Jeez, I wonder if he's sore at the whole me calling him Lurch thing.

"Yeah, Little Beast found Bree's phone out in the parking lot," I say as I hold it out for her.

A small spark of electricity flows through my hand as her soft, delicate fingers brush against mine to take the phone back.

"Little Beast?" she asks with a cute little quirk of her lips.

"Yeah, that's me," Casey says proudly. "It's going to be my ring name when I fight like Emmett and Chase do."

"Really?" she asks.

"Yep!" He beams at her.

"That's a good one." Chase grins at Casey.

"So—" I start to say, only to stop when I feel a sheer fucking amount of malice directed at my back.

I know who it is right away. Dammit

"Hi Bree," Dale says in that grizzly voice of his. "Mind if I borrow these two from ya?"

I wince at the words, and I'm betting Casey does too. We both know Dale's only nice to the people he's not training. Especially the little kids. But us fighters, he fucking hates us with a passion.

"Sure, Dale!" Bree smiles sweetly at him.

She's totally in that bastard's fucking thrall. She doesn't know his evil.

Heavy hands land on both mine and Casey's shoulders as he turns us away from Bree and Chase.

As Dale marches us away, I hear Chase's loud laugh.

Fucker's laughing at us, I just know it.

"So ya got yourselves a break, I see. Didn't even ask ol' Dale if he wanted to join ya. Nope, just left an old man like me to do all the work," Dale croons to us softly.

Casey looks over at me. "Can I say it now?"

"Only in your head," I grumble.

"Cheer up, boys, there's still lots of work you can help me with. But first we're going to have one of those heart to heart talks," Dale says as he leads us over to a quieter area of the gym.

"I'd rather you make me puke from working out," I groan.

"Oh, that comes soon enough. No, this one is of a serious nature," he says as he turns us to face him.

When all three of us are standing in a small triangle, he

says, "Bree only gave us enough information to get Chase to stop hounding her for the moment. I'm not happy with that."

The hackles on the back of my neck rise at his words. He's pissed, and so am I all of a sudden.

"I want the fucker's name who was messing around with her, understand me?" Dale says to me as he looks directly in my eyes.

I nod my head. "I want it too."

"Good, we're going to make sure trash like him don't mess with family," Dale says, and then looks to Casey.

"Okay," Casey says with a grin.

"You're old enough now to be a part of the gym and the guys. Don't fuck that up," Dale warns and then motions to the rings. "Go watch the ones I need you to look at."

Then, smiling at someone behind us, he changes his whole demeanor. Switching from the grizzled old bastard to some jolly fucking man.

Turning to see who's worked a miracle, I see Grace and her daughters walking toward us. Grace is beaming at Dale, while, if I'm not mistaken, Hope is giving Casey a devilish grin.

"We need to go," Casey hisses at me as he tugs my arm. "Like right now."

"What's the big rush?" I ask with a smile. "Don't want to talk to Hope?"

"I'll tell Dale you called him a pussy," Casey says, and then pulls even harder.

Fuck, a man can only take so much teasing, I guess.

"Alright! Talk to ya later, Dale!" I say as we rush past them and head for the fighting cages.

My head is fucking pounding, pain throbbing and pulsing behind my eyes. But like I've done in the past when everything is falling apart and I can't show the world what I'm really feeling on the inside, I force myself to slap a happy smile on my face as I sit behind the front desk.

Chase is hovering beside me like a mother hen, and the amount of anger simmering off him is so strong I find myself shivering.

He's pissed and rightly so. Someone attacked me outside his own gym. I get that. His pride has taken a hit. But I think what is really biting him is that I won't tell him who or why.

"Just give me a name," he mutters for the hundredth time as he squeezes his inhumanly large hands into fists.

It's tempting, so tempting to give him what he wants. To put it all out there. To put it in those hands of his so he can fight my battles for me.

But I can easily picture the consequences. Chase going after Tristan... Chase beating the shit out of Tristan...

Chase ending up in prison… Avery and their children suffering without him…

Our family completely and utterly ruined.

Unfortunately, with the shit I'm dealing with, violence isn't going to settle it.

Tristan's family is filthy, stinking rich.

Theoretically, I could file a police report against him, but his team of lawyers will just make it disappear. And if they don't, then there's all the judges they know…

When you have as much money as his family does, you don't have to play by the same rules as everyone else. You can use it to practically live like a god amongst us lesser mortals.

I know because I've been witnessing it for years.

They own the entire system we're all forced to live and abide in.

Really, the only thing I can think to do is wait him out because fighting back is not an option. I can't risk whatever he'd bring down on me, my mom, Chase… or even this gym.

Tristan will get bored eventually and move on…

I hope, anyway.

The heat simmering off Chase shoots up a hundred degrees as I press my lips together and refuse to answer him.

"I should call the fucking cops," he mutters, giving me a threatening look.

And once again, I can only hope it's simply that. An empty threat.

Because if he actually does it…. Fuck me… I don't even want to think about it.

Turning my face away, I hold my breath because it's the only way I can keep myself from hyperventilating.

Once again my heart is racing a million miles a minute, and with everything it's gone through today I'm afraid I might have a damn heart attack.

My eyes scan the crowd, searching for something to focus on. I need a distraction or I'm going to have an emotional meltdown.

As if my mind is subconsciously seeking him out, I find myself picking Emmett out of the dozens of faces in the crowd. With Casey beside him, he's standing outside one of the two cages that have been set up for today's exhibition. There's currently a fight going on inside the cage, and the two of them seem to be focused on it.

At once I begin to relax a little bit. It's almost as if simply seeing Emmett, knowing that he's close, has a calming effect on me. I try not to think about it too hard as I soak in every little movement he makes.

The way he lifts his muscled arm to point, the slight turn of his head as he talks to Casey.

I zero in on him, shamelessly using him as the distraction I desperately need.

He has a damn good jawline, I find myself musing. And I especially like that natural arched quirk of his left brow.

He might not be quite as fit as some of the guys around here, but he stands tall. His posture alone practically screams *don't fuck with me.*

I only had his hands on my cheeks for a minute or two, but even now I can't forget the sheer power his touch had over me.

Or the way those eyes of his seared into me as if he could see *me.* The real me.

Casey says something, his mouth moving, but the crowd suddenly begins to cheer and hoot.

Emmett leans down to Casey, putting himself at his level to give him his ear.

It's such a little thing, but out of the blue I have the most fucked up thought of my life.

Emmett would make such a good daddy.

Jesus Christ.

Mentally slapping myself, I jerk my head away.

Only to find Chase glaring at me.

Ugh, was he watching me watch Emmett the whole time?

Chase doesn't say a word, and he doesn't have to. The look on his face says it all.

My face burns with heat, and I try to think up an excuse to explain away what I was doing but come up with nothing.

Absolutely nothing.

With all the shit I'm in, you'd think I wouldn't have the time or emotional energy to become fixated on a guy of all things.

But that's exactly what I'm doing.

Shaking his head like he's disappointed, Chase turns away from me, directing his glare at Emmett.

Emmett must feel the weight of it because he glances back, his gaze colliding with Chase's. The two of them glare daggers at each other, neither attempting to mask their animosity.

And suddenly I feel like crying.

What am I doing? What am I causing?

What the fuck am I destroying?

My throat begins to close up on me, and I'm on the verge of saying fuck it all and making a run for it when my phone starts to vibrate and ring.

Glancing down at the screen, for a second I just want to

crawl into a fucking hole and *die*. It's the last fucking thing I need…

But maybe this is the universe's way of giving me the out I need.

Or punishing me even more for what I've been doing.

Snatching my phone up from the desk, I stand up.

"Where do you think you're going?" Chase asks without looking at me.

I try not to take his tone personally, given what's recently happened, but still bristle a little on the inside. "I have to take this call."

Finally Chase drags his attention away from Emmett to look at me. "You can take it right here, where I can see you and protect you."

Whatever irritation I was feeling immediately evaporates. He might be rough around the edges, but at his core Chase is truly a good guy. A good guy who doesn't really know me but seems to want to protect me.

If only he knew what he was protecting.

"I can't," I explain. "It's my father… I have to take it privately."

Chase continues to stare me down as if his glare alone will force me into submission. I have no choice but to lift my chin and stand my ground.

I can't give in on this, unfortunately. I have to speak to my father, and it has to be in private. If I don't, there will be severe repercussions.

Repercussions that are more frightening than anything that Chase could do to me.

My phone stops ringing, the call most likely going to voicemail, and I cringe. If my father calls back and I don't pick up, there will be hell to pay.

I count the seconds in my head.

One… two… three…

My phone begins to ring again.

Panic grips my heart. I don't even know how many damn rings I have left.

"Chase, please," I beg after the next ring.

I don't know if it's my tone or my pleading eyes that gets through to him, but Chase's face softens a little with sympathy.

Glancing away, he huffs out, "Fine, but take it in the office. I don't want you leaving the building alone."

Nodding my head, I grip my phone and make a dash for the back office. I probably look ridiculous the way I'm rushing, but it's the least of my worries right now.

My phone rings twice more before I make through the office door.

Slamming the door behind me, I hit the big green accept button on my screen and pant out, "Hello?"

There's a long pause before my father's irritated voice comes over the line. "Am I interrupting you, Aubrey? Is there something more important you need to do than talk to me?"

Shit. Here we go, starting the guilt trip already.

Leaning my head back against the door, I close my eyes and try not to sigh. "No."

"Are you sure? I could call back at a more convenient time…"

"I'm sure," I answer immediately, my head popping up and my eyes going wide.

I know that's not a sincere offer.

It's a threat.

"Very well, then," he says tersely. "I know you're *busy*, too busy for your father, so I'll get straight to it. I just got off the phone with Warren Yates."

There's another pause, and I don't say anything because I keep expecting him to go on while I hold my breath.

Finally, he asks coldly, "Is there something you want to tell me?"

Oh god, what does he know?

I didn't expect him to get wind of everything so quick. I don't think it's been an hour since Tristan was here.

Did Tristan go crying to his daddy right away?

Or perhaps my father doesn't know what happened today. Maybe he only knows about the split?

It's impossible to know. My father is being vague on purpose, and the question is completely loaded.

"I broke up with Tristan," I admit and try to mentally brace myself for his reaction.

I've been dreading telling him this, which is precisely why I haven't called him yet. There's no way he's going to be happy about this.

"You broke up with Tristan?" my father repeats as if he can't believe it.

"Yes, I caught him—"

Talking over me and not giving me a chance to explain the situation, my father's voice rises in pitch as he asks incredulously, "You broke up with the son of my biggest campaign contributor? The son of my biggest backer and supporter? The son of the man who has the power to make me or destroy me? The son of the man that could put me in the White House?"

With each question, his voice grows louder and louder with righteous anger.

And I find myself flinching.

I feared this would be his reaction, but a part of me, a

very small part, was hoping that he'd understand. That he'd support me once he knew the truth.

Again, I try to explain, "Yes, I caught him with—"

And again, he cuts me off by loudly talking over me. "Do you have any idea what you're doing? Are you intentionally trying to ruin me? Is this how you pay me back for everything I've done for you?"

Those words, *everything he's ever done for me*, cause a thick weight of guilt to tighten around my throat like a noose.

I've never forgotten for one moment everything he's done for me, and since he walked back into my life I've felt beholden to him.

Beholden for existing.

I try to defend myself, try one last time to explain it, but he's not having any of it. "No, I'm not trying to—"

"Do you know how much money I've spent on you? How many strings I had to pull to get you into your fancy school out in California? How much networking I've done for your sake? The sacrifices I've made… the time I've spent… the money I've spent… I've given it to you so you can have the kind of life you deserve, the kind of life you're enjoying right now. And this is how you repay me? You repay me by destroying what I've spent the last twenty years of my life accomplishing?"

The noose tightens, nearly choking me. I'm not trying to ruin my father or destroy his dreams, but I can see why he might think that of me.

Everything he said is true. He has spent a considerable amount of time and money on me. He's invested in me, but he hasn't necessarily done it selflessly. All the things he's done for me he's done because he gets something out of it. In fact, he used his money, power, and connections as a trap. Luring me in when I was at my weakest.

I'm not completely blameless, though. I knew when he walked back into my life when I was sixteen after abandoning me for fourteen years that he wasn't doing it out of a sudden sense of remorse or regret.

He needed me. Needed me to complete his perfect family image for the public.

After my mother divorced him, my father found and eventually married a wealthy heiress. An heiress who could help him achieve his dreams of winning a public office.

An heiress that unfortunately turned out to be barren.

Unwilling to adopt but knowing he was unlikely to win the Nevada governor seat unless he could portray himself as a family man, my father turned to the only child he had.

Me.

If I could go back, I'd shake myself. I'd implore myself to be happy with what I had. That what he had to offer wasn't worth the price of my soul.

But it's too late for that now.

I've made this fucking bed, and now I have to deal with all the shit hiding under it.

"Well, do you have nothing to say for yourself, Aubrey?"

Oh, am I finally allowed to speak?

I take a small, calming breath before I rush out, "Tristan cheated on me. I walked in on him yesterday fucking my best friend Ashley in our bed."

There. It's out. Maybe he'll back off now.

The line falls completely silent.

With each second he doesn't speak, I find myself growing increasingly more and more nervous.

My father is rarely, if ever, speechless.

After what feels like an eternity, I finally hear him take a deep breath.

Then he says, "I'm sorry you had to see that..."

For half a second, I start to feel relieved. Obviously, my father will be on my side. There's no way he could somehow condone or excuse Tristan's actions.

Then his next words make me feel like I've gotten slammed into the wall all over again.

"Tristan should have been more discreet."

Oh god, is he really defending him?

"I'm sorry?" I ask, wondering if I heard him right.

Without an ounce of shame, my father says, "It was inconsiderate and reckless of Tristan to do what he did. He's a big boy now, he should know better. He should carry on his dalliances where you won't see. I'll speak to his father so that this doesn't happen in the future."

The future? Is this a bad dream? One long fucking nightmare I can't wake up from?

He can't possibly expect me to stay with Tristan...

"I'm sure Tristan's future partner will appreciate that," I say, unable to keep the sarcasm out of my voice.

"If you're referring to yourself," my father snaps back, "I'm sure you will."

"No," I immediately deny. Then I repeat it again more forcefully. "*No*. I'm not referring to myself because I broke up with him. We're done."

My father begins to breathe heavily into the phone. "Listen here, Aubrey..." he says, before stopping and taking an audible breath to calm himself.

While I wait for him to finish whatever it is he's going to say, I mentally tell myself I'm not giving in on this. There's nothing he can say or do that will make me take Tristan back.

"You and Tristan are not done."

Before I can object, he continues, his voice firm and resolute. "Once I get off the phone with you, I'm going to call Warren. We're going to iron this mess out. I'll speak to Tristan myself and make it clear his actions are unacceptable."

"Unacceptable?" I repeat with disbelief.

"That's correct. Unacceptable but not unforgivable."

"I am not—"

"You will!" my father suddenly roars at me so loud I have to yank the phone away from my ear. "You will accept his apology if you know what's good for you, young lady!"

My stomach clenches and my heart thuds sickly with panic. My father has never been this angry or unreasonable with me before.

I'm going to puke, puke all over the damn floor.

"And if I don't?" I gasp out before I have to swallow down a throat full of bile.

"If you don't," my father snarls into the phone. "You will be solely responsible for ruining my career. You will be solely responsible for destroying all the good I've done for this state, for this nation, and the people."

But I haven't done shit to deserve that. If anyone should be to blame for that it should be Tristan.

"If you don't, you're no longer my daughter. I will no longer acknowledge you. I will no longer have any contact with you. I will fucking disown you. I will fucking ruin you. Do I make myself clear?"

Head spinning, I have to lean back against the door to steady myself.

"Well, do I?" my father demands harshly.

"Crystal," I somehow manage to choke out.

"Good. I'll call Warren now."

Without a goodbye, he hangs up, the line going dead.

For the moment, the world is silent. Uncomfortably silent.

Then his words buzz in my ears.

No longer his daughter… disowned… ruin me…

If only I didn't care. If only I could just walk away. But the weakest part of me has always needed his approval. Always craved his acceptance. Needed it to justify my existence.

Needed it to not feel so worthless.

The thought of meaning nothing again to the man that created me hurts me in a way I can't even explain.

When I was little, I tried to convince myself it was his loss when he walked out of my life. That it wasn't my fault because I didn't do anything wrong. But deep inside, I've always wondered why I wasn't good enough for his love.

The only reason I could ever come up for him abandoning me was that something must be wrong with me.

That unlike everyone else around me, I'm broken and flawed.

My own father didn't want me.

My own father didn't want me because I'm not good enough.

It wasn't until he strolled back into my life with his tempting promises that I started to finally feel as if I was worthy. That I deserved to take a place in this world.

I soaked in all the affection and love he gave me and used it to build myself up.

If I cut him off, if I refuse to do what he demands and he abandons me, will I return to that feeling that I'll never measure up?

Squeezing my hand into a fist, I dig my nails into my palm until I'm breaking skin and drawing blood. It's not until the bite of pain hits me that I can finally *breathe.*

Breathe and think clearly.

I'm not going to figure this out standing in this office, hyperventilating. I need to get the fuck out of here before someone sees me.

Releasing my fist, I glance down at my bloody palm then wipe it against my shorts. If I'm quick, nobody will notice.

Nobody will notice me cracking and breaking.

Turning around and grabbing the door handle, I feel like I'm operating purely on automatic mode. My brain begins to focus on only the things I need to do.

I need to walk back to the front desk to grab my purse. I need to tell Chase I'm sick and I need to go home.

I need to get the fuck out of here.

Slipping my phone into my pocket and pulling the door open, it's simply a matter of putting one foot in front of the other to walk down the hall. There's no need to think. No need to agonize over the past twenty-four hours.

It's nothing…

Hold it all in.

It all means nothing until I can deal with it in private.

I've got everything inside me completely locked down tight until I turn the corner and set eyes on Emmett heading for the men's room.

Suddenly, as if just the sight of him has thrown my system into complete shock, my legs stop working and I'm glued to the floor.

Emmett glances at me then looks away as if he didn't see me at first.

I hold my breath, watching him and hoping he continues to walk by none the wiser.

Then he looks back to me in surprise and stops dead in his tracks.

I try not to shake, fighting off the trembling my bones want to give in to as his eyes rake over me from head to toe.

Too late, I squeeze my fingers together and slap my fist against my shorts.

"Bree?" he asks softly, his brows knitting together as he jerks his attention back to my face. "What's wrong?"

What isn't wrong?! I want to scream, but only end up shaking my head.

He takes one step toward me and I cry out, "Don't!" as I stumble back.

For the love of god, don't get near me. If you knew what was good for you, you'd run far, far away.

You'd forget me.

Ignoring me, he stalks toward me, the look on his face growing darker. Once again, I find myself having this unsettling feeling that he can see right through me. See right through to the very depths of my soul.

I take a step back for each one he takes forward until I've trapped myself against the wall.

Using his bigger body to block me in, Emmett reaches down as if he's going to grab my hand but I jerk it out of his reach.

"Don't touch me!" I snap.

A look of hurt passes over his face and I experience an immediate pang of guilt.

Oh god, the last thing I want to do is hurt him of all people.

We stare at each other in surprise before he shakes his head sharply.

"Fuck, I'm sorry," he says and reaches up, raking his fingers through his hair as he takes a step back. "I don't know what I was thinking. I'm sorry for bothering you…"

Dropping his arm down to his side in defeat, he turns his back on me and begins to walk away.

I want him to leave… and yet I don't. In fact, something inside me begins to panic as he walks away.

After what I just did, he'll probably never speak to me again.

"Everything turns to shit," I whisper.

The words just slip out of me on their own as if my soul is sending a distress signal.

I press my lips together, horrified that my thoughts are starting to leak out, and hope he didn't hear it.

"What was that?" he asks, whipping around to face me again so quick it's as if he was ready for me to call him back.

When I refuse to answer, he walks toward me again, quickly closing the distance between us.

"What was that?" he repeats and his gaze bores into me, willing me to answer him.

Unable to resist him, I find myself explaining, "Everything I touch turns to shit… so please, don't touch me."

Shock. Pure, unadulterated shock appears on his face and stares back at me.

And I wish I could shrink into something small. I wish I could disappear into the wall.

Then the shock fades away.

What it leaves behind, I can't even explain. But it's suddenly like I'm the one staring into his soul.

Staring at someone who's just like me.

"That's okay, baby girl," he says with a mixture of both tenderness and sadness as he reaches out his hand and cups my cheek.

His palm is warm and a little rough, but I find something about that touch of roughness soothing.

"I'm already shit," he says as he leans in so close his breath hits my face. "I've been shit for a long time."

It's my turn to be shocked as I look up at him. Is he messing with me? How could he possibly believe that? Especially after what he did for me today?

Hating the expression on his face, I tell him honestly as his thumb strokes against my cheek, "You're not shit to me."

His thumb suddenly stops, and my heart skips a beat, afraid he's going to pull away or dismiss me.

Before he can disagree, I blurt out, "In fact, I think you're pretty fucking great."

An unwanted blush blooms on my cheeks and heat creeps down my neck. I'm not the least bit eloquent, but I couldn't live with myself if he walked away thinking he's lesser than he is in my eyes.

Still trapped in his penetrating gaze, I watch a transformation take over his face. What little bit of tenderness that was there disappears, replaced something fierce and hard.

Something that both terrifies me and takes my breath away.

Suddenly he makes this deep, rumbling sound in the base of his throat and his fingers curl possessively around my cheek.

Before I can prepare myself or pull away, he's pushing into me and kissing me.

The first press of his lips against my lips is downright electrifying, and I swear my entire body lights up with a sizzling, crackling heat.

As if he's just as surprised, he stiffens up for a moment. Then he's groaning and pushing me up against the wall.

The first press of his lips was hard and possessive, as if it was meant to claim me, but the next pull of his mouth is done like he's a man that's been starving.

Starving for me.

There are so many reasons I shouldn't be doing this, so many reasons to push him away, but I find myself grabbing at him. Grabbing at him like I'm afraid he's going to suddenly disappear like a phantom from a dream.

His kiss is better than any drug… better than any self-inflicted pain.

With his hard body pressed up against mine, fitting like it was always meant to be right here, the rest of the world is falling away.

There's only him and the way he makes me feel.

And like this he makes me feel… free.

Even with his body acting like a cage, trapping me against the wall, my soul is soaring.

Hand sliding from my cheek to the back of my head, his fingers thread through my hair. Then he tugs, arching my head back so he can further devour me.

His lips push and pull, urging me to open for him. Urging me to give the last bit of myself to him for safe-keeping.

I resist at first, afraid of where it will lead.

As if he can sense my conflict, his kiss suddenly softens, becoming tender and loving. With his mouth, he shows me I can trust him.

Trust him to keep me safe.

Melting against the wall, all my insides turn into mush. And no longer conscious of what I'm doing, I give into him, parting my lips so his tongue can sweep inside.

The first touch of his tongue against mine is so intense I find myself jolting in surprise.

His fingers tighten in my hair to keep me in place.

If I thought the simple press of his lips was earth-shattering, his tongue stroking against my tongue is downright mind-blowing.

Each rub of his tongue feels like he's lighting all these tiny sparks inside me.

And a craving like no other takes ahold of me.

Craving for more of his touch, craving for more of his taste.

Craving for more of his safety.

Fingers gripping at his shirt, I try to pull him closer. Try to pull him *inside* me.

I moan into his mouth, partly in pleasure and partly in frustration, unable to get what I need.

Perfectly in tune with I want, he suddenly grinds his hips into my hips, his hard bulge grinding into my pussy.

Pure liquid heat shoots through my veins and my knees go weak.

As I start to slide down the wall, his hand is there to catch me. Grabbing me by the thigh, he lifts my leg up, locking it around his hip.

Then, rocking his hips in a fluid motion, he moves against me.

Caught up in the friction, I find his rhythm, chasing the sensations building inside me. And I'm so close, so close to what I want, what I need. It's there, just out of reach, when the sound of someone gagging penetrates the haze.

"Ewwww, get a room," Casey says, and my entire body goes cold like someone dumped a bucket of ice water over me.

Reality comes rushing back in like a tidal wave and embarrassment sinks its claws in deep.

Oh god, what the fuck was I doing?

Giving into my first instinct, I shove Emmett away.

He stumbles back, confused, his eyes still hooded and glazed.

Glancing between Emmett's confused face and Casey's disgusted one, I've never felt more ashamed.

I don't know what came over me. I've *never* acted in such a way before.

Not with anyone else…

Shaking his head and straightening, Emmett shoots Casey an irritated look then focuses his attention back on me.

"Bree, ignore him," he says, and reaches his hand out to me. "It's okay."

I take one look down at his hand, at what he's offering, and do the only thing I know how to do.

I flee.

"Bree!" Emmett calls out as I take off running.

Running as if my life depends on it, I pray that he doesn't chase after me.

By the time I reach the front desk, I've run myself so hard that when I stop I'm gasping.

A quick glance behind me shows me though that Emmett didn't follow me. Grabbing up my purse, I fling it over my shoulder and head for the front door, only to be stopped by Chase.

"Yo, where you going in such a hurry?" Chase asks as he steps into my path.

Oh shit, if Emmett comes, Chase might find out what we did…

I can literally feel myself going white as I pant out, "I feel sick. I need to go home."

Thank god Chase doesn't question me.

He simply nods his head, immediately accepting the excuse. "I'll walk you to your car."

I swallow back a sigh of relief and follow after him, all the while afraid Emmett might pop up behind me at any second.

When we reach my car and there's still no sign of Emmett, I count my lucky stars and say a quick goodbye to Chase.

He stands in the parking lot as I pull out, determined to watch my car until I can take my left turn onto the main street.

Once the light turns green, I glance into my rearview mirror and lift my hand, meaning to wave goodbye to Chase, but catch sight a looming figure standing in front of the main doors.

Emmett is standing there, watching me with a resigned look on his face.

Dropping my hand, I hit the gas a little harder than I mean to and squeal out into the street.

Forcing myself to drive only ten over the speed limit, I crank my radio up and fill my car with music so loud it's impossible to think.

By the time I pull up in front of my stepfather's house, my head is splitting and my ears are ringing.

In my rush to get inside the house and safely up to my room, I almost forget my purse twice. Once I have my car locked up, I dash up the front steps, taking them two at time.

I make it through the front door and all the way up to the base of the staircase before my mom pops out of the dining room with a smile on her face.

"Hey honey," she says cheerfully. "How was your first day?"

S ometimes the things we want most in the world are the things that will destroy us.

I wanted to be the champ. I wanted the accolades, the lights, and the glamor. I've always had the chip on my shoulder that I needed to prove something to the world and my shit parents.

Maybe that's why I feel this huge fucking crushing weight on my chest when I watch Bree drive away from the gym.

I really do believe one damaged soul can recognize another. It's something in the eyes and the way we carry ourselves. The way we carefully guard our words and actions.

I want to be her champion. I want to be her fucking rock. And I know without a doubt that the douche who pushed my fucking girl to the ground was an ex who hasn't gotten the memo.

He'll get it, and it's going to be one he'll never fucking forget.

Screaming the dirtiest words I know in my head isn't

going to do anything to fix this shit, though. I feel like a fucking ass for letting her go, for letting us get separated. Not that I blame Casey for it. Little dude was right, we needed a room right then.

The way she was moving against me…

Shit.

I've got her phone number though, and I've got her location too. I'm probably a dick for snooping on her, but my ass isn't stupid enough or drunk enough to think for a second that her ex is going to let her go easy.

He's hurt her at least once, and I'm betting he'll try that shit again.

That fucking kiss, though. Fucking man alive, it shot adrenaline straight to my heart. It took me to eleven out of ten. Her lips, her taste, just her fucking presence in that kiss…

She didn't kiss me with some fucking shy little peck.

Hell no, she put her soul into it.

And the way she pressed her body right back against mine, clinging to me in desperate need of something I barely understand…

It was like offering a life raft to a drowning man.

Fuck, my life is spiraling out of any semblance of control. Casey, Bree, me. Three huge new developments. Myself, being probably the biggest.

I can feel the cravings, the yearnings, and delusions starting. The deep, dark part of me wants to go back into a bottle. It would sure as fuck be easier to let myself slip back into that eventual suicide of the mind and body

Fuck the world.

Fuck the kid.

And fuck any chance at romance.

But there's another part of me that's slowly waking

back up and calling that dark part of me a little bitch. It's telling me I need to do better. I need to stop being a fucking pussy. That I'm not finished, and I'm not ready to tap the fuck out yet.

I'll be that guardian for Casey.

I'll be the champion Bree needs.

But I'd be lying if I didn't admit the darker part of my soul doesn't have a stronger grip on me right now.

Shaking my head, I retrace my steps back to Casey. We need to pack it up and get out of here. Shit's going to be rough for us as we figure out how to get past Tommy's ghost and my failings as a decent human being. Maybe it's not the ghost we need to get past, but maybe it's the one we have to come to terms with.

"You know you'll be taking a couple of physicals and drug tests over the next couple of months. Probably the sooner the better," a voice says from behind me.

Dammit. Yet another person I know that has seen the shit side of me.

Turning around, I slow my walk to a stop. "Hey Avery, I wasn't…"

"Chase has his own big brother hang-ups that he has to deal with. Big muscles and big brains don't always agree with each other," she says with a laugh before holding up a hand to stop my protesting. "I'm more of a Friar Lawrence type of person, not the overbearing parents and cousins…"

What the fuck? Was that a Romeo and Juliet reference?

"Um…" is about the only word I can get out of my mouth.

"Don't worry. Mum's the word on you two needing to get a room," she says with an exaggerated wink.

Ah, shit.

"Avery…" I say, and I feel this need to protect what has just started between Bree and me.

My hackles are raising at just the thought of us having any sort of interference.

I'm not ashamed though of what she saw or Casey. It wasn't what I would have liked to do in public, but it is what it is. I've never felt anything like that before. Ever.

Fuck, I've never straight up practically made love to a woman through just one kiss. Especially on the first day we meet. That's never fucking happened to me before.

That was some serious me, Tarzan, you, Jane, let's go back to the cave and mate for life shit right there.

Avery takes my arm and pulls me slowly to the side of the gym. "Relax, Emmett. I just want to honestly talk to you about Casey before you get in too far over your head."

From where she has us angled, I can see Casey shouting encouragement to one of the fighters we were tasked with looking over. He's so in the element surrounding us, it's almost easy to forget all that's been going on with him.

Easy to forget the gigantic storm cloud that's been circling over his head.

"He's… He's going to need a lot of emotional stability. He's going to need a person in his life who can take the abuse he might give. He needs someone who's going to be there and help him transition from this broken little boy into a man," she says quietly.

My first gut reaction is to tear her apart, to ask her how the fuck can she call Casey *broken*.

But I don't because I know he is, just like me. But he's worse because I carelessly left him broken. I allowed this to become the dark stain on his soul that it is.

"I'm going to try to do every—" I manage to say before she cuts me off.

"I could use a Yoda metaphor like I do with the kids who come here needing help, but honestly... Don't fucking just *try* Emmett. *Trying* won't help him grow and learn to be the person he needs to become," she says quietly, but with more vehemence than I've ever seen her have before.

"I know, he's got the fucking weight of the world on his shoulders," I say, and the reality is maybe setting in.

I'm going to be taking care of a child that's not my own, that has been royally fucked over with life, and he's had no support from one of the most important people in his life.

"Take some of that load, show him he's not alone in his guilt for being left alive while the one parent who gave a damn in his life is now gone."

Nodding my head, I really don't have any words for what's going on in my thoughts. She's right on all counts, and I need to step the fuck up.

"Good. Now back to the other part, you're going to be doing drug tests and physicals for the fight board. Your body from here on out belongs to the gym," she says with a grin.

"What do you mean?" I ask, and I can feel that little part of my brain again screaming at me that something is about to fuck my world over even more. "The fight board doesn't give two shits about me raising a kid."

Avery motions to my pocket. "No, but your contract does. You might want to check your phone when you get a chance. I'm pretty sure it's about to explode."

"What the fuck?" I ask as I pull it out.

A sickening urge to vomit hits me as I open up my

phone. I always keep my phone on do not disturb when I'm at the gym. Even now I have to turn on notifications. It's a holdover from when I was in training. It kept all the distractions at bay.

But now that the notifications are turned on, my phone starts lighting up like fucking Christmas. Dings and pings are going off from missed calls and texts that aren't in my contacts. My email app shows that I have over a hundred unread emails. The text app has just as many, if not more.

What the fuck?

"Dale has contacted the company and he's put in your official request for a rematch. He's also let it slip to a couple of key news outlets," Avery says with a wide grin.

"What the fuck?!" I shout at her.

They have no fucking right to do something like that. He's not even my official contact for the company. I can feel the heat of my anger rising up my chest and flooding my face with pure rage.

"You guys can't fucking do that!" I all but yell, and remember too late where the fuck I am.

"We can't do what?" Chase asks with a pissed off look on his face as he marches over to where Avery and me are talking.

"Fuck you too, fucking Frankenstein's creation asshole," I spit out at him. "You guys don't have the right to act like my manager. That's Tommy's…"

Shrugging his shoulders, Chase moves to stand next to Avery. "We did and you will be fighting. Dale's already got the schedule for you. Avery has her classes for Casey scheduled for the times you'll be here, as well. So it's going to be a family affair thing."

"I… shit," I mutter. So they'll be using Casey to keep

me in line. "What's the timeline? I don't think I'll be ready for a fight in the contract's allotted time frame."

"Two months," Dale says from behind me.

I'm going to fucking puke, I can feel it right now. Bile is rising up my throat. Holy fuck. Two fucking months. There's no way. I haven't prepared or trained in six months. I'll be fucking killed out there in the ring.

Casey will lose two people if I agree to the fight.

"There's no fucking way… I mean… I…"

Fuck me.

Dale claps me on the shoulder from behind. "Sink or swim."

"So, tomorrow your system should be clear enough to do the first preliminary drug tests," Avery says. "Unless there's something besides booze in your system."

Fuck, I almost wish there was. That would be an easy way to get this shitshow of a circus to come to a grinding halt. "No, just alcohol."

"You sure?" Chase asks as he peers into my eyes.

"Yeah, just the alcohol," I say.

"Any pain meds?" Dale asks.

"Nah, I took the pain meds from the surgery, but then self-medicated with alcohol."

"When was the last pain med you took? Ibuprofen, Tylenol, Aleve?" Chase asks.

"Two weeks after the surgery," I say.

Looking to Dale, Chase says, "Notify the board about that. Give 'em the down and dirty facts. No sense in hiding anything. This way they don't have any surprises. They'll contact the USADA, and we need to as well to make sure there's not any complications."

"You'll have to get the medical records from the surgery. They should have been sent over, but we need to make sure we have copies. If we need to explain why something is in his system, that'll cover it all, I think," Dale says.

It's like I'm a fucking child all over again. They're talking about me as if I don't even have a choice in all this shit.

"Do I get a say in any of this?" I ask.

Knowing that they're doing something for my benefit like this is infuriating and comforting, I guess. But fuck, I'd really like at least some input.

"Not really. Starting tomorrow, your ass is mine," Dale says before walking away to ruin someone else's life.

"Go get Casey home, fed, and settled. You guys have a lot on your plates, and tomorrow both of your worlds start anew," Avery says as she flashes a smile at me before walking away.

Chase smirks at me before he walks away too. "I don't let runts date my sister."

"I'm going to fucking kill him," I mutter.

Walking into the house with Casey in tow is an odd feeling. Besides the guys today, it's been a long time since anyone's actually been here. So long that I immediately feel that awkward shame people get when someone sees their dirty home. It's not like I've had any real reason to take care of the place, but I still feel the embarrassment of having a kid see I can't keep my shit together.

Casey wrinkles his nose. "Grandma would kill me if I ever left my room like this."

He's got a point. Now that I've been away from the place for more than a couple of minutes, I can smell the copious amounts of alcohol and grime that have taken over. This place smells like a fucking dump, and my stomach starts churning at the thought of all the alcohol.

"Kinda smells like the arena after a fight," he continues as he walks around the living room. "Looks like it too."

"Yeah, yeah, yeah," I grumble as I move past him, motioning for him to follow me. "Let's get your room set up, then we'll order some food. I need to take out the trash too, I guess."

Mercifully one of the three spare bedrooms in the house is clean and relatively empty except for a couple of old boxes of workout gear. Leading him into it, I turn on the lights and show him the private bathroom.

"All yours… Beast," I say while opening up my arms and spinning around the room.

I'm pretty proud that this room is setup nice enough that it's livable. It's got a bed, a couple of dressers, a big tv, and even the bathroom is stocked up on the necessities.

Back before my shoulder got wrecked and everything turned to shit, my house was pretty fucking nice. I didn't subscribe to the whole bachelor pad thought of mind. I kept my shit clean and looking good. I wanted to make it as much of a real home as I could.

Lots of things were different back then. I had a stable home here. Tommy and Casey would come by all the time and stay the night when it got too late. It was like our own little family.

Tommy's mom even helped me decorate the rooms.

I wanted to make it as real as I could. I wanted the warmth that her home always had, wanted it to be the exact opposite of what I lived through with my real family. No more eviction notices, drugs laying out in the open, empty refrigerators and cabinets. Fucking hell, I wouldn't have to put up with passed out strangers invading my space ever again.

Casey drags his bags up onto the bed and starts to pull his clothes out. "Can I bring my gaming systems over?"

"I don't see why not," I say as I pick up a couple of piles and help him with opening up the dresser drawers.

"Grandma said this was a working summer break, so I wasn't sure I'd be allowed."

That throws me a little.

"Huh? How long has this been in the works?"

"Since right before school let out, I guess," he says.

I don't even know how long ago that was. If I'm being honest, I don't have a firm grasp on where exactly I'm at on the calendar.

"How long ago was that exactly?" I ask and put another stack of shirts in the dresser.

"What do you mean?"

"Like… Shit. When was that?" I ask and feel like an even bigger asshole lush.

"Grandma and Avery started talking about you three weeks ago. Two weeks before I got out," he says like I'm an idiot.

"Oh," I say brilliantly. And yeah, that kind of gives me more information. "When do you go back?"

"Home?" he asks, and there's a hitch in his voice when he says that word, home.

"Well, I meant school, but either."

I really and truly almost don't want him going back home. It's fucked up how weird that is to think.

"I get nine weeks for summer break then I head back. I'll be going into gifted seventh grade," he says with a small shrug of his shoulders.

I give him a light punch to the shoulder. "Damn, man, that's awesome."

"Not really, I don't like gifted classes. Everything is so much faster, and it's like they're trying to shove books directly into my head. Every night it's homework and computer work. And since I'm really good at math and science, they drown me in it," he grumps out.

"Yeah, but you'd be bored to tears in the regular classes," I say, trying to find a bright lining.

Casey throws the last of his clothing in a drawer with a huff. "That's what Grandma says, but I miss my old friends. Not like it matters. Grandma left me here with you until I graduate college."

Fuck.

"I seriously doubt it's like that, Casey…" I say but trail off because I don't exactly know what it is like.

Fuck. Me.

Information would be so helpful right now. I could especially use a timeline of what the fuck I'm signed up for.

Casey just grunts and plops down on the bed. "She and Avery both want me here. They said I needed to have a new perspective on things. I probably shouldn't have called Grandma a bitch, either."

I drawl out the word, "Yeah." Then I shake my head. "That might have been a bad move."

Nodding his head, he looks up at me. "Do you think she hates me?"

How many times do I have to look into those eyes and see Tommy staring back at me?

"No, Little Beast, not at all. She couldn't hate you any more than she could force herself to stop breathing. She loves you with every ounce of her heart," I say as I take a seat next to him.

"Then why did she send me here?"

Fuck, I wish I knew the answer to that because for the life of me I can't think of what I have to offer.

"Because I'm family and she thinks we'll help each other heal," I say and wrap my arm around him.

"Maybe."

The knowledge that there's so much more going through his head and heart eats at me. Eats away at my heart just like all the pain and hurt I've buried deep down inside.

"We will, one punch at a time. I'm a big fan of fighting my way through bad shit," I say and raise my hand up to him, showing him my knuckles.

There's a lot of scarring on them. Lord knows, I've kept my past pretty damn secret, but there was a time I didn't fight in the legal bouts.

"I thought you had to wear gloves," he says with confusion.

"Yeah, those scars aren't exactly the good kind. I fought through just about everything I could to get the hell out of what I was living in," I say, and I did.

I fought for my daily bread at times when I couldn't face the prospect of going back home to my dad.

Tommy's parents took care of me as much as they could, but the law still insisted I went home as much as my dad wanted me there. I was his little welfare check.

I still needed new clothes and sparring gear though when I was hitting my late teens, so I fought in the underground circuits for a couple years. I made quick money for myself, even if Tommy was begging me to go legal. But shit was needed.

No need for Casey to know all my past misdeeds, though. Maybe when he's older he'll understand.

"Point is, you and me are the same. We're going to fight through all the shit and pain we have coming at us. We're going to punch and kick our way out of this shit, and when we can't see anything else besides the pain, we'll be stronger for it," I say before wrapping my arms tightly around his shoulders.

Sometimes I wonder if I have that magic that Helen had when she'd hug me and I'd feel the strength and will to keep going.

"Promise?" Casey asks.

"I promise, but it's going to hurt us every single step of the way. Every single one. I wish I was able to lie to you and say it won't. Can't though, because working out alone is going to kill us both."

"Um, why am I going to be working out? I thought you were talking figuratively just then," he says with a slight groan.

"Cause we both fucked up too much. We need to get back on the straight and narrow."

"Doesn't explain why I have to work out."

Pulling away from him, I spend a long time looking at his eyes and the small features of his face. Am I doing the right thing right now? Am I projecting?

Fuck, I wish Tommy was here just for three minutes. Just long enough to hear his voice tell me what I should do. What his hopes and dreams were.

Did Tommy ever want me to quit fighting? To give up this life and try for something else? Would he want his son to be anything like me? I see so damn much of Tommy in Casey right now. So damn much that I can barely keep my eyes open without fucking waterfalls coming out of them.

Casey isn't Tommy though, he's his own self. He's got a life ahead of him that Tommy doesn't. One that's on a path of his own choosing. Should I give a kid his age the choice to be who he wants?

"What do you want to do when you get older?" I ask.

"Huh?" he asks like I'm crazy.

Standing up from the bed, I pull him with me. "What do you dream about when you think of growing older?"

"I don't know?" he asks and says at the same time, his shoulders rising in a shrug.

Motioning for him to follow me, I head out of the bedroom and back down the hall to the kitchen. "What if I said you could be a fighter like me? Or a teacher? Maybe a computer game designer. Firefighter? Police Officer?"

"Honestly?" he asks.

Entering the kitchen, I walk over to the pantry and start searching for garbage bags. "You look in the fridge and cabinets. Start loading up any bottle with alcohol on the counter."

"Why?" he asks.

Damn, this kid likes monosyllabic responses.

"We've got shit to do. You called Helen a bitch, what was the punishment?" I ask as I locate the bags and start pulling out multiple ones.

I'll have to use one of those delivery places to restock this kitchen.

"Oh… I lost my PlayStation for a week," he says with a shrug of his shoulders.

"And you were shipped off to me because of that?" I ask with doubt in my voice.

"I… I don't want to talk about it," he mumbles quietly.

"Fair enough. Well, we're going to clean this house up. This is part of your punishment for calling her that."

"Fair enough," he says right back.

"Good, since this is your new home for the foreseeable, I want us to keep it like a home. Not the gutter I've been treating it."

"Okay," he says and gives me another shrug of the shoulders.

"Back to my question, though. What would you want to be when you grow up? Don't worry if you can't pick something, but think about it. We're going to get you there. I've never wanted anything more than to be a fighter, but that's not what I am right now."

Fuck, I feel like I've got diarrhea of the mouth and brain. Maybe I'm preaching more to myself than the choir though.

"What are you now?" he asks.

"A broken, lush, waste of space," I say immediately, and I feel like I'm being a little too damn honest.

"Wow," he says. "Grandma doesn't like it when I say bad things about myself like that."

"You should never say bad things about yourself, only honest things. Right now, *I am* those things, but I'm not going to let myself be that anymore," I say and start pouring out the bottles of alcohol into the sink.

My brain feels like it wants to go down with all the sweet, blissful numbing chemicals.

"So why are you forcing me to work out with you?" he asks.

"Because I saw the fire in your eyes when you were at the gym. You've got the bug in you."

The same exact one I used to have in me.

Training montage, training montage, training montage. Those are the two words that keep running through my mind as the ringing in my ears grows louder and louder.

I wish I was in some fucking movie right now. Something where I could do a superfast time-lapse of the pure fucking hell I'm in.

Five-thirty in the morning came way too early for me, and getting Casey up at six wasn't a pleasure either. Little guy has a mouth on him at that time of the morning. So do I, though, so we made it through our pre-run warmups without threatening too much violence.

It was when I dropped him off at the mile-and-a-half mark around the house that I knew I was in for hell today. I haven't run five miles in months, and it fucking showed. I'm pretty sure when I barfed in some poor sap's bushes at the three-mile mark that I left part of my spleen. I didn't eat much the night before, but damn, I sure did throw up everything I had in me.

The forced breakfast of eggs, bacon, and plain baked chicken… sucked. Protein, protein, protein.

Ugh, fuck.

"Keep your damn legs up!" Dale screams at me just as I feel my core screaming its final death notes.

"F… Fuck you!" I grunt out at him.

"That's right, pansy boy! Talk some smack, that's all you've got," Dale cackles as he drops a light weight ball on my stomach.

The air threatens to woof out of me as I try to maintain a clenched core and keep my legs up in the six inches of hell position he has me in.

"You smell that, Chase?" Dale asks the big asshole beside him.

"What's that?" Chase asks.

"That's the smell of pussy coming out of his pores!" Dale cackles again.

"Dale!" Avery shouts from the other side of the gym.

"Dammit," Dale grouches before looking down at my panting ass.

Oh shit.

"Pushups, and don't you let that little beer gut touch the floor!" Dale snarls at me.

"What the fuck?" I ask as I try to slowly roll over to my stomach.

I think I'm fucking dying.

He snarls. "You got me in trouble."

"But..." I wheeze out.

"That's ten more, asshole. And if I get in trouble again, I'm just gonna keep adding," Dale says before he shouts, "Casey, get your sticks over here now!"

Well, at least I'll be in good company, I think as he tells Casey to drop.

"What did I do?" Casey whines.

"You think I didn't hear about what you said to that sainted woman, Helen?" Chase asks.

"Shit," Casey whispers to me.

Unable to help myself, I snicker at Casey. "Yeah, this is probably going to hurt."

"Up!" Dale shouts.

Shit.

"Stay there, gentlemen. And I'm using that term loosely," Dale says.

"Crap," I grunt when I'm up.

I figured I'd be doing pushups. Nope, Dale is going for pure torture.

"Down," Dale says, then without giving us a break, "up!"

Fuck. I keep reminding myself I'm doing this for all the right reasons. Bree's watching, and for the life of me I can't let her see me fail.

Something about that damn kiss yesterday has set my ass on fire. It's like all the pain, the hate, the self-doubt, the black abyss, was pushed far away from me.

She burned something deep down inside of me with the way she connected to my soul.

Last night, while lying in bed, I was tormented by the past and future. I could see so many ways that everything could go wrong. And I could see all the horrible ways they could maybe go right.

Casey, no matter what, will be in that picture though. Can Bree accept that?

I know he's supposed to be here for the summer, but I'm thinking I need to keep him a bit longer. He needs to have a male figure in his life that can keep up with him. One who he knows will keep him in check. His grandparents were doing the best they could, but they need to heal and be able to rely on someone too.

I don't know what the future will hold, but I want to keep Bree and Casey with me.

That's another thing I keep forgetting.

Looking up when I hope I won't get caught, I get to look at Bree for the briefest of moments. And looking at her fills me with the energy I need to raise and hold myself in position.

She's fucking beautiful, and it's like her lips call to my soul. They call for me to get up, go over there, and sweep her up into my arms. They call for me to kiss the living fuck out of her and then drag her back to my cave and…

"What the fuck are you looking at, runt?" Chase snarls

into my ear as I feel his big meaty paws pushing down on my shoulders.

"My fut—"

The fucker starts to push even harder down on me.

My arms start to fucking shake from his weight, but one more look at Bree and I lock them and hold strong.

"My future… you fucking fat bitch," I say with a very forced laugh.

"I don't think so," he growls so deep in my ear it fucking vibrates me.

Before I know what happens, he pushes all of his fucking weight down on me and I collapse onto the ground.

"Fucker," I grunt.

"Did I say you could collapse?" Dale barks at me. "Casey, go to the bags. You need to give me fifty kicks with each leg and then sixty punches with each arm."

Fuck, little dude gets off easy.

"Up!" Dale shouts at me.

Chase is still holding me down as I struggle to raise myself back up, but at least it feels like he isn't pushing his full weight on me now.

"You want to actually try yet?" Chase asks. "You know Jamey's not taking this fucking lightly. He's out there right now planning on ripping your other shoulder off."

"Fuck him!" I snarl and push all the way up.

"Down!" Dale shouts, then, "up!"

With each reputation Chase growls out what Jamey's doing and it only infuriates me more. I'm going to fucking tear that piece of shit limb from fucking limb. I'll fucking kill Jamey in the damn ring. I'm not going to just go for the win. I'm going to punish him every single second and every single round.

"Stand up!" Dale shouts at me.

Getting in my face, Dale stares at my panting, ragged ass. Long seconds pass between us as he searches my soul. "You want to fight now? You want to hurt him?"

"Yes," I snarl.

"You want to use all that hatred and rage? You want to face every single fucking demon in you out there on the mat? Are you ready for that?" he asks so fucking quietly I can barely hear him over the ragged gasps of air that come from my lungs.

"Yes," I say after I think about everything I'll have to actually be in order to do that.

"Good," Dale says before turning away from me.

Raising my hands to the back of my head, I take in huge lungfuls of air.

Fuck, I feel like I'm dying.

Looking at the backs of Chase and Dale as they start to walk away, I feel that doubt they have in me. I feel the mistrust they have for my words. They think I'll fucking fall, and they'd be right if I didn't also see Casey kicking the heavy bag with all his heart.

I'd fucking fall down if it wasn't for him and Bree.

Casting a glance at Bree, I spot her looking at me with worry, like she's afraid I'll keel over at any minute.

Not going to happen. I have to make sure I put my body through hell now so that when I finally get those legs of hers around my waist, I ruin any chance of her finding any other man worthy.

She's fucking mine, that kiss sealed the deal. I'm not sure if she knows it yet, but she will. Hopefully she's good with the readymade family that's coming her way.

Casey and me are a package deal.

Doesn't matter if it's before I fight Jamey or after, I'm

also going to get that little bitch that tried to hurt her. He'll be fucking lucky if I don't put him in the ground.

"Did I say you were finished?" Dale turns back to face me. "Get on the fucking heavy bags. One hundred strikes from each arm and foot."

Well, shit. This is going to be a long fucking day.

But with Bree in my sights, nothing's going to stop me.

CHAPTER TEN
BREE

When my head finally hit the pillow last night, I had the foolish hope that when I woke up everything would be better in the light of morning. That I'd somehow be able to fix everything if I got some rest and could think clearly.

After all, they say sleeping on a problem is the best way to solve it.

Unfortunately, when I woke up and remembered everything that happened, I still had no answers.

If anything, with all my problems crammed together, they loom even larger.

Tristan, my father…

Emmett.

Together, they're a mountain I'm afraid I don't have the strength or stamina to scale without plummeting to my destruction.

But I know if I don't even try, I'll be left here, dangling, on the constant brink of slipping, of losing my grip and falling…

At least that's what it feels like at the moment.

Especially as I stare at Emmett. Stare and watch as he pushes his body to the breaking point.

I've managed to avoid him all morning. Managed to avoid all the sharp, questioning looks he was throwing my way. But now that I'm stuck at the front desk on door duty, there's no pretending what happened last night didn't happen.

There's no pretending as his eyes lock on mine, burning with a promise that we're not finished yet.

I don't know if the guys are purposely trying to humiliate him or make a spectacle, but they've got him set up front and center in the gym as they hurl challenge after challenge at him.

I try in vain to look away, to not watch, to focus on something else. I shift in my chair, pick at my nails, and check my email.

I even log into Facebook.

But time after time, I'm drawn back to Emmett. Drawn to him like I'm drowning and he's my only hope of salvation.

It's foolish, beyond foolish to get involved with him. Selfish to drag him into my mess. I'd be the biggest bitch if I fucked his life up. Could I live with myself if he ended up collateral damage? After watching him rise up and conquer everything the guys are throwing at him?

After what he did for me?

Probably not, but that selfish part of me doesn't want me to think about it. Doesn't want me to worry about what could happen.

She wants me to throw caution to the wind and dive in head first, despite the potential consequences. To take what I want for once in my life.

To *live* on my terms.

To finally be happy.

The longer I watch him, watch the sweat dripping off his shirtless body, his muscles tightening and flexing with tension. Watch him stare at me with an intense focus, like he's proving to me in the most primal way possible that he's the perfect mate, it's getting harder to ignore her.

Harder not to give into the impulse to run up to him and throw myself at him.

"Earth to Bree!" Avery shouts beside me and I jump about a foot off my seat.

Tipping her head back, Avery laughs as I hit the chair and slap a hand over my chest.

"Shit, you nearly killed me," I gasp as my heart races.

Dropping her chin, Avery's eyes sparkle at me as her laughter quiets to a musical giggle. "I've been standing here for five minutes, saying your name."

"What?" I ask dumbly.

There's no way. She's probably just messing with me.

"Five minutes," she repeats, her glossy lips stretching into a grin. "For five minutes I've been trying to get your attention."

My entire face instantly lights up with warmth and I find myself mumbling. "I... I..."

I really have no excuse. Yet again, I was caught staring at Emmett like a teenage girl that can't help herself.

What the fuck is wrong with me? I've always had good self-control.

It must be all the testosterone in the air...

Avery gives me a consoling pat on the shoulder then turns her head to look in Emmett's direction. "It's okay, I don't blame you for being distracted. They're putting on quite the show."

I turn my head to follow Avery's line of sight. The guys

have now moved over to the area with all the different types of bags they punch and kick.

"I think they might be trying to kill him," I mutter quietly as I watch Dale and Chase take turns shouting at Emmett.

For his part, Emmett remains focused on the bag in front of him, his face set hard with concentration.

I can't believe he hasn't decked one of them yet.

Avery sighs. "It's for his own good. He has a big fight coming up and only a short amount of time to prepare for it."

Standing in front of a heavy bag, Emmett gives it a quick one-two, punching first with his left fist then his right. But when he lifts his leg to deliver a kick, he seems to struggle, obviously flagging.

I've been watching him work out for what feels like hours, and I'm surprised he hasn't just keeled over from exhaustion. I would have been flat on my face after two minutes of what he's been through.

But do either of the guys give him a break? No. Dale steps right up to Emmett, yelling something about him being an out of shape pussy.

And I find my hands clenching into fists in response. Part of me wants to stomp right over to Dale and punch him in his face to show him who's the real pussy.

"Yeah, but do they have to be so mean about it?" I find myself growling.

Avery chuckles and gives my shoulder an affectionate squeeze. "If they're nice and ask politely, he probably wouldn't push himself past his own limits. If they don't push him past his limits, he won't win."

"I get that," I admit begrudgingly, "but it still seems

like they're being unnecessarily hard on him. Chase, especially."

Earlier, it looked like Chase was going to kill Emmett when Emmett was trying to do his pushups. The way he shoved Emmett down... I didn't think Chase would let him back up.

Now he's taunting Emmett, smirking as he says something I can't quite hear but have no doubt is insulting.

Avery is quiet for so long I start to think that she didn't hear me. Glancing up, though, I see that her mouth is pulled down in a frown and her brow is furrowed with thought.

"Chase is harder on the ones he cares the most about," she finally says and gives my shoulder another squeeze before pulling away.

I scoff. "So they're both being dicks because they care about him?"

Her grin returning, she nods her head. "Yep."

I shake my head in part disgust, part confusion.

Avery laughs at my reaction. "You'll get used to it."

"I doubt that," I grumble before her words really hit home.

Get used to it? What exactly does she mean by that? Get used to the guys abusing Emmett? Or the way they train people in general?

Before I can ask, Avery goes on. "Anyway, I came over here to let you know that you're free to go to lunch. I'll watch the desk."

I'm still tempted to ask her what she meant, to clarify that statement, but as she stares down at me expectantly, I decide I really don't want to know the answer.

I don't want to know if everyone else can see what is

going on between us. Because if they can, then I'd have to face it.

And if I have to face it, I'll have to own it. I'll have to make a more permanent decision.

Grabbing my purse off the floor, I roll my chair back and stand.

Emmett lets out a grunt so loud I can hear it clear across the gym.

Jerking my head in his direction, I watch him shove the heavy bag away from his chest as Dale yells at him.

"Eyes on the bag, lover boy!"

Heat returns to my cheeks as Emmett's eyes meet mine, tired now but still full of intensity.

Still full of promise.

Just as Dale gives the bag another shove, sending it for Emmett again, I rip my attention away from him.

Emmett let's out another loud grunt behind me, and knowing I was the cause of that grunt, I can't run out of the building fast enough.

I'm so stuck in my head, so mentally messed up, I end up driving ten minutes down the street, heading for my step-father's house, before I realize I can't go home yet.

It's only lunch and I still have half of my shift left.

And fuck me, I don't know how I'm going to survive it.

How am I going to survive being in the same place as Emmett? Breathing the same air as him?

He hasn't said a word to me yet, but his presence alone is screwing with my head. After only four hours, I'm struggling. Seriously struggling with a mess of confusing emotions.

Every time I look at him, I can't help but remember the kiss. Remember how for those few short moments of bliss I finally felt at peace. I finally felt like I had found my place in the world.

And it scares the hell out of me.

It scares me more than my father or Tristan ever have.

He has a pull over me. Some kind of strange, supernatural pull that I don't understand how to counter yet.

Until I can figure out how to resist him, I need to keep my distance. But how can I do that if he's in the gym?

The idea of giving Chase my notice is tempting as hell. Especially as it dawns on me that I'll probably see Emmett every day I work for the rest of the summer as he trains for his upcoming match.

Just the thought of seeing Emmett every day, half-naked, glistening with sweat as he pushes and molds his body into a powerful fighting machine, is enough to drive me to the brink of madness. And if he does what he's been doing today, staring me down like he's a damn predator and I'm the prey he has his sights on, I might seriously fucking lose it.

Making a U-turn, I head back toward the gym and stop at the first place that looks like it has food. Still toying with the idea of quitting and trying to figure out exactly what to say to Chase so he doesn't look down on me, I end up ordering two different meals in the drive thru.

Two meals and I have no damn clue what's even inside them.

By the time I make it back to the gym, I have a huge sack of food and absolutely no desire to eat any of it. There's a huge ball of anxiety sitting in the pit of my stomach, taking up all the space, as I walk back through the front doors.

Avery waves at me and smiles. I give her a nod and manage to force my own smile before my eyes search the gym, seeking out Emmett.

When I fail to spot him, instead of feeling relieved, I find myself somehow feeling disappointed.

Dammit.

Pulling up my shoulders as soon as I realize they're slumping, I make way over to the front desk.

Avery eyes the huge plastic bag I'm carrying and her face lights up with amusement. "Hungry?"

The words *not really* almost pop out of my mouth before I catch myself.

"A little," I sigh as I plop the bag down on the desk.

Chuckling, Avery stands from the chair. After flipping her long, sleek black hair over her shoulder, she slips on her purse.

"I have to go pick up the girls from Grandma's and take them to ballet class. I probably won't be back today, but if you need anything Chase will be here."

I nod in acknowledgement as she comes around the desk.

I'm just about to head to the chair and sit my butt back down when she suddenly stops beside me.

Turning to me, her face is serious, almost grim, as she says, "Thank you for helping us out, Bree. We sincerely appreciate it."

My first instinct is to brush it off, to let her know it's not a big deal. But looking at her face, it's plain to see that to her it is.

She is truly grateful that I'm helping her by working here.

Knowing that any kind of dismissive response would

be insulting, I struggle at first to think up something to say.

Then it comes to me.

Smiling at her, I say, "No thanks needed. We're family."

At first, Avery looks a little taken aback by what I said.

Then her entire face lights up as she beams a smile back at me. "That we are."

Reaching out, she gives my shoulder an affectionate squeeze, lingering for a moment that's longer than necessary before she pulls away and walks past me.

Turning, I watch her as she walks out the front doors, my heart squeezing with a strange sensation that's soft and fuzzy but also a little painful.

I can still feel her warmth on my shoulder as I take my seat. Still see the brightness of her smile as I look at the big white plastic bag in front of me.

Dammit.

So much for quitting. I can't walk away now, not when I know how much it means to Avery.

Untying the bag, I fish out a couple of sandwiches and salads and set them out on the desk. Then I stare at the food, trying to come to grips with the emotions swelling inside my chest.

For once in my life I'm needed, truly needed.

I don't know how long I stare at the food, lingering and savoring the experience, before I notice someone approaching the desk.

"Hey Bree," Casey says and gives me a little wave as he wanders over to me.

Freshly showered, his damp hair is combed back, though one stray strand keeps falling into his eyes.

"Well, if it isn't my hero," I smile at him and watch with delight as a blush creeps up his neck.

"I'm not a hero," he grumbles as he stops beside the desk.

"You'll always be my hero," I tell him and have to bite my lip to keep from giggling as his blush deepens.

Reaching up, he rubs the back of his neck and shifts on his feet as if he's uncomfortable. Then he grumbles something beneath his breath, but I can't hear it over the loud growl suddenly coming from his stomach.

"You hungry?" I ask.

"Yeah, a little," he admits as he drops his hand.

"Want a sandwich? I have no clue what's in it, but it's probably good," I say as I nudge one of the two sandwiches toward him.

"How do you not know what's in it?" he asks as he picks up the sandwich and unwraps the end.

Before I can shrug my shoulders, he's taking a big bite out of it.

"I think they gave me the wrong thing in the drive thru," I answer.

Chewing with a thoughtful look on his face, he swallows then grins at me. "It's an Italian, my favorite."

I grin back. "Awesome."

Standing from my chair, I give it a little nudge, rolling it toward him. "Here, sit while you eat."

Already chewing another big bite, he shakes his head in refusal.

"Sit," I order, "or you'll get indigestion."

"Yes, *mom*," he says irritably and drops down in the chair.

I gasp. "I'm not that old."

Casey snickers before taking another bite.

"You're what? Ten? Way too old to be my kid," I say as I perch myself on the inner corner of my desk.

"Twelve," he corrects me after swallowing then he takes another big bite.

The entire footlong sub is nearly gone now.

"Yeah, definitely way too old to be my kid," I say and pick up one of the salads.

"How old are you?" he asks, peering up at me curiously.

I waggle my finger at him and smirk. "You should never ask a woman that question."

Rolling his eyes, he finishes off his sandwich then balls the wrapper up and tosses it into my little garbage can.

"How old do I look?" I ask as I peel the lid off the salad.

Eyes lighting up with mischief, he crosses his arms and leans back in the chair as he says, "I dunno, all you grownups look old to me…"

I snort and he laughs.

"But if I had to guess, I'd say thirty."

I reach down, grab a plastic fork out of the bag, then wave it menacingly at him. "Thirty? Are you sure that's your final answer?"

Uncrossing his arms, he holds his hands up protectively in front of him, but the mischief in his eyes spreads to the grin on his lips. "Thirty-five?"

"Why you little…" I mock growl, toss the salad to the side, and slide off the desk.

Casey jumps up from the chair with a giggle as I point the fork at him.

"I'm sorry!" he cries out as he moves behind the chair, putting it between me and him.

And as he looks at me, on the verge of another giggle, my heart swells with joy. It swells because all that anger he seems to be carrying around is gone from his face and he finally looks his age.

He finally looks like a happy twelve-year-old *boy* and not a child who was forced to grow up too soon and pretend to be a man.

I jump a little to the right and he jumps to the left.

"I'm sorry," he repeats with another giggle. "I got it wrong. You're forty!"

"Oh my god," I cry out and stomp around the chair until he's now the one standing in front of it.

"I'll have you know I'm only twenty," I say as I narrow my eyes and point the fork at him.

"Oh," he says, his eyes going wide with surprise. Then that little mischievous grin returns. "You look soooo much older."

I let out a little shriek and chase him around the chair again, his happy giggles music to my ears. "I'm so going to get you for that!"

We make it three rotations around the chair, with me purposely trying not to catch him, before he stops, giggling so much he's nearly out of breath.

After grabbing his stomach, he gives me his best puppy dog eyes and juts out his bottom lip. "But I thought I was your hero."

My phone suddenly dings behind me and the sound jolts me back to reality, but I manage to catch myself before I completely ruin the moment.

Bringing the fork up, I tap it thoughtfully against my chin. "That's right, you are…" I let out a big sigh. "I guess I can't hurt you then."

I take a step back, then another, and wave at his chair. "You're safe, my hero. I promise I won't stab you with this fork."

Casey eyes me suspiciously, like he's not buying my act, and remains behind the chair.

"What? A big boy like you is afraid of a little old lady like me?" I smirk, goading him.

Snorting, he drops his arms and puffs out his little chest. But he still comes around the chair cautiously, afraid I'm going to jump him at any second.

And he's right to be afraid because as soon as he's close enough, I pounce on him.

I don't stab him with the fork, though. No, I drop it and wrap my arms around him, giving him the biggest hug I can give.

His entire body stiffens up in response.

But I don't care, for two seconds I manage to push some of my love into him before I jump back and cackle.

"I never said anything about not hugging you though!"

As I move to the desk and hop back up to sit, Casey just stands in place with this shell-shocked expression on his face.

An expression that starts to worry me.

Did I seriously fuck up?

Not knowing what else to do, I cackle at him again and say, "You have my girl cooties now!"

That seems to bring him out of it. Shaking his head, his eyes return to focus and he pouts at me. "Ew. You don't play fair."

Completely unapologetic, I smirk and pick up my phone. "You can pay me back next time…"

Glancing down at my screen, I see a long text message from my father.

Fuck.

My eyes quickly scan across all the words before the preview disappears, and my heart drops to my stomach.

My father wants me to meet him, Tristan, and Tristan's father at the Bellagio for dinner tonight.

A shadow passes over my phone a second before Casey asks, "What's wrong?"

Jerking my head up, I blink in surprise to see Casey suddenly standing close to me.

"Oh, nothing…" I mumble and turn my phone over before he can read it.

Casey scowls and the look he gives me has me instinctively bringing the forced smile I seem to be wearing more and more these days to my mouth. "It's just my dad. I'll text him back later."

"Oh," Casey says as if he's a little surprised and then a strange expression passes over his face.

An expression that seems to be a mixture of envy and sadness.

I have the sudden, intense urge to hug him again. To wrap my arms around him and hold him until that expression disappears.

What the hell happened to him? How can a boy so young be filled with so much sadness?

"I think they gave me cookies. You want a cookie?" I stumble out and lean over to dig into the plastic bag.

Yeah, I feel like the biggest idiot as I pull out the two cookies that came with everything I ordered and hold one out to him.

But I don't know what else to do.

I don't know how to fix him.

Hell, I don't know how to fix myself.

"Yeah, sure," Casey says with so little enthusiasm as he accepts the cookie, you'd think I was handing him a head of broccoli or something.

"You're giving out free cookies?" Emmett asks behind

me, and my heart jumps back up from my stomach to land in my throat.

Just hearing his voice ramps up all my senses, instantly putting my body on high alert.

"Free cookies and sandwiches," Casey grins smugly over my shoulder before taking a big bite out of his cookie, sending crumbs flying everywhere.

"Damn," Emmett says, "I'm missing out."

I smell him before I can bring myself to turn around and look at him. Smell that clean, crisp, male scent that tells me he's also freshly showered.

A big hand comes down on the desk beside me and my world begins to shrink down as I sense him moving into my personal space.

All the little nerves in my body light up as if they've suddenly come alive. Afraid I might start to hyperventilate, I focus on keeping my breathing steady even though the beat of my heart is racing so fast I want to gasp for air.

I knew that I'd have to face him today, but I was hoping it would remain from a distance.

Slowly, oh so slowly, I turn and tip my head to look at him.

His face is mere inches away from mine, so close my lips begin to tingle, remembering his kiss.

This close, his face becomes my entire world. My entire existence.

It would take no effort at all to lean in closer and see if he still tastes like I remember him…

The corners of Emmett's mouth pull up as if he knows exactly what I'm thinking and his lids lower.

Those eyes of his, those damn beautiful, intense eyes of his begin to suck me in, drawing me closer to the point of no return.

Then he asks, "You got any cookies left for me?"

I blink in surprise, the question yanking me out of my trance.

Realizing that I'm leaning into him, I jerk back.

Now it's Emmett's turn to look smug, as smug as Casey looked a moment ago.

And he's not done yet.

Leaning in, he follows me.

I begin to panic, afraid he's going to kiss me right here, out in the open.

Flustered, I ask, "You want my cookie?" and thrust my hand out to stop him.

Emmett finally breaks eye contact with me, glancing down at my hand before he chuckles. "Yes, I want your cookie."

Fucking hell, I walked myself into that one.

My entire face burns with mortification as he plucks the cookie out of my hand and carefully lifts it up to his mouth.

Before his teeth sink in, I cut my attention back to Casey, using his presence to plant me firmly back in reality.

"So, you got any plans after this?" I ask, hoping to dissolve the tension in my bones with small talk.

Casey shrugs his shoulders and looks to Emmett.

I resist the urge to glance back and look at him too.

Yeah, I'm not falling for that trap again. I've already made a fool of myself enough today, thank you very much.

I can hear Emmett wiping his hands together before he says, "I was thinking we'd get some pizza and catch a movie. You down for it?"

Casey's face lights up and he's quick to answer, "Yeah!"

Happy for Casey, I find myself smiling at his enthusiasm.

Then Emmett's voice brushes against my ear. "How about you, Bree?"

"Me?" I blurt out in surprise.

Emmett chuckles. "Yes, you. Are you up for catching a movie with us?"

My first instinct is to tell him no, sorry, I'm busy. I have to wash my hair tonight and I seriously need to shave my legs.

But Casey turns his full attention on me, eyes pleading with me to accept.

I don't know why he wants me to come out with them, but the thought of letting him down makes me feel a little sick.

Shit.

"I don't know…" I murmur and squirm a little on the desk.

I'm supposed to have dinner with my father and Tristan tonight. If I don't show up, my father is going to be absolutely livid.

And besides, the last thing I want to do is spend an entire evening with Emmett, especially when I need to be doing the exact opposite. I need to avoid his ass.

"Please?" Casey asks and the look he gives me causes my heartstrings to tighten.

Oh my god, how can I say no to that face? Right now, he looks so sweet and innocent, I can't stand it.

Damn it all.

Emmett did this on purpose.

I guess it comes down to who am I willing to let down more? My father or Casey?

Sighing over all the shit this is going to cause, I answer reluctantly, "Okay. I guess I'm down for a movie."

"Yes!" Casey exclaims as he bounces up a little and beams at me with pure happiness.

I try to smile back but now I feel sick at the thought of not only being in a dark theater with Emmett but also pissing off my father.

"Great," Emmett says as if he expected that answer. "I'll pick you up at your house at six?"

I shake my head, immediately shutting that down. "I'll meet you at the theater."

There's no way I'm getting in a car with him.

"Yeah…" Emmett drawls out, and I brace myself for what's going to come out of his mouth next. "That's not going to work. We're going to get pizza first, and it will be easier to pick you up than give you directions."

Some of Casey's happiness begins to fade away, replaced by a touch of concern as he looks between us.

Ugh. I no longer have the urge to kiss Emmett.

No, I want to strangle him as I clench my teeth together and try to hold a smile.

I can't keep arguing with him though because it's obviously upsetting Casey, and upsetting Casey completely defeats the purpose of agreeing to go in the first place.

So I have no choice but to accept his terms. "Fine. Pick me up at six."

"Alright, it's a date," Emmett says, and I jerk my head in his direction just in time to see the smug, self-satisfied grin on his face. "Come on, Casey, it's time to go. We'll see you later, Bree."

Oh, that dirty, rotten, no-good, cocky bastard.

"It's not a date," I correct, but he only chuckles at me.

"Bye Bree," Casey smiles and waves.

I manage to wave back without giving Emmett the middle finger. I even manage to not to call him a jerk out load.

But I stew over his underhanded move for so long, I almost miss a crucial detail before he and Casey walk out the door.

I turn and call out, "Hey," just as Emmett grabs the handle. "Don't you need my address to pick me up?"

"Nope," Emmett answers and lifts up his phone. Waving the phone at me, his grin grows wider. "I've got it right here."

Confused, I don't get what he means at first, and before I can get some clarification, he walks out the door.

What the hell? How does he have my address in his—

He didn't.

Remembering he had my phone yesterday, I quickly unlock the screen and check my contacts.

After scrolling around a bit, I find him. The cocky bastard is right there in my list.

And, as if that's not bad enough, he had the gall to add himself as: My Future Husband.

Sometimes in life there are decisions that you know right away are bad decisions. Decisions that will fuck your life up and have long lasting consequences.

Going out with Emmett tonight definitely feels like one of those fuck-my-life-up bad decisions.

Staring at the mess of clothes on my bedroom floor, I wonder what the hell I'm doing.

Am I a sucker for punishment?

With all the other shit going on, why am I doing this to myself?

Casey's pleading face flashes in front of my eyes as a reminder.

Oh yeah, for Casey…

But is it really only for him? Or deep down, do I want this to be more?

Do I want this to be the start of… something?

Turning to the face the mirror hanging on the back of my door, I tug at the skirt of the little blue sundress I have on.

Ugh, it's too cute, and makes it look like I'm treating this like a date. And it's totally not a date…

Ripping the dress off and tossing it to the side, I stomp over to my closet and push my hangers around. I have a wardrobe that could put most girls my age to shame. Gucci, Prada, Chanel, Burberry… From my tops to my bottoms, it's designer everything. But it's all stuff bought with my father's money, and the thought of wearing any of it out tonight doesn't feel right.

It doesn't feel like *me*.

With the time I have left before Emmett gets here ticking in my ears, I push myself through the mass of clothes to get to the back of my closet.

The only good thing about Emmett being able to track me through the find my friends app on my phone is that I can also track him. When I checked two minutes ago, he was ten minutes away.

Which means he's eight minutes away now, and I still need to brush my teeth…

Shit.

Desperate to find something, I start to dig through a box full of clothes I haven't worn since high school. As I pick through the pieces, memories threaten to distract me, memories of happier days, but I shove them away.

After sorting through a bunch of worn-out stuff that I bought at Target, back when that was all I could afford, I finally stumble across a black band shirt and tug it on. It's a little tight in the boobs, but it still seems to fit. Knowing my ass won't squeeze into any of my old jeans, I settle on wearing a pair of red running shorts I'd normally wear to the gym and push my way back of out of the closet.

Standing in front of the mirror again, I take myself in. I

look casual, like I really don't care, which is exactly the look I'm going for.

Yanking out my hair tie, I run my fingers through my hair until it falls down my shoulders.

Makeup or no makeup?

Peering at myself, at the dark bags appearing under my eyes, I decide no makeup. I don't want to give even a hint that I'm trying.

I stare one more time at my reflection then put my running shorts to good use and make a dash for the bathroom. After quickly brushing my teeth and pulling a brush through my hair, I'm ready to go.

I check my phone and the app shows me that Emmett is two minutes away.

Perfect timing. Just enough time, in fact, to get my butt down the stairs and out the front door before Logan or my mom wonder what's up.

Grabbing my purse, I throw it over my shoulder and make it all the way to the front door before my mom calls out from the kitchen. "Aubrey? Is that you?"

"Yes, Mom," I call back as I pull open the right side of the double doors. "I'm heading out for a bit. I'll be back later tonight."

A black Jeep Wrangler pulls up in front of the house just as I pull the door closed behind me.

Emmett hops out of the driver's seat and comes around to open the passenger door for me.

And damn, if the way he's dressed in his muscle-hugging black t-shirt and tight blue jeans doesn't have me almost stumbling down the front steps to land on my face.

With his hair slicked back and his clothes ironed and wrinkle-free, he looks like he's doing exactly what I don't want to be doing—going on a date.

I'd pause for a moment and take in the sight of him, but I'm afraid I might freeze in place, never wanting to do anything else again.

Emmett lets out a low whistle between his teeth as he takes in the mansion behind me. "Nice place you have here."

I'm not sure he intended to do it, but that remark has my defenses immediately shooting up.

"Yeah, it's not mine," I say and flash my teeth at him before I slide into my seat.

That left eyebrow of his quirks up and he looks a little surprised as he shuts my door for me.

Watching him walk around the front of the Jeep, I almost forget we're not alone, when Casey says behind me, "Hey Bree."

Twisting around, I offer him a smile he doesn't see as I say, "Hey Casey."

Nose pressed almost against the glass, Casey gawks out the window at the house like he can't believe what he's seeing. Twisting back around, I look out my own window, trying to see the place with his eyes.

When did such luxury and opulence become normal to me?

"Whose house is it?" Emmett asks as he slides into the driver's seat and shuts the door.

The way he asks it has me cutting him a sideways glance. Did I detect a touch of jealousy there?

He just stares out the front windshield as he puts the car into drive and pulls us out of the driveway.

"It's Logan's and my mother's," I answer and smother a grin.

I don't know why the possibility of him being jealous makes me happy, but it does.

"Who's Logan?" Casey asks from the backseat.

I glance into the mirror to look at him as I answer. "He's my stepfather. Chase's dad."

Out of the corner of my eyes, I see Emmett's shoulders visibly relaxing.

"Oh…." Casey drags out as if he's just figured it all out. "So that's why Chase was calling you his sister."

"Yep," I say and lean back in my seat. "His dad and my mom got married last spring."

"Cool," Casey responds, sounding both distracted and bored at the same time.

"Yeah, cool," Emmett mimics and looks over at me, smirking.

Our gazes meet, and I experience that little jolt that's beyond unnerving, especially as it settles deep in my belly. This time, though, instead of smiling nervously at him, I simply shake my head and roll my eyes at him.

"What movie are we going to see?" I ask and turn to my window.

Peering through the glass, I pretend to watch the scenery while I'm truly just trying to disengage myself from Emmett and all the confusing feelings he's stirring inside me.

Emmett begins to tap his fingers against the steering wheel. "There are three choices. The new Avengers movie, the new Spider-Man movie, and the new X-Men movie."

Three superhero movies, great… I was super-heroed out like a year ago, but I guess those are the only movies that would interest Casey.

Emmett stops tapping his fingers and I feel the weight of his eyes on me. "Which one do you want to watch?"

Shrugging my shoulders, I find his reflection in the

glass. "I'm good with whatever has Chris Hemsworth in it."

I watch all the humor fade from his face and have to bite my lip to keep from laughing as he growls, "The new Lion King it is."

"Great," I say and turn in my seat to face him. "I totally love Mufasa's voice."

Emmett's expression grows darker as I smile at him, then Casey chimes in from the backseat. "But we didn't get—"

"I know, it's just a joke, Casey," Emmett says quickly, cutting him off and shooting him a pointed look.

That pointed look has my spider-sense tingling.

Looking between the two of them, I can't help but feel like there's something they know that I don't.

Casey shrugs his shoulders and plops back against his seat, crossing his arms over his chest. "Just sayin'."

It's my turn to arch a brow at Emmett. Is he planning to do something sneaky? After the whole Future Husband thing in my phone, I wouldn't put it past him.

Avoiding my eyes, Emmett reaches for the dial on the radio. "So, you like classic rock?"

"I guess," I answer with a frown, not happy that he's changing the subject.

Emmett finally glances over at me as he comes to a stop at a light, but he only looks at my face for a moment.

His eyes drop down, scanning across my chest. "You guess? You're not really a Def Leppard fan? I didn't take you for a poser."

I look down, following his line of sight, and then feel my face warm. "Oh… yeah… this…" I mumble and then clear my throat. "I went to see them like four years ago with my mom."

I wasn't aware of my breasts a minute ago. Seriously, I completely forgot they existed. But after one little innocent look from Emmett, they feel warm and heavy. Tingling with every little breath I take.

"Ah, so your mom is the fan," he says, the corners of his lips tipping up as he cuts his eyes back to the road.

"Yeah," I answer as I give into the urge to cross my arms.

"What kind of music do you like?" Emmett asks, tapping his fingers against the steering wheel again. "No... let me guess—"

"Taylor Swift!" Casey cackles, cutting Emmett off.

I could honestly care less about Taylor Swift, but I'm curious to know why Casey would think liking her music is funny. Is it because she's a girl?

"What's wrong with Taylor?" I ask defensively.

"I knew it!" Casey exclaims and cackles some more like it's the funniest thing.

Brow furrowing, I look to Emmett for an explanation.

"There's nothing wrong with Taylor Swift..." he hedges, and the way he's looking at everywhere but me, it's obvious something about this is definitely making him uncomfortable.

"*But*?" I push, again feeling like I'm being left out of the loop and not liking it one bit.

"He thinks you look like her!" Casey supplies before doubling over in a fit of laughter.

It takes a second for Casey's words to fully sink in, but when they do I find myself rounding on Emmett. "You do?"

Emmett drops his chin and shakes his head, still refusing to meet my eyes as he mutters, "Dammit, Casey. Is nothing sacred?"

Uncrossing my arms, I reach over and poke him in the side. "Hey, I asked you a question."

Turning off the road, Emmett pulls us into a driveway and parks the car in front of a house before he finally turns to face me.

I thought I was prepared for his full, undivided attention. After all, I did poke him and ask for it…

But as he gives me that look, the one where his gaze cuts through all the walls I've built up, straight to the core of me, I regret my boldness.

"Yeah, I think you look like her," he answers slowly, his gaze never wavering. "But prettier."

Prettier… It's such a small compliment, easily discarded, and of absolutely no importance, yet it hits me hard.

When was the last time I heard a compliment? A true compliment that wasn't given by my mom?

I can't even recall it's been so long.

The only compliments I ever got out of Tristan were backhanded and meant to make me feel self-conscious. He especially liked to pick on my weight. And my father… has he ever complimented me? When I think about him, all I can think of is all his demands.

"Prettier?" I find myself repeating as my eyes search Emmett's eyes, looking for any sign that he's teasing me because I want to believe him.

I want it more than I should.

Emmett leans toward me, his face serious, and suddenly I can't breathe.

Reaching out, his fingers brush a chunk of my hair behind my ear as he says, "A thousand times more beautiful, baby girl."

The tips of his fingers drag down my cheek to the line of my jaw, and my entire face tingles from his touch.

I find myself trapped, unable to move as I try to savor the feelings he creates so easily inside me. Savor them like a sweet piece of candy that's going to melt away before I'm done with it.

Because I'm not supposed to have this… or him…

But I want it anyway…

At least for the moment.

Drinking in his face, I watch his eyelids grow heavy until his lashes are nearly fanning his cheeks.

Completely forgetting myself, I begin to lean toward him, following some deeply buried instinctive need to be closer to him.

Then Casey clears his throat loudly. "Are we going to sit here all night, or are we going to watch a movie?"

I jerk away from Emmett in shock, dropping like a rock back to reality.

Shit. What the hell was I doing? What came over me?

Emmett's eyes widen at first, as if he's also surprised, but then a cocky grin spreads across his face as he takes in my burning cheeks.

Seeing that cocky grin of his and the knowing in his eyes, my blush burns so hot I feel it creeping down to my toes.

Dammit. Why do I keep forgetting myself whenever I'm around him? I can't even control myself with Casey sitting behind us.

I'm totally and utterly shameless.

Scooting as far over in my seat that I can, I try my best to cool down, while Emmett's voice sounds like he's on the verge of laughter. "Yeah, yeah, hold your horses, buddy."

Well, I'm glad one of us finds this amusing. Actually, no I'm not.

From the backseat, Casey whines with youthful exasperation, "What does that even mean?"

Emmett shoots me a look that says, *can you believe this kid*. "It means wait a minute."

Casey groans. "Why didn't you just say that?"

Emmett's eyes sparkle with mirth. "I did… when I said hold your horses"

Casey makes a sound of disgust then pushes his door open. "Whatever. I'm waiting by the door."

Once Casey slams the car door shut, my brain decides it's ready to function again. Why did Casey get out of the car here? And why is he waiting by the door?

Looking out the windshield, all I see is the brown stucco house we're parked in front of and the two houses beside it. Glancing into the rearview mirror, I search for some sign of a theater, but only see more houses. There's not a mall or business to be seen on the horizon.

Giving Emmett the benefit of the doubt, I wonder if we're only stopping here before we head out to get the pizza and movie he promised.

"I thought we were going to catch a movie at a theater…" I say as I glance back and watch Casey walk up the steps of the house we're parked in front of.

"We are," Emmett says as he twists the key out of the ignition. "We're going to watch it in my home theater."

And there it is… That's why Emmett shut Casey down so fast when we were talking about movies. It's because he had this up his sleeve and he didn't want me to know about it.

He totally tricked me into this on purpose.

Keys jingling, Emmett palms them, then reaches over me and opens his glove box.

I press myself back into my seat, barely avoiding his arm as he pulls out three plastic DVD cases. Pushing the glove box shut with his knuckles, he finally pulls his arm back and opens his door.

Getting out, he's comes around the front of the Jeep and opens my door for me.

"You coming?" he asks as I just sit where I am, trying to figure out how I'm going to get myself out of this mess.

Is there even an excuse at this point to bail? Because if there is, I can't think of it.

The thought of being with him in his house though is starting to give me heart palpations.

It was one thing to be with him in public… but in his private house, where he has complete control?

A shiver of excitement slithers down my spine and I shut that shit down quick. I have no idea where it came from, and I really, *really* don't want to examine it closely.

"Bree?"

I glance at the house again and bite my lip. This feels like another one of those fuck-my-life-up bad decisions. I can feel it in my bones that nothing good is going to come from this.

Nothing good will come from getting closer to him.

I could say no. I could say take me home right now or I'm calling an Uber. Especially since he tricked me into this situation in the first place.

But seeing Casey pacing eagerly in front of the front door…

How bad could things possibly get if he's here? It's not like Emmett can pounce on me in front of the kid.

"Yeah, I'm coming," I grumble and shoot Emmett a dirty look.

He knows what he did, but the cocky bastard doesn't have an ounce of shame or remorse. No, his grin grows even more smug and pleased as he walks beside me up the front steps. There's even a little bounce to his normal swagger...

Or maybe that's just my irritation over the situation.

Dammit. If I could get away with it, I'd totally stick my foot out and trip him so that smug smile ends up plastered on the front porch.

Stopping beside Casey, I try hard not to glare daggers into Emmett's back as he unlocks the front door. Try and fail. Thankfully, Casey doesn't seem to notice.

No, he's so excited, he grabs my hand and tugs me into the house. Emmett barely has time to step to the side before Casey is half-dragging me, half-leading me through the door.

"Emmett bought a new TV today to watch movies, Bree," he says excitedly. "You have to see it, it's huge!"

I never knew kids could talk so much. I swear Casey hardly stops to breathe.

Still pulling me by the hand, Casey leads me through the house, giving me a tour while he talks my ear off. The first thing he shows me is the new TV Emmett bought. It is indeed huge, a gleaming seventy-two-inch, top of the line.

After the TV, though, Casey shows me to his room. The room lacks a personal touch, and I find out he moved in with Emmett only last night.

We don't stay in the bedroom for very long. Casey seems determined to show me every bedroom and bathroom in the house, and while he does it a hundred different questions pop into my mind.

Why did Emmett buy that TV? Why did Casey move in with him? Who are they to each other?

I never got a chance to ask Chase or Avery…

Thankfully, in his excited, nonstop chatter, Casey fills me in on everything. I get his entire life story. He tells me about his grandparents, and how his grandmother brought him to the gym so she could drop him off to stay with Emmett while his grandfather recovers from an illness.

He also tells me about his mom, a deadbeat drug addict who can't get her act together. He hasn't seen her since he was a baby and can't even remember what she looks like.

The most shocking revelation by far though is when he tells me about his dad, Tommy. Tommy passed away a few months ago. His car was hit by a semi-truck that crossed the median on the highway.

By the time Casey finishes, dropping my hand so he can dig into the pizza Emmett ordered, I'm close to tears.

It explains so much about Casey, and all the little things that have been bothering me. His anger… the way he carries himself at times like he's a little man and not a child. He's been through so much, at such a young age.

My heart aching and on the verge on breaking, all I want to do is wrap my arms around him and hold him tight. To be there for him. To offer what support I can give.

But do I even have a right? Do I have a right to insert myself into his life? Especially when I have no intention of staying?

Feeling sick to my stomach, it's everything I can do to pretend to be interested in the movie, but I try, for Casey. Sitting beside him on the couch, I try to share his excitement every time one of his favorite superheroes comes on the screen. I eat all the popcorn he shares with me. I even cheer with him during the big action scenes.

About halfway through the movie, he begins to lean into me. Somehow his head ends up on my shoulder. Afraid to move, afraid it will cause him to pull away, I freeze in place. Ten minutes must pass before I work up the courage to relax and accept his weight.

Another ten minutes or so passes with Casey leaning against me before Emmett motions for me to look over at him.

Glancing over, I see Casey sleeping.

He fell asleep on me.

So many emotions well up inside me, but I think the strongest one of them all, the one that feels the best yet hurts the most, is knowing that he *trusts* me.

Standing from the recliner he was sitting on, Emmett walks over to me.

"I've got him," he says quietly before bending down to pick up Casey.

I don't want him to take Casey away from me, selfishly I want to keep him next to me all night, but seeing Emmett lift him up into his arms, cradling him carefully, I find myself feeling at ease. Just the way he holds him leaves no doubt in my mind that Casey is cared for and safe.

Standing from the couch, I follow behind Emmett as he carries Casey to his bedroom. Halfway there, Casey seems to stir a little, his arm dropping, dangling at his side, as he murmurs something.

All it takes is a few whispered words from Emmett and Casey is curling into him, falling back to sleep.

Heart in my throat, I watch from the doorway as Emmett lays Casey on his bed, removes his shoes, and tucks his little body under the covers. Before he straightens, Emmett takes a moment to tenderly brush Casey's hair back from his forehead.

And the look in his eyes…

I don't think I've ever seen anything like it.

It's love incarnate.

Then he's facing me.

And that look doesn't disappear.

For a heartbeat, I let myself imagine that look is meant for me. I let myself indulge in the fantasy that he cares about me and loves me.

To be loved by him… to be cared for and protected by a man like him… What a life that would be…

Then I shove it far away.

As Emmett approaches, eyes still locked on my face, I retreat into the hallway. Seeking cover in the darkness. Hoping all my emotions aren't out in the open. And if they are, hoping he doesn't see them.

Without looking behind him, Emmett grabs the handle for the door and closes it quietly.

Still retreating, the urge to run, to hide from him comes over me. Even in this dim lighting, I can see that look in his eyes hasn't faded. If anything, it's grown in intensity.

"I should probably go," I stammer out nervously.

Emmett's voice is a quiet rumble in the dark as he says, "You probably should."

In any other situation, I'd take that remark as an insult or a sign that I'm not wanted, but the way he says it, the way he keeps stalking toward me, it's clearly a warning.

A warning that what I've been afraid of all night, what I've been avoiding is about to happen.

Reaching down, I dig into my pocket, fingers fumbling to grab my phone. "I'll just order an Uber…"

Apparently, I can't retreat and grab my phone at the same time. Finally stopping, my fingers wrap around my phone and I whip it out.

My thumb swipes my phone open and I click on the app, bringing it up, but before I can do anything else, Emmett's hand is on me, stopping me.

"Bree," he exhales, my name coming out with sweet adoration, and it's everything I can do not to look up at him.

Because I know if I look up at him, I'm a goner. I won't be able to resist him.

I don't know what it is about him that makes me weak, that draws me to him, but I'm powerless to stop it.

He's the cliff and I'm the car barreling for him, and I can't stop no matter how hard I pump the brakes or try to turn in another direction.

My eyes burn as I stare down at the bright screen, but I don't pull away. I can't bring myself to do that again. I remember all too well the flash of pain in his eyes yesterday, and god help me, the last thing I want to do is hurt this man or make him feel like I don't want him.

The problem is I want him too much.

Unable to pull away, but also unable to take the next step, I remain paralyzed, frozen in place, before Emmett makes the decision for me.

He gives a gentle tug on my phone, a testing tug, and my subconscious must make my decision for me because my fingers open, letting him have it.

I don't know what he does with my phone. I don't look up to see, and I can't hear over the sound of my own breathing.

But seconds later, his fingers are wrapping around my face, cradling my cheek. There's a tenderness to his touch, the same tenderness he was using with Casey, but instead of comforting me or putting me at ease, it actually makes me a little angry.

Angry because he's making it so much harder for me not to give in.

If he had grabbed me or tried to manhandle me, it would be so easy to push him away.

But treating me like this? Like I'm something that he cares about, something that he treasures? How am I supposed to react to that?

Lifting my lashes, I force myself to peer up at him. Force myself to meet that intensity head on.

"You tricked me here," I accuse and watch doubt and guilt pass over his face.

That intensity of his flickers, and I half-expect it to go out completely.

Then it flares back to life, even brighter than before as he asks, "Would you have come if I didn't?"

Of course I wouldn't have come because I knew this would happen.

Us alone, and me ready to make the biggest mistake of my life.

I've thought about this a lot over the past twenty-four hours. Entertained the thought of giving in to the attraction. Letting things play out how they would. But after it's done, how could I go on? How could I possibly live the rest of my miserable life, doing my father's bidding, after having a taste of what Emmett could give me?

"No, I wouldn't have come," I admit.

"That's exactly why I did it," he says in a tone that's completely unapologetic.

The lack of apology has my anger rising. I try to jerk my face away, but he manages to grab my chin, pulling me back to him.

"I did it because you wouldn't have come otherwise and Casey needed you."

Wait. What?

I'm so surprised by that revelation, I can't help but repeat it. "Casey needed me?"

Eyes locked on my eyes, Emmett nods his head without looking away. "Yes, he needed you, Bree."

Before I can completely come to terms with that, Emmett hits me with another bombshell.

"I need you, Bree."

Those words, those four little words cause both joy and terror to war inside me.

And ultimately, terror ends up winning.

I'm the last fucking person anyone should need, and if Emmett knew what the hell was good for him and Casey, he'd stay far away from me.

I try to pull away again.

I try to save him.

But, instead of letting me go, he pulls me closer. Wrapping his arm around me tight, his expression darkens.

"Tell me you don't need me," he demands, his breath washing over my face. "Tell me after that kiss yesterday, you don't feel like you've finally found what you've always been missing."

If he were Tristan, I'd be downright scared for my life right now.

But he's not. He's not that jerkface. And despite the pissed off look on his face, despite the way he's trapping me, keeping me from fleeing, I know, I *know* deep down in the marrow of my bones, Emmett would never hurt me.

That's why I have to end this now. That's why I have to force these words that slice like razors out of my throat.

"I don't need you," I croak, and brace myself for his reaction.

For his disgust. For his disappointment.

But it never comes.

I expect his arms to fall away, for him to take a step back. Maybe even bright white shock to appear on his face.

What I get is him drawing me even deeper into his embrace as his lips crash into me.

I try to resist at first. Try to pretend his taste, his touch, his smell, has no effect on me.

But it's all in vain.

He kisses me like a man possessed. Like a man fighting for his life.

Like a man trying to prove a point.

And despite how long I try to hold out, how long I try to persevere, I'm drowning and he's the breath of air I need.

Pushing his mouth into my mouth, he growls before saying, "Liar."

Then he kisses me even harder.

Pulling back again, his teeth scrape against my lips. "Stop lying to yourself."

Head swimming, I grab onto him as the force of his next kiss threatens to knock me over.

"Stop lying to me."

Clutching at his shirt, I open my mouth, ready to tell him off, but he pounces on the opportunity. His tongue sweeps into my mouth to dance with my mine.

My toes curl inside my shoes at the first stroke, a bolt of pure electricity flowing through me.

And god help me, before I even realize what I'm doing, I'm kissing him back. I'm kissing him like I'm about to die and this is the last kiss I'll ever have.

Because it feels like it.

After this I'll be dead, utterly dead. Emotionally, mentally, physically.

Because I'll never be kissed like this again.

"You need this as much as I do," he growls into my mouth, the sweet vibrations rolling through me.

And I do. Fuck my life, I do. I've never needed anything more than this spark igniting between us.

This connection I have with him. This feeling of belonging.

Desperate to hang onto it, my hands tear at him with a mind of their own. Grabbing his shirt, I try to lift it over his head.

Reaching down, he helps me, taking the fabric from my hands. He breaks our kiss only long enough to rip the shirt off.

Then his lips are on me again as my palms explore his skin. Learning all the hard planes of his body by touch.

But it's not enough. I need more of him. I need to feel more of his skin against my skin.

As if he can read my mind, as if he has the same frantic need, his hands grab my shirt, pulling it up between us.

Then my chest is against his chest and we're finally skin to skin.

My bra the only thing between us, I feel his deep rumble of pleasure through the fabric.

And my nipples tighten at the sensation.

Wrapping my arms around his neck, I tug at him. Desperate to have him closer because he'll never be close enough.

Hands molding around my ass, he lifts me up and I automatically wrap my legs around his waist.

Somehow he manages to carry me and kiss me at the same time. Only stopping from time to time to push me up against a wall and grind his hips into me. Rubbing his erection against my clit.

By the time my back hits a bed, I'm so worked up, so needy and wet, I begin to grow frustrated.

Everything is happening fast, but as he works on pulling off my shorts and his pants, it's not fast enough to sate the ache pulsing between my legs.

Or the deep, sudden need to have him inside me.

I need him now, before I remember why I shouldn't be doing this.

Before I remember everything this is going to fuck up.

Once the last of our clothes are gone, he settles himself between my open thighs, but he doesn't enter me. No, he breaks the kiss to move his mouth down to my breasts.

I groan with impatience as sucks my nipple into his hot mouth, his tongue toying with me.

Any other day… but not today.

Deciding to take matters into my hands, literally, I reach down between us and find his cock bobbing between us. He stiffens, his mouth sucking tight as my fingers wrap around his warm, velvety skin.

I arch my back in response, my nipple tightening so hard it borders on pain, until he finally releases me with a groan.

"If you don't stop, you're going to unman me," he warns, his mouth still hovering over my breast.

"What does that even mean?" I pant and flutter my lashes at him, playing innocent as I stroke my hand slowly up and down his length.

Emmett groans again, deeper this time, and closes his eyes as my stroke makes it up to his head. Wetness seeps across my fingers, slickening my grip.

Making it easier to quicken my pace.

Eyes flashing open, his jaw tenses as he tries to maintain his self-control.

"Keep going and you'll find out," he grits out.

Another warning.

"Okay," I say without stopping.

Growling, his head dips back down, his teeth scraping across me as he tries to jerk his hips away.

I tighten my grip.

"Goddammit," he tries to growl, but his voice cracks with weakness.

Knowing I'm getting to him, I lift my hips until the crown of his cock is pushing through my lips.

Suddenly he stiffens above me, his body taut with tension.

But I don't stop. I can't stop.

Having already come this far, I use him for my own pleasure, grinding my hips as I work him against my clit.

Above me, he begins to tremble. Then, like a rubber band stretched too far, he finally snaps. Making a noise that sounds almost feral, he reaches down, grabs me by the wrist, and yanks my hand away.

Just as I open my mouth to complain, he slams his cock home inside me.

"Is this what you want?" he grunts as his hard length pushes through my tightness.

Completely shameless at this point, I throw my head back and moan out, "Yes," as my body tries to adjust to suddenly having him inside me.

Stretching me.

Filling me.

Almost breaking me.

Fuck, he's so big, so much bigger than I'm used to. If I wasn't so wet, he would probably split me in half...

Pulling back his hips, he begins to slowly slide out of

me, and I can't hold back the whimper that makes it past my lips.

"Is this what you need?" he asks, then slams back inside me.

Overwhelming me with too much incredible sensation.

I knew being with Emmett would be intense, but fuck, I never expected this. I never expected my entire world to be utterly and completely upended.

Head dropping down, his lips capture my lips as he pumps himself in and out of my body. And with each deep stroke, with each rolling grind of his hips against my clit, I lose myself a little bit more.

I give more of myself to him.

Until there's nothing left.

Nothing left but the desire to spend the rest of my eternity just like this. With him above me and inside me, filling up every hollow, empty space and little crack.

Breaking our kiss, he's lets out a soft, drawn-out groan before he declares, "Fuck, you feel so good. So fucking good, baby girl…"

Suddenly his pace increases and his breath comes fast and heavy as he drives himself into me with a frantic purpose.

"I could spend the rest of my life like this. The rest of my life buried inside you," he declares.

And I didn't realize I closed my eyes until this very second.

Popping them open, his face, tense with pleasure and strain, peers down at me.

"Could you spend the rest of your life like this?" he grunts, his skin slapping against my skin. "Could you spend the rest of your life with me, Bree?"

Maybe, at any other time, under different circumstances, I'd be able to answer him in a sensible way, fully aware of the consequences my answer will carry.

But at this moment, experiencing the most exquisite pleasure of my short, pitiful life, with him staring intensely down at me, half-asking, half-demanding, "Could you?"

I can think of no other answer but, "Yes."

A million times, yes.

"Thank fuck," he says with a look of relief.

But that look is short-lived. It's quickly replaced by something that's wild, something that's untamed.

Reaching down, he grabs me by the back of the knee and pulls my leg up. Already on the verge of an orgasm that's intense but something that's close to what I'm familiar with, the pressure inside me suddenly changes.

His cock pounding even deeper than before, everything becomes too much as I struggle to process sensations so intense and strong it feels like they're going to fucking kill me.

"Because I can't let you go… not now… not ever…"

My eyes start to roll back into my head as I'm swept up and carried away by the most powerful orgasm of my life.

Over the roar in my ears and the rush in my veins, I'm hear him say, "You're mine. Fucking *mine*."

And as crazy as it is, at this exact second in time, with his warmth flooding through me, there's nothing else I want to be.

I want more than anything to be *his*.

Early dawn light filters through the curtains as my alarm starts to screech beside my head.

"Fuck," I groan quietly and try to swing an arm at the nightstand to silence the shrill noise.

But my arm doesn't fucking move, it's weighed down by a warm, breathing mass of sexiness. Now normally, or at least in the distant past, I wouldn't be too happy about having a girl wrapped around me like a boa constrictor, holding me down to the bed like I'll float away. But right here and right now?

I'm absolutely fucking digging this.

Bree's so warm, and she's latched on to me like her life depends on it. It's comforting, it's fucking amazing…

It's maybe…

"Urgh," she grumbles before reaching toward the noise, swatting at it.

"I've got it," I whisper to her as I reach over and slap down the button on the alarm.

"What the fuck?" Bree gasps suddenly and bolts away from me.

"Uh," comes my brilliant reply.

Probably not the smoothest thing I could have said.

"What time is it?" she yelps while jumping out of bed.

She starts to frantically scramble around the room.

"Um, five-till-six," I say as I turn on the lamp beside the bed. "What are you doing?"

"Where are my panties?!" she yelps as she keeps rushing about, picking her clothes up from the floor.

"No clue," I say with a chuckle.

She's not getting those back.

"My socks?" she asks as she yanks up her running shorts.

"Same answer," I say, and this one I'm telling the truth about.

Though if it would keep her in this house for the rest of our lives, I'd hide every item of clothing she owns.

Wrapping her arm across her incredible breasts, she says, "Stop staring, you've probably seen a thousand pairs before."

"I've seen the stars a million times, yet I still stare whenever I get a chance. Perfection deserves the attention," I say with a small growl.

My mouth is watering just at the memory of tasting her flesh, licking the pale skin of those delicious breasts. She has tan lines, and for some reason they are one of the sexiest things I've ever seen. Same with the mismatched socks that she lost.

Just about everything on her is sexy and beautiful to me.

"Oh god." She groans and rolls her eyes so hard, I'm not sure she didn't pull a muscle in there somewhere.

"What?"

"That was horribly corny," she says as she bends over to swipe up her t-shirt.

I frown as I watch her cover her chest. "Don't need a bra today?"

"Shit!" she squeaks before she dives back to the floor to continue her search. "Help me, dammit!"

"With what?" I ask as I sink to the floor, completely naked and semi-aroused.

"I need my bra at least! My mom's going to kill me! I can't believe I let you get me in this situation," she spits out hastily as she snags the bra I hold up for her out of my hand.

Yanking her shirt back over her head, she does that weird feminine thing where she puts it on backwards and then twists it before yanking the straps over her shoulders.

Fucking hell, those breasts don't need to be covered.

It's really fucking tempting though to give her panties back just so I can see her take those shorts off again.

"What situation?" I ask. "You got a curfew?"

Glancing down, I don't see a monitor on her ankle.

"No... but..."

She trails off as I move to stand in front of her. She's moving and jittering so bad that I feel like she's about to explode.

"Bree," I say quietly.

"I..." she says.

I gently rest my hands on her shoulders. "Bree, *breathe*. Breathe in and out three times."

She gives me the stink eye, but I stare down into her eyes and take slow steady breaths. No matter what her situation is, I'm here. She's got me now. I'll...

She's midway through her third breath when I say, "Shit."

"Shit? Shit what?"

Well fuck, is she on the pill or something? Is it bad that I'm really hoping she's not? It would make things so much easier if I knocked her up. There would be no reason for her not to marry my broken-down ass at this point.

I keep my hands on her shoulders just in case she wants to try and kill me. "Not sure this is the right time to say this, but we didn't use protection last night."

Her eyes widen for a moment before she rolls them again. "I'm on the pill, we're good."

Breathing out a sigh of disappointment, I grumble, "We'll have to fix that."

"What?" she asks, eyeballing me again.

"What?" I repeat back.

Pulling away from me, she bends over to grab her shoes. I'm about to grab her hips and fucking hump her before I realize now might not be the best time for that.

"You need to get me home!" she growls right before she plops down on the side of the bed and begins to yank her shoes on.

"Poof, you're home," I say as I cross my arms over my chest. "I haven't forgotten about what you said last night."

Confusion flows over her beautiful face. "What?"

"You said, and I'm quoting here, you could spend the rest of your life with me here," I say.

"Are you fucking insane?" she asks in astonishment.

"Not that I know of, but if I was, would I really know I was?" I ask then shrug my shoulders. "That's not really the issue though... Do you have short-term memory loss? I should probably know if you do. I mean, I don't want you to forget that spectacular orgasm."

"No, I don't have any kind of memory loss! You just can't hold me to some promise I made in the heat of the moment!" she practically shouts before I start motioning for her to keep it down.

"Don't wake, Casey," I murmur.

"Shit!" she squeaks and all of a sudden her cheeks turn bright red.

"What?"

"He's going to know I stayed the night!" she whispers harshly.

"As loud as you were last night, I'm pretty sure he knows already. He may have thumped on the walls for us to keep it down a couple of times," I say with a smirk.

"Holy fuck! He did not!" she whispers, turning even more red.

I shrug my shoulders. "So? Are you taking back your promise?"

"What promise?" she whispers loudly at me.

Standing up from the bed, she stomps her way over to stand right in front of me.

"You know full well you said yes," I say.

"You asked me that right before I had one of the… Before I came!"

"One of the what?" I ask with another smirk, and I swear I can hear her grinding her teeth.

"Shut it. You asked me a life-altering question mid-coitus. I would have sold you my liver at that point in time."

Did she just say *coitus*?

I can't help the chuckles that ripple through me. "Coitus?"

"I'm going to kick your ass," she snarls at me before punching me in the chest.

"Ouch," I say with another one of my charming smirks.

"Yes, it was a moment of weakness! It doesn't mean we're fated to the stars or something."

She stares up at me with those words ringing in my head.

"Bullshit," I say and stare right back.

"What?"

She glares at me, and I know I'm right, and so does she.

"You had every chance to bail from the moment you met me, you didn't."

"Oh, for fuck's sake!" she snaps at me.

There's a loud knock on my door followed by Casey yelling, "Can you two shut up? I was supposed to get thirty more minutes of sleep!"

Well fuck, that wasn't expected.

Both of us stare at each other for a long moment, each lost in our own embarrassment.

"Oh my god!" Bree whispers before she starts to giggle, giggle like a madwoman.

"Fuck!" I start to snicker as I try to hide my partial hard-on from her.

Even arguing with this chick gets me hard. I didn't even notice how close I got into her personal space before Casey yelled at us.

Looking down at Bree, I tug lightly at her chin so that she looks up at me. "You said yes, no take backs."

Before she can argue with me, I lean down and kiss those lips of hers that have tormented me. Those plush, silken lips.

Last night I was in dire need of filling that void in my soul, to raise my soul back from the depths of the dark abyss. I know I can't hinge my recovery on her, but it feels right to make this connection. To fill the empty spaces with her life.

To take hold of her hand and never let go.

My hands gently caress her cheeks before sliding to the back of her head and pulling her deeply into the kiss. The resistance I felt last night was a wall I wasn't entirely sure would ever come down.

Now it's gone.

I don't have the words to describe the emotions she puts in the kiss, but it's more than anything I've ever felt before. Her hands grab at my chest as she molds herself into me, and for a split second I think, *fuck the world outside of us.*

Reaching down, I pull her shirt up and push my hand under her silky bra. Cupping her generous mound of breast, I give it a light squeeze.

Moaning so quietly I almost miss it, she pushes even harder into me.

"Hey! Who's cooking the eggs and bacon?" Casey yells. "I don't think you guys want food poisoning, but I can try."

Bree pushes my hand out of her shirt and pulls away from me. "Shit!"

"Fuck," I growl and start stalking toward her, my throbbing cock leading the way.

Wide-eyed, she looks down at my cock and then back up at me. "No way!" She darts for the door. "Get dressed!"

"Get back here," I growl at her.

She says, "No way, no how," before she dashes out of the room and slams the door behind her.

"Motherfucker."

~

Gym shorts are not the best clothing to wear with a raging hard-on. I have to tuck my dick up behind the waistband like I'm some damn kid in high school.

Trudging down the long hallway, heading for the kitchen, I can't help but smile though.

She's so mine, that fucking kiss proved it. She wanted it and needed it as badly as I did.

The smell of bacon and eggs hits me as soon as I walk into the kitchen, and it's startling to notice the difference. Gone is the smell of booze and stale pizza. Casey and I did a pretty good job when we rushed to clean the house yesterday, getting it ready for Bree. We even got the fancier toilet paper.

Can't have her using the sandpaper I was buying before.

"Damn, that smells good!" I groan, rubbing my stomach.

"Right?!" Casey groans as he looks at Bree, rubbing his stomach too. "Emmett is a horrible cook compared to you."

"Really?" Bree looks over at me with a huge grin. "Thanks."

"Watch it, Casey. I'll start buying turkey bacon if you keep that up," I grumble at him.

He's right, though. The smells coming from the pan top anything I could make.

Laughing at Casey's horrified expression, Bree says, "Turkey bacon isn't that bad."

"Oh, yes it is!" Casey says, sliding away from Bree as he holds up his fingers in a cross. "That stuff is for bad people who go to jail or something."

"He's right on that. Turkey bacon can't compete with real bacon," I say.

Rolling her eyes, she looks at us both. "It's a healthier bacon, guys."

"Ew, that's just wrong," Casey says, and I nod to agree with him.

~

Breakfast was fucking amazing. Just the three of us stuffing our faces with food as we sat around the table, laughing and joking. I had a heavy thought though when it was over, right after we cleaned up the table.

What if we were a family and Casey was ours?

It fucking wrecked me.

I was able to get away from them before they could see me just about lose my shit. And thankfully I made it to the hallway bathroom before I threw up everything I just ate.

Tommy swam in my blurry vision when I looked up from the toilet and into the mirror. Fuck. I'm not supposed to be raising Casey with some chick I just met. That's not how any of this shit was supposed to go.

This is far past who I was ever going to be. This isn't who I ever thought I could or would be. I'm in unknown territory, and it's scaring me that it feels so easily right. Is it? Can I even know the difference?

Driving Bree back to her mom's house, I think she can feel the vibe that must be oozing out of my pores.

Fuck.

She grabs my hand on the center console and gives it a tight squeeze while tugging it toward her.

Glancing over at her, I see that there's concern in her eyes.

Casey is just chattering away behind us, oblivious to the drama unfolding in my head.

Quietly, so that only I hear, Bree asks, "What's going on?"

I shake my head because I can't even explain the long, twisted thoughts that are flowing through my mind. The one thing, though, that lingers in the background of all those thoughts is that I have her here, right now, by my side.

Her and Casey, here in the now.

And I'm not letting her get away. I don't care what I have to do, I'm fucking keeping her ass.

Keeping her and never fucking letting go.

"Tell me later?" she asks, and she gives me a small smile, showing me how fucking warm her heart is.

Showing me how deep her emotions must run. That she can read me and see that I'm twisted up shows. Fuck, this girl is something special.

Nodding my head to her, I mouth back, "I'll try."

"So guys, anyone want to place bets on whether Dale makes Emmett puke today or not?" Casey asks.

"I hate you right now," I growl out at him.

"I'll tell him you said that." Casey snickers at me. "I'm safe, he likes kids and women."

"Well… keep it up and we'll see," I say.

I don't have a comeback. He's probably right about it all.

Squeezing my hand tightly, Bree gives me that warm and mushy feeling all over again. It's fucking jarring and settling at the same time. It's also so unfamiliar, I just might fall into it and not come back out.

Last night was… I hate to use the term, but it was fucking magical. I don't know how else to describe the pleasure I gave and received. I don't know how to describe the connection we formed. The only thing I've ever experienced that comes close to it is the peace I feel when I'm in the ring. And even that isn't the same.

I'm actually happy that she's beside me right now. I'm happy and I feel guilty as fuck for it.

How the fuck do I deserve to be happy?

The ride to her mom's has my head swaying from happy to guilt to confusion. Fuck, I'm a goddamn mess.

When we pull up in front of her house, my hand seems to have a mind of its own. It simply doesn't want to let her go. I even have to do an awkward reach over my body with my free hand to put the Jeep in park.

"I'm going to need to take my hand with me, Emmett," Bree says with a laugh when I refuse to let her go.

"Fine, but only if you agree to come to dinner with us," I say with a smile. "Unless you want me dragging you to the gym with us right now in your clothes from yesterday."

Growling, she yanks on her hand, but I refuse to let go without the promise. "Fine, dinner, but you have to cook."

"Works for me."

I smile and let go of her hand. If she knew how much it costs me to let go, I doubt she would have made me just yet.

Pulling her hand away, she looks back to Casey. "How bad is it going to be tonight?"

"Depends, they have food poisoning vaccines yet?" he asks.

"That was one time. One goddamn time and it was like four years ago," I growl at him.

Casey groans. "Dad and I almost died!"

My stomach drops when silence fills the car.

The weight of the world is crashing down on me.

I look back at Casey though and try to give him a smile as I grab his knee and give it a small squeeze.

"I won't make fish, I promise," I say with fake cheerfulness.

"I can't even go to Red Lobster anymore because of you," Casey says back with a sad smile.

His dad said the same thing to me every time I mentioned cooking around him.

"How… How about HotStop Wings?" Bree suggests.

Poor Bree, she doesn't know what she just did.

"Who's buying?" I ask with a real chuckle.

"You should buy since you're the one who asked me to come back." She looks between the two of us. "Why are you guys smiling like that?"

"She's never seen a growing boy eat hot wings, has she?" Casey begins to laugh.

"Remember, we probably need to wear bibs," I say and wink at Casey.

"That's what the to-go bag is for. You just rip it a bit and tuck it down your shirt to catch the droppings," he says.

"Genius," I say, grinning at him.

"You guys are worrying me," Bree says with a giggle.

"You're just lucky it's me buying. I don't think you could afford the two of us. We have, lets say, large appetites," I say as I grab her hand again and pull her toward me.

"I'm starting to think that after seeing how much you two ate at breakfast."

She leans into me, and she must be more comfortable with me in front of Casey now because she doesn't get upset when I give her a quick kiss on the lips.

I let her hop out of the Jeep without stopping her, and

Casey takes her place. He elbows me in the shoulder when I don't stop watching her sexy ass walk all the way to the front door.

Damn, running shorts look good as fuck on that ass of hers. It swishes and jiggles in the perfect way.

"Dude, you're drooling," Casey says.

"Just making sure she gets into the house," I say and look at him. "When you start dating, you always wait until they make it into the house before you leave. And if it's dark, you walk her to the door. It's a safety thing."

"Doesn't that seem kind of creepy? You watching them walk up their driveway or whatever?" he asks, and takes a quick look to make sure Bree got in.

"No, and if a guy doesn't think of his girl's safety first, he doesn't deserve her," I say as I put the jeep into drive. "Oh, and never honk at a girl's house, expecting her to come out. That's just douchey. She isn't a dog that responds to whistles."

My phone starts to blow up again as soon as I turn it on in the gym's parking lot. And by blow up, I mean texts, emails, and phone calls coming in one right after the other.

Fuck, what the hell is going on now?

I don't have time for shit like this, not one fucking bit. I need to get focused on training and taking care of Bree and Casey.

Those are my two priorities.

I turned the motherfucker off for a reason last night. Everyone who needs to get a hold of me knows my house phone number for emergencies.

Getting out of the Jeep, I toss my phone to Casey. "Silence that fucker. I don't want to hear about it until after training today."

"Yes, sir," Casey says with a laugh as he starts fooling around with it to make all the chimes and dings stop. "You want to know what it's all about?"

"Nah," I say, "it's probably bullshit anyways."

Casey drawls out, "Okay."

And I get the feeling maybe I should find out what's going on.

But as I walk into the gym, I don't think I'll need the help.

Chase, Bear, and Dale are all standing near the front desk, looking up at the large TV that plays the sports updates. Once I see what they're watching, my entire body starts to go numb with deep-seated rage.

Turning to see who came in the door, Chase gives me a pissed off look. He motions for me to get over to him before he points up at the screen.

Dale spits out, "Fucking Silva."

Over the clatter of the men and women working out around us, I hear the sportscaster talking about something Silva did on some social media platform last night.

Last night while I was having one of the best nights of my life, this douchebag was talking major shit.

I stick my hand out for my phone and Casey hands it to me quickly. Swiping it on, I check to see what I'm missing. It doesn't take me long to find it, Brett sent me a link through text.

Opening the link, my hands start to tremble as I watch a video of Jamey reenacting the end of our last match. Except whoever the fuck he has acting like me is howling and screaming like a girl about his arm.

The fuckers even reenact the part where Jamey knocked out Tommy, calling him a dead little bitch.

I stare at the phone long after the video ends, the craving for the dark, blackout stage of being drunk calling to me.

"I'm going to fucking kill him," Casey whispers beside me.

"I get him first," I growl and throw my phone across the gym, sending it slamming into an empty wall.

"Shit!" Casey winces as he chases after it.

I hope I broke that fucker, but knowing the case I bought for it, I doubt it.

"Well, I guess you know the first thing I wanted to talk to you about," Dale says as he walks over to me.

"Yeah, what's the second?" I ask, staring at him.

"The company called this morning. Seems they had a cancellation for next month's match. It was supposed to be a title fight, but one of the guys got a bad staph infection. They want to know how you feel about moving your match up a month," Dale says in a way that I'm positive he already knows my answer.

"I want a bigger payout for beating him," I say, and then look around me.

Chase is still pretty pissed off, and I bet I know the reason why.

Dale laughs in his harsh, almost raspy, way. "Already did, figured I'd act like I gave you an option."

"Anything else or can I go get changed?" I ask.

"Yeah, were you the reason why Bree didn't make it home last night?" Dale asks and his voice has this deadly calm to it.

A calm he only gets when he's ready to hurt someone.

Only a fool would think he can't fight. Being a trainer doesn't mean he can't dish out a serious ass-whooping.

"I was, and she'll be staying at my house for the fore-seeable future," I answer.

To be honest, if he or Chase wants to push the issue one fucking inch, I'll fucking break 'em both.

"She in love with you?" Dale asks.

"She doesn't know it yet, but yeah. Just as much as I

am with her," I say before walking away and heading to the locker room.

I need to get ready. Pounds are going to be shed and muscles are going to be worked until they're hard and lean.

I know when Bree arrives because the moment she steps into the place, I can feel her presence in my mind. Like she's rooted there.

Chase notices it too though, and the dirty ass look he gives me lets me know he's going to make my life a living hell.

Fuck it though, she's worth the hell and pain. She's worth everything.

"Hey Dale," I call out after a very long set of burpees. "Casey said you wouldn't punish him too hard because he's a kid. Sounded like he called you a pussy to me, but I could be wrong."

"Casey!" Dale shouts out across the gym, and I would snicker if I wasn't worried about getting in trouble.

Casey, poor kid, was sitting on the desk next to Bree, reenacting something for her. And I can tell by the way his head turns toward us, he's scared.

Yep, little turd shouldn't have fucked with me.

Stopping my burpees exercise, I bend over at the waist, taking a couple of deep breaths. Burpees don't look hard on the body, but they are, and they fucking suck. Do enough of them and you'll wanna die.

Casey jogs over to us and gives me the stink eye. "Yeah?"

"I'm a pussy, huh?" Dale asks with a growling snarl.

Casey's eyes go wide. "What? I... I never said that."

"Place your bets, ladies and gents," Dale shouts to the

gym. "We're going to see who can last the longest, Casey or Emmett. First one to puke has to mop up the mess!"

"Wait, what?" I ask in horror. "What the fuck did I do?"

Dale cackles as he looks around at the growing crowd. "Burpees, boys. Ten sets of ten to start off!"

"I just did twenty sets of ten!" I mutter loudly.

"I hate you, Emmett," Casey groans as he gets into position.

"This will teach you both about the value of being a good role model. And it's good for your testicular fortitude," Dale laughs. "Now start!"

Fuck. Me. I'm going to die.

I can see Bree over at the desk, watching in growing confusion as all the guys and gals around her start betting money, workout routines, and just about anything under the sun.

"This is gonna hurt," I whisper to Casey.

"I really hate you," Casey groans as we both drop down into our first set.

The first ten reps aren't too bad. I just remember the video I was shown earlier this morning, replaying Jamey Silva's words in my head.

Dead little bitch.

That keeps the fire in my stomach more than anything else. I let those words heat me up. I let them slither and writhe all over my brain, encompassing me with rage and disgust.

At the fifteenth repetition, Casey falls to the mat, gasping for air and telling Dale he taps out. Looking over at him to make sure he's not seriously dying, I keep going.

My body is shaking by the twentieth rep, and I can feel

my stomach wanting to hurl from the abuse I'm pushing myself through.

After finishing up, the crowd is staring at me with a strange mixture of bemusement and acknowledgement. Not a lot of people can make it through what I just did. I've had a full day so far with my workout and training inside the ring.

My body hurts in places I don't remember existing, but I still have the drive to do something else.

To punish something.

Eyeing Dale with annoyance, I say, "I'm heading to the bags."

"Twenty-five elbows strikes, thirty punches on both arms. Then the same for the knee strikes and kicks," he says, and I just nod.

He knows I've got the anger again in me. I'll be worth shit tomorrow, but right now I need to blow this steam off any way that I can.

Bree's soft voice comes from over my shoulder. "You okay?"

Nodding my head yes, I don't turn around. "I'm good."

"You sure?" she asks, and then out of the corner of my eye I see her sit down beside me on the curb of the sidewalk.

I chuckle ruefully. "Yeah, might have overworked myself in there."

I fucking just about killed myself in there. Even now, my arm barely wants to move enough to reach over and hold her hand.

"Was it about the video they keep looping on the sports channel?"

"Yeah, a little. Maybe a lot."

I look over to see her big blue eyes so full of sympathy it almost breaks my carefully held together shell.

She grips my hand a little tighter as she scoots closer to me, her hip and shoulder bumping up against my own. "Want to talk about it?"

"Not yet, I can barely think clearly," I say with a huge groan as I stretch my spine back, trying to pop out the tension that's resting between my shoulders.

"Tonight?"

"Yeah, after Casey's asleep. He doesn't need to hear all the shit that's rumbling around in my skull."

"Okay. I don't know half of what's going on here right now, and the stuff I do know…"

She trails off quietly.

"I feel like an asshole, Bree. I know I shouldn't drag you into a life that's…"

She turns my head to face her. "That's what?"

"Complicated as fuck. A life that's not going to be easy. I have a kid now, I guess. He's going to be living with me for the foreseeable future. We're a package deal, and I don't want that scaring you off."

She doesn't answer right away, but when she does, she smiles. "He likes me more."

"That's because you feed him," I say and laugh loudly at the thought of it.

"If only all our problems could be solved by just feeding them food, huh?" she says with chuckle.

"Yeah, if only," I say, and then I imagine myself force-feeding Jamey Silva a huge pile of dog shit, one turd after another until he fucking died.

~

Bree looks at both Casey and me in utter astonishment. After rubbing her eyes, she takes another look at all the discarded bags and empty boxes littering the kitchen table.

"I… I… How is any of this possible?" she asks, clearly confused. "I thought you ordered so much for leftovers or something."

Resisting the urge to let out a massive, house-rattling burp, I frown. "I'm still feeling kinda peckish, actually. How about you, Casey?"

Casey leans back in his chair and rubs his slightly bloated stomach. "Eh, I could go for some pie right about now."

"What?!" Bree looks at us both with revulsion. "You both ate more than I weigh and you want more food?!"

Casey looks over at me and I can tell what's coming before he's able to stop himself. A massive burp that actually shrinks the size of his stomach bursts from his lips. Poor guy doesn't stop with one, either. A second one comes out and it's even longer than the first one.

"Excuse me, I'm so sorry," Casey says with an idiotic grin. "Yeah, some apple pie would be amazing right now."

"Dude, I'd go for some brownies. Maybe the ones with nuts and chocolate chips," I say and lick my lips.

God, I'd actually kill for a brownie right now. All those hot and spicy barbecue wings have got me needing something sweet.

"Oh my god!" Bree mutters as she turns in her seat, away from us, and starts rubbing her temples. "You two ate at least twenty wings each."

"Twenty-three," Casey says with pride. "So can we order pie or what?"

"Twenty-nine. Would have been thirty but you ate one of mine, Bree," I say with a smirk.

"Are you serious?" She turns to give me a dirty look. "You're begrudging me one of your wings? Counting yours, I had six."

I shrug my shoulders. "Not my fault you're a lightweight."

"A what?" she asks with a growl.

"I think she's a flyweight," Casey says, and slumps back in his chair.

"Eh, strawweight," I say while looking at Bree with grin.

"What the heck are you two talking about?" she asks.

"What weight class you'd be in if you fought," I say.

"Oh god, you two need to get a… Hey, wait a second. Are you discussing my weight in front of me?" She crosses her arms over her chest, peering at us both. "Are you?"

Shit.

"Ummm, I need to see what movie we got for tonight," Casey says before hopping up from the table and running out of the kitchen.

Fuck. I'm too old and sore to move as quickly as he did.

I offer her a grin, hoping it will placate her. "Only in the best of terms."

"Oh really," Bree says entirely too sweetly. "So let me ask you a question."

I'm a dead man.

"Um, go for it," I say carefully.

"Just how much do these strawweight and flyweight classes weigh?" she asks and it's like she put powdered sugar into her voice.

"Uh… well…" I stammer out because she's looking really funny at me.

She grins. "I could always ask my much older and much bigger big brother, and his best friend Dale."

"Well, you see… a flyweight is… um… around…" I start to say before she cuts me off.

"Oh, shut up. I met Chrissy today and she taught me a lot about weight classes. It's pretty damn intimidating thinking of all the stuff she can do," she says with a shake of her head.

I roll my eyes in relief. "Yeah, but she's also a champion, and she works just as hard as any of the guys. She's scary fast."

"I knew she was fighter, but didn't know how far she was?" Bree says.

"Yeah, she's the reigning champ of her weight class right now. She's got speed and good striking abilities. Her grappling is also pretty damn good. I'm hoping to get some time in the ring with her so I can go against someone close to Silva's speed."

I'm counting on Chrissy giving me a good preview of Silva's speed. Chrissy is a little lightning bolt when it comes to punches.

"Wait, you're going to fight a girl?" Bree asks with such an expressive face that I bet she's a horrible liar.

"Yeah, but not like you're thinking. We'll be in full protective gear and won't be hitting each other with all of our power."

I'm betting Bree thinks I'll be beating up a poor little girl. If only she knew the truth.

"I promise you, it's not as bad as it sounds. She'll be more than happy to help me tune up my speed, and I'll be good practice as someone who's takedown skills are superior to hers. We'll be helping each other."

"Wow. It's just that I've caught glimpses of real matches on TV, and it looks so brutal," she says with a small amount of awe.

"Oh, it's brutal as fuck, but it's something you kinda get used to," I say with a small shrug of my shoulders.

"You get used to getting beat up?"

Laughing, I shake my head. "I wouldn't put it like that exactly, but yeah you get used to taking some pain in order to give a shit ton of it."

She shakes her head. "I'm not sure I could ever do what you guys do."

I smile at her and stand up from my seat. "Definitely takes a certain kind of mind frame, I think."

I grab the garbage can near the back door and haul it over to the table so I can start sweeping the food bags and containers into it.

"Can I help?" Bree asks as she watches me quickly cleaning up the mess.

"Nah, I got it. Though you can go make sure Casey picks something that might interest you too. We might get stuck with another superhero movie if ya don't," I say.

She looks a little surprised as she asks, "You're not a superhero movie fan?"

I shrug my shoulders. "Eh, I've seen so many of them I'm starting to root for the bad guy."

"Oh, so you're kind of like a bad boy then, huh?" she says, smirking at me as she leaves the kitchen.

Casey falls asleep during the movie again, and I'd high five the kid if I thought he knew how much of a favor he is doing me.

But damn, this little guy is heavy as I pick him up from the couch.

"You okay?" Bree asks as I come to a stop to make sure I'm not going to keel over.

"Yeah," I say, and straighten up fully so she doesn't see that my ass is feeling like roadkill right now.

Bree giggles quietly before she steps to the side. "Okay, but you sounded like you were about to die."

"Little fighter is getting heavy is all," I say, and try not to let my wobbly arms wake Casey.

I pushed it too far in the gym today. I know better than to do that, but I couldn't help it. Fucking Jamey Silva knew what he was doing when he made those videos.

He knew it and did it to get under my skin.

I'll fucking beat him when I get my chance to put my hands around his neck, I know it. If I don't kill him that is. That's a fucking temptation that's way too appealing right now. I know it shouldn't be, but I really do want to cause the fucking asshole some pain and suffering.

Just thinking of him has the muscles in my arms twitching in anticipation of the war we're going to have.

Dropping Casey into his bed as gently as my shaky arms can manage, I turn toward Bree's presence. I'm half-fucking surprised she isn't gone already. I know I've made a lot of promises to her, but she hasn't yet reciprocated the promise of staying with me.

I need her to be here with me, I know it.

I know it as deep down as I know that Casey is a permanent part of my life now.

Casey needs me and I need him. I need the reminder that there's a life outside of all the pain and misery I've been living in.

I need Bree too.

I need that light that's in her eyes right now, and the soft smile that appears when she watches me put Casey to bed.

And I can't wait for that look to be in her eyes every day. I know she's got some shit going on outside of us, but whatever the fuck it is we'll fix it together.

That or I'll figure out how to hide the body of the douche who knocked her down. The desert is a big place and it has lots of forgotten holes.

Moving quietly through the room, I reach out to take Bree's hand, and lead us out. "Dude's been falling asleep pretty damn easily lately."

"I noticed. He seems pretty happy and content right now. Like he's finally feeling safe," she says, and a fleeting emotion flashes across her face.

It's a mixture of sadness and something else. Hope, perhaps?

"You okay?" I ask and pull her toward my bedroom.

She doesn't even put up a token resistance. "Yeah, just tired."

"Long day?" I ask.

Moving up until she's beside me, she pokes me in the arm. "Yes, but nothing like yours. Did you try to kill yourself out there?"

"Maybe," I say, "but I have to be ready for whatever war I'm getting ready to step in. Fighting Jamey is going to be a war, no peace talks. He went way too far."

She nods her head. "I could tell, though I have to tell you the truth, I've never followed MMA before I met Chase, and even then, I haven't given it more than a few glances. I know Chase was the world champ when he retired, and from what my mom says, he was one of the best and scariest fighters out there."

Despite our differences over his sister, I still have a shit ton of respect for Chase. "Yeah. He was called the Reaper for a reason. When Chase fought, he buried guys in the mat. He put 'em down and made sure they stayed there. He has some fights that they still talk about."

Bree smiles at me. "What do they call you?"

"Waste," I say with a laugh. "Or at least that's the latest one."

"What?" she asks, confused.

"I haven't exactly been on the straight and narrow as of late," I say with a shrug.

Pulling my shirt over my head, I toss it at the dirty clothes hamper.

"Avery told me a bit about what happened, and from what Casey has talked about… Emmett…"

Turning to her, I let her see me in all my scarred glory. "I failed to get back up after losing the match and losing

Tommy. I let all that dark negative shit consume me, and I let it keep me down for far too long."

Closing in on me, I watch as she stares at my chest. Her eyes run all over the muscles that are slowly beginning to come back. They don't linger on where my abs used to be, but the way her little tongue peeks out to moisten her lips has my cock ready to stand at attention.

"I know a little about dark stuff clouding over you. It's pretty hard to see outside of your own world sometimes, isn't it?" she asks as she looks up into my eyes.

Nodding my head, I reach out and pull her to me. "Want to tell me about it?"

She moves into my arms. "Not tonight. I don't think I can think about stuff like that right now…"

Leaning down, I softly kiss her lips. "We're going to need to lay our cards on the table soon. We need to come in with clean slates. This isn't going to be a fling, baby girl."

He eyes widen and then close as I lean back down to give her a longer, slower kiss. My tongue slips past her lips, eager to dance with hers. Eager to deepen our connection.

She tastes so damn good, so damn good I can't get enough of her. I can't get enough of her taste. I can't get enough of her scent. This close, it's fucking intoxicating.

I'm already a fucking goner and she's still dressed.

Her arms raise for me as I pull her shirt up and over her head.

And I can't stop myself from looking down and admiring the bra that cups her lovely breasts. "Fuck, you're so goddamn sexy."

Blushing, she bows her head and shakes it. "I don't know about that. I don't feel like I am."

Moving her chin up so that I can look in her eyes, I say, "You're the sexiest woman I've ever seen."

She shakes her head. "I don't—"

I cut her off. "No, you are. You're so fucking beautiful and sexy, the moment I saw you I felt my heart drop in my chest. It felt like my soul connected to yours the instant our lips touched. You're the woman of my dreams, Bree."

A faint blush rushes up from her chest to her cheeks.

It's so damn cute, I have to kiss her again.

Pulling her body tight to mine, my hands slip to her back. And even though I just did this last night, the damn things start to shake at the prospect of unlatching her bra and releasing her breasts.

I have to break our kiss again and move back so that the lacy bra can fall between us. Once it does, I catch a peek of her pale pink nipples tightening as if they're ready to be licked.

Reaching down, I move with a speed I didn't even realize I had and push at the waistband of her shorts. My tongue lashes out against her breast, hungry, needy, as I bend to shove those stupid shorts off her slender hips.

Her body shudders toward my questing tongue before I sink further down to the floor.

"Stupid fucking clothing," I growl out while yanking her shoes and socks off.

Laughing, she places her hands on my shoulders for balance. "You're going total caveman now, aren't you?"

She doesn't even know the fucking half of it.

Rising quickly to my feet, I sweep her off hers and carry her wedding style before tossing her through the air.

Shrieking, she lands on the bed with a bounce before she starts to laugh at the sight of me stalking after her.

"Bree, I don't know what the fuck it is in your

pheromones that drives me insane, but you've got me. You've got me completely hooked," I say when I reach the bed.

Grabbing her by the ankles, I pull her to me. "Come here, you."

Gasping, she looks up as I shove my pants off my hips and push everything to the floor.

She glances down at my throbbing cock and back up to my face. "Completely?"

"Without reservation," I say, and then sink to my knees between her thighs.

I wanted to taste her so badly last night, but I couldn't keep a grip on my self-control. I was unhinged, unable to fight the desire to stake my claim.

Unable to keep my shit together when she stroked me dangerously close to release.

I can control myself tonight, just enough to take the time to do what I've been thinking about doing every time I look at her thighs.

Spreading her legs, I start kissing her stomach, my tongue circling around and dipping into her bellybutton.

"What are you doing?!" she nearly shrieks and starts pushing at my head.

"I'm tasting you. Last night was too damn fast," I say with a grin.

"No way! You can't do that!"

She pushes at me again, but I don't budge.

"Oh yes the fuck I can. You haven't figured it out yet, but you're mine completely, and that means you've got to take it when I want to give you pleasure. Now relax and let me get back to tasting you," I order.

"But... I've never..." she starts to protest only to stop and freeze up when I dip my head back down.

Finally, I let myself experience the taste I've been craving all my damn life. Craving and didn't even know it.

My tongue swipes her from the bottom of her wet pussy lips up to her little clit.

Fuck, she tastes so damn good. She tastes like fucking heaven.

"Never what?" I nearly rasp, pausing only long enough to savor her sweetness.

Looking down at me with wide eyes, she seems to struggle to speak before she finally gasps out, "Never had that…"

"Man, guys are fucking stupid," I say before taking another swipe at her delicious pussy.

It's not enough though to just slide my tongue through her lips and flick it at her clit. I don't want to just sample her, I want to fucking devour her and ruin her for any other man.

Grabbing her by the hips, I hold her in place and use all of my mouth to show her what's she been missing without me in her life.

Lapping, flicking, and sucking, I feel like I'm turning into a fucking starving beast that's attacking her, but I just can't get enough.

Can't get enough of her taste.

Can't get enough of her hands tugging at my hair.

Can't get enough of her juices as she finally shudders and comes against my mouth.

She cries out, "Fuck," as my mouth locks down on her clit and sucks up every drop.

Half-crazed with my need of her, I can't stop until she begs me to stop.

I have to physically pry myself away from her in order to get to my feet.

Eyes closed, Bree is spread out on the bed. Her breasts rising and falling with her pants.

Staring down at her, I'm nearly overwhelmed with the urge to feel those breasts crushed against my chest.

As I climb over her soft, limp body, her eyes finally pop open. "That... That was fucking amazing," she croaks.

I grin down at her as I nudge my way between her open thighs. "We're not even done yet."

I grab her thigh with one hand, yanking her leg up, while my other hand grabs my slick cock and positions it at her entrance.

My cock is wet as fuck. It started leaking all over the damn place when she came against my mouth.

"Emmett," Bree gasps up at me as I sink myself into her warmth.

Fuck. Fuck. Fuck.

She's way too fucking tight. Way too fucking perfect.

I'm way too fucking close to blowing my load.

Knowing I'm losing the last shreds of my control, I grab her other leg and yank it up, positioning her until both of her ankles are over my shoulders.

"Oh my god... Oh my fucking god, it's too much. I can't..." Bree moans and squirms.

Dipping my head down, I pull a quick kiss from her lips and tell her to, "Hold on tight, baby girl."

I give her two seconds, two fucking long ass seconds to grab onto my forearms before I give into my inner beast again and start pounding her with my cock.

Eyes rolling into the back of her head, I have to smother her screams with my mouth.

With each deep thrust, with each slap of my hips, I know without a doubt I'm hitting her fucking g-spot.

Slamming everything I have to offer, everything I have

give, into her, it only takes a couple of minutes for her to reach her peak.

Her tight, warm pussy clamps down in a death grip on my cock.

Finally free to let go, I drop the last remaining shreds of my self-control and explode.

Roaring my fucking victory into her mouth.

Bree whimpers and twitches beneath me as I pump her full of my cum.

And when my dick is empty, I can't find any desire to stop.

No, I want to keep going. I want to stay inside her for the rest of the night. I want to stay inside of her for the rest of my fucking my life.

"I'm fucking dead. You fucking killed me," Bree groans when I finally release her mouth.

Grinning because she thinks this over, and it's so not fucking over, I let her legs slide back down to the bed and give her moment to catch her breath.

"What the fuck, Emmett?" she squeals when I get tired of waiting and flip her over to her stomach.

"Are you ready to tap out?" I growl. "Because I'm not fucking ready to tap out."

Grabbing her by the hips, I get to my knees and pull her ass up into the air.

Fuck, her ass is juicy and beautiful.

"Oh my fucking god," she groans but doesn't fight me. "I don't know if I love you or hate you right now."

"Love," I grunt as I bend over her, ready for round two. "Don't even try to deny it because I fucking love you, baby girl."

The last two weeks have been hands down both the best and worst two weeks of my life.

Spending my days at the gym and my nights in Emmett's bed…

I've never been happier.

So happy, I almost feel content.

But I know from personal experience, nothing good ever lasts.

In Emmett's arms, with his kisses pressed against my skin and his whispered words of sweet devotions echoing in my ears, I can push it all away. I can shut out the rest of the world, focusing on only us and where all our broken pieces connect.

I can completely immerse myself in the fantasy and pretend that what we're doing can go on forever… that this is our love story and we're guaranteed a happy ending.

But real life doesn't work like that.

Fuck, my life never works like that.

I feel it every time I'm away from him and remember

all the shit I still have waiting on my plate for me. Problems that don't go away when left unattended. Problems that only fester and mold the longer they're left sitting there.

It's been three days since my father has sent me a text. I haven't had the balls to speak to him since I gave him a flimsy excuse for standing him up for that dinner at the Bellagio. He's tried to schedule five more dinners since, and I've ignored every single one of them, knowing full well that it would eventually come to back to bite me in the ass.

So, when I drive up the driveway to my mom's house to pick up some clothes for the week, I'm not surprised to see his limo parked out front. Not surprised, but devastated nonetheless.

I thought we'd have more time…

God, I just need a little more time with Emmett and Casey. A little more time to feel like a normal human being. A little more time to bottle up some of this happiness. To preserve it and cherish it.

I haven't even been able to work up the courage to tell Emmett the truth yet. Fuck. He has no clue.

My foot eases down on the gas, my body carrying out the impulse to speed away before I even comprehend what I'm doing.

But then my father's driver pops out of the limo, waving his arms frantically to flag me down. Before I can swerve past the limo, the crazy bastard actually jumps in front of my car, forcing me to slam on my brakes.

Jerking forward, I let out a scream and my arms tighten to keep me from going into the steering wheel. Bouncing back against my seat, I blink stupidly out of the windshield, my heart and breathing racing with a rush of adrenaline.

Shock still buzzes through my brain as the driver, palms planted on my hood, calls out, "Ms. Madison, your father would like a word with you."

The door beside me suddenly pops open and my father's personal bodyguard, Aaron, reaches across me and pushes my gear stick into park.

"What the hell, Aaron?" I snap out, still struggling to accept the shit that's happening as he reaches down and expertly and efficiently unbuckles my seatbelt.

Jaw tightening, he grits out, "You heard him, your father wants to speak with you."

Then he grabs me by the arm and hauls me out of the car.

Never, *never* in my life have I ever been treated like this. Treated like I'm not a person, but an object to be moved.

I try to jerk my arm out of Aaron's hand, but his grip only tightens painfully around me as he drags me across the driveway.

What the fuck is happening. Seriously, *what the fuck is happening*?

The driver, now standing at the back of the limo, sniffs and gives me a contemptuous look as he pulls the door open.

I only have a split-second to gawk at him before Aaron shoves me roughly into the limo and closes the door behind me.

Hands and knees landing on the backseat, my father's cool voice hits me just as I push myself up. "Hello, Aubrey. So glad you could finally make time for me."

So many foul words want to scream out of me. Words

asking what the fuck he thinks he's doing… words that want to tell him we're not living in some kind of messed up mafia movie…

But I manage to find the strength to swallow them back down as I sit up and push my hair out of my face.

Giving myself a moment to get my anger and breathing in check, knowing full well if I start screaming at him this fucked up situation could get even worse, I stare at him before I start to say, "That was completely unnecessary—"

Only to cut myself off when the car starts moving.

I glance at the window in numb horror. Is my own father kidnapping me?

"I'm afraid you gave me no choice," my father says calmly, almost as if he's bored.

I jerk my attention back to him and meet his eyes.

His mask of composure breaks as his top lip quivers like he's fighting back a snarl. "You've been ignoring me for the past two weeks."

I'm completely in uncharted waters right now and I have no idea how to navigate my way out of this.

I always knew my father could use his money and power against me at any time, but I never dreamed he'd do it in such a way.

Staring at his cold, handsome face and wondering why he doesn't look as awful on the outside as he is on the inside, I say as meekly as I can manage, "I'm sorry, I've been busy."

Maybe if I'm meek and contrite, I can cool his anger and convince him I won't do what I did again. Maybe he'll let me go, and then I can grab Emmett and Casey and we can run away…

"Yes, I know," he says, his voice dripping with disgust. Reaching beside him, he grabs a folder off the seat beside him and throws it at me. "Busy in the gutters, fraternizing with the *rats.*"

The folder hits my chest and papers flutter around me before I manage to catch a couple of out of the air. Gripping the one in my right hand, I pull it up to my face, and feel the bottom fall right out of me.

There, on glossy paper, is a picture of Emmett, Casey, and me outside Emmett's house. The picture is candid, taken as we're smiling and walking up to the front door.

I stare at it for a long time, mentally pinpointing the time it was taken, and feel the hairs on the back of neck rise.

Forcing myself to tear my gaze away, I lift up the one in my left hand to see a picture of just Emmett and me. We're sneaking a kiss behind the gym, away from prying eyes.

"You've been spying on me," I say so softly it's almost a whisper full of horror and accusation.

"Spying?" my father says then makes a dismissive noise. "Hardly. I've been keeping an eye on you for your protection."

Shaking my head, I slip the left picture over the right then look to the others around me. So many moments of the past two weeks surround me. Moments of happiness, moments mostly involving Emmett and Casey.

They're scattered on the floor and seat like they're trash, like they're nothing…

Anger rising inside me, I finally lift my eyes to my father and ask, straight to the point, "What do you want?"

My father, being the established politician that he is, doesn't give me the direct answer I desire.

Reaching to his side, he grabs a glass full of what I have no doubt is his favorite gin and takes his time sipping from it before he decides to speak.

"I should disown you," he states and watches for my reaction.

Unfortunately for him that threat doesn't pack quite the punch it used to, and I just look back at him calmly.

When I show no signs of distress or worry, his eyes harden and he takes another sip from his glass, drinking deeper this time.

Lowering the glass, a strange glint enters his eyes as he says, "I should, but I won't. I won't, not because you don't deserve it, you certainly deserve it, but because I understand."

This, unlike the threat, surprises me. And when the surprise makes its appearance on my face, his lips finally give into the snarl he's been suppressing.

"I know what it's like to go, as they say, *slumming*. To see how the other side lives. After all, I did it myself. In fact, if I didn't do it with your mother, you wouldn't even exist."

His words hit me like a slap in the face and I feel myself rear back.

"What did you say about my mother?" I hiss.

He completely ignores my question. Instead, his face lights up with this sick kind of glee as he goes on as if I didn't speak. "And given that half of you is white trash like your mother... It was probably even harder for you to resist that sweaty gym rat. Like attracts like, doesn't it?"

I shake my head in dismay. I'm so angry, so damn angry, tears sting my eyes. My father has said some pretty nasty things to me over the years, but they're usually barbs that are cleverly disguised to hide the intent.

This... this is just outright nastiness.

"Wouldn't that make you trash as well?" I snap, throwing his stupid, messed up logic back at him.

For a second, his eyes flash with anger, but it quickly fades away. He takes the time to drain the rest of his glass and then carefully sits it beside him. "No, because as I said, I was simply experimenting. Sowing my wild oats. I come from good stock, so it was only curiosity on my part. Once I realized my mistake, I quickly rectified it, and I've been happy ever since."

As far as I'm concerned, the gloves came completely off when he insulted not only me but also my mother, and I don't even try to stop myself now from speaking what I truly think.

"Are you?" I ask skeptically, narrowing my eyes at him. "Are you truly happy? You look like a miserable old bastard to me…"

My father flinches, actually flinches as if my words hurt him, then his jaw ticks. Reaching over, he picks up his empty glass, and without looking at it, tries to take a drink. When only ice clinks against his lips, his expression grows darker and he tosses the glass to the side.

I jump a little when the glass hits the door, making a loud noise but not shattering.

My father gives the ice rolling onto the carpet a look of disgust, as if he wasn't the one who just threw his glass, then turns his attention back to me.

"As I said," he says roughly then clears his throat. "I understand what it's like, Aubrey. I do. I understand because you're still half me. And for that reason, and that reason alone, I'm willing to forgive you."

After all the nastiness he just spewed, I'm pretty sure his idea of forgiveness isn't a good thing. I don't say that out loud though. Not when he no longer has a glass to throw.

When I don't respond in any way, he sighs heavily. "I

forgive you, Aubrey, but it stops now. It all stops now. I've let you have your fun, I've let you have your little fling. Now it's time for you to step up and fulfill your responsibilities."

Trying not to focus on the whole *let me* crap he's spewing, I have to clear my own throat, the damn thing trying to close up on me. "And what exactly are my responsibilities?"

My father's eyes and voice sharpen as he glares at me. "Don't play stupid, you know very well your responsibilities. You will marry Tristan Yates, play the good wife, and produce a couple of children, uniting our two families."

God, what is this? Have I accidentally stepped into an alternate reality?

"Don't roll your eyes at me, young lady," he says, his face flushing with anger. "You're lucky to have this opportunity. There are dozens of other families that would give everything they possess for their daughters to be in your position."

When my eyes roll again, he growls in frustration then adds as if it's some kind of consolation that will convince me to submit, "If you do as your told, after you produce a couple of children, perhaps you'll be permitted to do as you wish."

"And if I don't?" I challenge as I cross my arms over my chest.

There's nothing, nothing in this world he could threaten me with at this point to make me agree to any of this craziness.

A slow smile starts to creep over my father's mouth as he leans back in his seat, and I realize too late that I've walked myself into his trap.

Shit.

"I wanted to do this the nice way, Aubrey…" he says ominously as he reaches over and grabs another folder I didn't notice until now.

Just like the other, he tosses the folder at me. "But you give me no choice."

Quickly uncrossing my arms, I scramble to catch the folder before its contents join what's already scattered around me. When I do finally have it safely in my hands, I realize I had no reason to worry. The stack of papers inside have been clipped securely to the folder to keep them from spilling.

"What's this?" I ask as my eyes scan over the top paper.

It looks like some kind of legal document. A court case or something like it.

"All the background information I dug up on your gym rat and that little boy he's taking care of," my father says smugly.

Icy cold dread washes over me, and I quickly scroll through all the text on the paper I'm staring at until I find Casey's name. After reading a couple of sentences, it quickly becomes obvious that I'm reading a custody agreement.

There's nothing shocking in the agreement, custody awarded to both of his grandparents after his father's death, so I flip past it and move on to the next paper. The next paper, however, isn't a paper at all but another glossy picture.

A picture of Emmett clearly trashed. He's passed out on his back porch, surrounded by empty liquor bottles and beer cans.

I suck in a breath and my father chuckles.

"That photo is only a few weeks old, and given his

upcoming match, the photographer was hesitant to sell it to me before it's printed, but I managed to convince him."

I slant a dark look at my father over the folder and he chuckles again as I flip to the next paper. Great, another picture, but this time Emmett is passed out in his front yard.

"Tell me, did you know he's a drunk before you hooked up with him? Was that half of the appeal?" my father taunts, and the folder begins to crumple in my hands as my anger starts to get the best of me.

I flip to the next picture, then the next. It's just picture after picture of Emmett trashed in some fashion.

Utterly disgusted, I only make it halfway through the stack before I snap the folder shut. I've seen enough.

"So what?" I ask as I lower the folder. "So what if he used to drink?"

It's not news to me. And despite how disturbed and heartbroken I am by what I've seen, I'm determined not to let my father get to me.

"You didn't make it to the back," my father says with a flick of his hand.

Sighing, I shake my head, not taking the bait. "I'm tired of these games. Why don't you get straight to the point?"

My father's face tightens with anger and I hear his teeth grinding together. All that expensive dental work at risk because of me...

I've never, in all the years I've been in contact with him, given him so much defiance or resistance before and it's clearly getting to him. In the past, I've always bent to his will, submitting quickly and easily out of the fear he'd walk out of my life again. I've carried out his bidding for the past four years.

I've been his pretty little obedient doll. Bending, almost breaking, in the ways he's used me.

But not today… goddammit, not today.

"Very well," my father grits out. "Since you refuse to look, I'll describe the contents for you. In the back of that folder you will find the most recent bank documents for Mr. and Mrs. Babson, Casey's grandparents."

If I thought the bottom fell out of me before… well, my entire existence drops as I immediately realize what my father intends to threaten me with.

Flipping quickly through the pages, I end up accidentally tearing a couple in my haste to reach the very papers he's talking about.

"It seems Mr. Babson has had some medical issues lately. Some very expensive medical issues which have put a strain on their finances…"

"Don't," I warn, looking up from the papers. "Don't you dare…"

Ignoring me, my father continues, a smile beginning to creep across his face. "Their house is about to enter foreclosure. And being that they're on a fixed income, there's little hope they'll be able to pull themselves out of the financial hole they've found themselves in."

God help me. Gripping the folder, it's everything I can do not to shake and tremble like a fucking leaf.

"Soon, they'll be without a house, unable to care and provide for their dear grandson…"

For a foolish second, I hope that my father forgot that Casey isn't in his grandparent's care, he's in Emmett's.

"Concerned, as a father myself, and as the governor of our great state Nevada, I took it upon myself to do a little investigating. Casey, that poor boy, has had such a tragic life, and I'd like to do all in my power to help him. I was able, through a little luck and perhaps a little divine intervention, locate his mother, Amber. Her picture should be right there with the mortgage documents."

Bile rises in my throat and my fingers shake as I force myself to flip through to the very picture he's speaking of.

It's a mugshot of a woman who looks nothing at all like Casey. Nothing like him that is until I force myself to look past the crazy hair, vacant eyes, and sad expression, finding the similarities.

"She, herself, has had quite a life. She's been in and out of jail and rehab for over a decade…"

Snapping the folder shut, I close my eyes and take a deep breath, gathering my composure before I say, "And your point is?"

I think I know what he's getting at, but until I hear it from his lips I can't be sure.

"My point is, Aubrey, I'm very concerned for Casey. His father's dead, his grandparents are unable to care for him. His mother is a drug addict who can't get clean, and he's been left in the care of an alcoholic who has no relation to him. Perhaps the courts should be made aware of his case…"

Somehow I manage to open my eyes and look at my father. Somehow I manage to continue breathing as the full gravity of what he's threatening me with completely crushes me from the inside out.

If his threats were directed at me or Emmett, I could live with the fallout. I could handle and deal with whatever came.

But I could never live with myself if he hurt Casey… I… just… *couldn't*. And I'd do anything, *anything*, to keep that from happening.

Even if it means doing my father's bidding and

marrying Tristan.

"You're a monster," I hiss as the full force of my sadness, of my fucking grief hits me.

I think it would hurt less if he'd fucking stabbed me. Stabbed me in the heart until nothing was left.

My father makes a *tsking* noise and shakes his head. "I'm simply a concerned citizen, Aubrey."

There are so many things I could say, but it would all be a waste of breath. I already know from what he's said and from what was in the papers he gave me that he's put a lot of thought, time, and effort into this.

And he has no shame, no honor, if he's willing to hurt a child for his own personal benefit.

Eyes aching with the need to burst into tears, I suck in another breath, trying my hardest to keep myself together.

But I can't stop my voice from cracking as I say, "I'll do whatever you want... just leave Casey alone. He's fine where he is."

Triumph lights up my father's eyes and the look on his face makes me utterly sick. "Are you sure? I cannot, in good conscience, abandon the boy."

Everything inside me, the pain, the anger, the despair, swells to the surface, and it hurts. It hurts so fucking bad I can't think straight. I can't think of a way to make it stop.

"I'm sure," I say, just wanting to get this nightmare over with.

But even after everything he's already done to me, my father isn't done yet.

"Very well, that's relieving to hear, and I'll take your word for it," he says, then relaxes in his seat. "Now that this unpleasant business has been settled, let's go home, shall we? The Yates will be joining us for dinner tonight. We have a wedding to plan."

The bottle sitting on the table in front of me is no longer looking like an *if* but a *when*.

I spent three days searching for Bree. Three long fucking days frantically searching the city for her before her phone finally gave me a ping on her location.

Betrayal doesn't even begin to describe the feelings I have raging through me right now. I'm not some neanderthal who doesn't understand the fucking internet. I know who her father is, and I know where she is.

She's in his fucking house.

What I don't know is why. Why the fuck did she leave us? It's not just *me*, it's fucking *us*.

Her promises were bullshit.

Fucking bullshit.

Everything that came from her eyes and lips was nothing but fucking lies. She's disappeared from my life as fast as she walked into it, and all I've got left is a kid who's falling into the abyss.

Casey's sleep has been tortured, and I spend more time racing from my room to his because of his night terrors than I do actually sleeping. He's got demons crawling inside of his body, and there's nothing I can do but sit beside him as he shakes the whole bed in fear.

One week gone and I can only stare at her location. It's as if she's a star in the sky now, there to see but completely unobtainable. I fell for her hard. I can't even say it wasn't love. I'd be lying to myself and the universe if I did. But did she love me? Or was I just some passing ship in the night?

She told me she couldn't do this, that she wasn't good for me. Was this what she meant? Was this what she knew would happen?

One long week and I haven't touched a single drop of alcohol. One long fucking week I've forced myself through the punishment from Dale and Chase. They hold me accountable for Bree leaving.

It's all my fault, I can see it in their eyes.

I see it in every pair I eyes I meet, the look of blame. It's just one more fuck up to add to my already growing list of failures.

Even Avery doesn't look at me the same. There's this look of anticipation in her eyes, like she's just waiting for me to make my last fuck up. To fuck up Casey so she'll have to come racing in to save him.

Helen hasn't made an appearance yet, but I figure it'll be today or tomorrow that she comes and snatches my kid away from me.

Then I'll have nothing left in me but this hollow fucking shell.

I shouldn't call Casey my kid, but he is now. He's mine as much as he's Helen's. Tommy's gone so he's stuck with me.

Until I'm forced to give him up too.

Last night, Casey and I finally had out the storm that's been brewing on the horizon. We went at it like two heated rivals in the ring. He used words even I don't say around him. There was enough blame in his words that I felt the sting of every single syllable. He's right, I fucked it up.

I let her leave.

I've been here all night on the back porch, been here all night with a bottle of rum. Rum's been my best friend these last few months, and I can't figure out how much longer it will be before I follow it down to the bottom.

The sun starts to peek over the horizon.

Fuck it, might as well start now.

I reach for the bottle but it's no longer there.

With a look of pure rage, Casey turns and throws the bottle as far as he can.

The bottle slams into a tree and explodes in a dazzling shower of amber liquid and shards of glass.

Standing up to face him, I yell, "What the fuck, Casey?!"

"Fuck you, Emmett! You're going to be just like everyone else!" he screams as he gets right up in my face.

He might be shorter than me, but right now he's posturing up like he's about to throw down.

Last night obviously wasn't the end of this little hurricane.

"How the fuck am I like everyone else?" I yell right back at him.

"You're just going to fucking leave me like everyone else does! Dad, Grandpa, Grandma, and Bree! You had to run her off! Now she's gone! Gone! She left me just like you want to do! You think I don't know what will happen if you drink? Grandma comes and gets me, then I get shoved into another fucking home with some relative I don't know!" he belts out.

Every name he speaks hits me like a sucker punch to my already barely functioning heart.

Pushing up hard against my chest with his hands, he shoves me when I don't respond. "You think I'm stupid, don't you! I know about my mom. A junky who couldn't stand the idea of having me! Dad was the only one who really wanted me and now he's gone!"

"Casey…" I say as I grab his hands and yank him close to me so that I can wrap my arms around him.

"I hate you! You made her go away! She was good to me!" he yells into my chest.

I can feel hot pools of tears leaking through my shirt and burning my skin. "Casey, I'm so sorry."

"No one wants me! Why does everyone leave?" he asks, and I know he's no longer talking to me.

He's venting out all the vile, self-hating thoughts he's been holding inside of him since Tommy died.

After venting about God, and even wondering if there is a God, his words become too choked with sobs for him to continue.

And I keep holding him, knowing he's finally breaking through all his walls.

"Fuck, Casey," I say when his sobs lessen enough for him to hear me. "I'm not going to leave you. Never. God himself would have to end the world before I ever leave you by yourself."

"Bree wasn't supposed to leave either," he whispers.

Fuck, I know he grew to care for her, but I fucked up thinking it would be just me who got attached.

I remember something Helen once told Tommy and me

about dating single mothers. She told us not to do it unless we were willing to break two hearts.

Fuck, she was right.

I'm a single fucking father with a kid who's suffering a broken heart.

Pulling away from him, I nudge his chin up so that his red eyes stare back into my own red eyes. "I don't know why she left, Casey, but it wasn't because of you. If it was my fault then I fully accept the blame for this, but we will not let this break us. We can't. There's too much at stake."

"I know, Emmett," he says quietly. "I know it wasn't us, but I just can't help how it feels. My head is so messed up, I don't even know what to do anymore."

Fuck me. I might finally have the answer to one of his questions.

"I do," I say.

"What?" he asks as he pulls away from me.

He needs his space, I get that. Doesn't mean I don't want to keep him wrapped up tight so I can keep all the dark shit in life away from him.

"We go get our shoes on," I say, pointing to his bare feet and then mine.

"And?" he asks incredulously.

I smirk at him. "We get donuts."

"Yeah, right." He laughs for the first time in days and I relish in the thought that I made it happen.

"Seriously, we go get donuts. We don't eat them, but we take them to the gym and put 'em in Chase's office. We should be able to get there before Dale does," I say, and I can tell Casey is starting to see where this is going.

"Can I take like a bite of one? I'd give up my Playstation for like a week if I could get like half of one," he starts to beg, pulling my leg.

"Maybe, but if you do, you better hide any evidence. We can't get caught," I say with another smirk.

I love the smell of a good prank in the morning, and after what we've gone through, this one's going to be so fucking worth it.

I put my fist out to knock knuckles. "We're family, Casey, and nothing will break us apart. Your dad used to call me his wife sometimes when we were taking care of you, and you know what? He was right. I'm never going to be able to replace the man you lost, but I promise you I will always be in your corner. Father, mother, or whatever you want to call me. We're here together. Fuck the rest of the world if they don't get it."

Casey stares at my hand and I know somewhere in his soul he's making a choice. I just hope he knows how much he means to me. I don't care what I have to do from here on out, from now on he's my top priority.

Slapping my hand to the side, he gives me a tight hug, his arms trying to squeeze the shit out of my ribs. Hugging him right back, I don't let go for a long time.

We need this and this right here is going to be our salvation.

One day at a time, one fight at a time, until we're through it all.

"Thanks, Mom," he snickers before racing away from me.

"You little fucker!" I bellow out at him as I chase him to the shoe pile next to the front door.

～

We're not dressed for the gym, but that doesn't stop Casey and me from setting the box of donuts on Chase's desk and running for the locker room before anyone can see us.

We both slow down though, only a little, to see if Bree is back at the front desk, but keep going when we see her chair is still empty.

Fuck if it doesn't pull at my soul to think she left us, left us and didn't even say why.

I've sent her a shit ton of texts, hoping one of them would get her to text back. I've even sent her declarations of my love...

And all I get is silence. Fucking silence.

I know I should chase after her, but for what? She made it pretty clear when she disappeared that she didn't want to have anything to do with us anymore.

I think even Casey texted her with his phone a couple of times, and it fucking kills me to think she's stonewalling him too. She probably has us both blocked.

She's blocked us and ghosted us.

What can I fucking do?

Thankfully Casey and I both have a spare set of workout clothes to change into because while we were planning our prank, we also talked about my ass getting back to the grindstone for the upcoming fight.

The world is burning down around us, but it won't stop us from moving forward.

Every time I think of slowing down this week and maybe pulling out of the match, I can't do it. Something inside me has been growing every day since I came back to the gym, something angry and violent. This isn't about payback for the first time Jamey and I fought each other.

No, this is about his videos and his little taunts.

He's doing shit like this to get a reaction. He's trying to

get into my head and fuck with it. But every time I see an interview with him, I feel my body getting closer and closer to what I've been working toward.

Closer to being able to dish out some serious fucking damage.

"I don't know whose fucking donuts those are!" Chase yells from the front of the gym.

And Casey and I start shaking from the fucking giggles before we can get a hold on ourselves.

Thankfully there's no one around to see us. We've been in the back corner, using the rowing machines for the past fifteen minutes.

"Don't give me that, Chunky!" Dale shouts back at Chase. "I wanna see you sweating today! We're going to work off some of that pansy Avery's let you get away with!"

"I'm not one of your fighters, old man! This is my gym, you can't go bossing me around!" Chase bellows back.

Ducking his head down, Casey looks like he's seen a ghost as he whispers, "Did he just call Dale an old man?"

Dale growls, "I can't, can I?" so loud suddenly every fighter in the gym is busy with whatever they're working on.

"Ah... *fuck*, Dale," Chase sputters before he heads for the locker room.

If I didn't recognize the murderous tone in Dale's growl, I might be stupid enough to laugh. Dale's face is so red though, I know to keep my head down.

"Casey," I mutter out the side of my mouth, "this was never us."

"No shit!" Casey whispers just as quietly and quickly goes back to rowing like his life depends on it.

Yep, if this shit gets out, we're going to end up red

smears on the asphalt after Chase runs us down. But fuck it, it's been a long time since I've seen Chase work out like he has us doing. He hasn't gone to fat or anything like that, but it's been a long time since he's been put through the paces.

I might be punishing Bree unknowingly through Chase, but I think I'm okay with it.

I don't have time to drop back into a depression right now. I've got a kid and a fight to deal with. I need my head in the fucking game.

Fuck it.

After this fight, I'm going to her dad's house and yanking her ass out of there. I can't get arrested before a fight, but afterwards… Yeah, that'll work…

Shit.

I feel almost fucking bipolar. Bouncing from resentment toward her to not giving a shit, she's mine.

The more I row and feel the muscles in my body straining, the more me chasing her ass down sounds like a good idea. And if I get arrested? I've got enough money to make that shit disappear.

"She's not getting away from us, Casey," I say to him as I yank extra deep into the machine.

He's breathing heavy and sweat drips off his forehead as he leans forward to take a mini-break. "No?"

"Nope, were going to go drag her ass back to where she belongs," I say, and pull hard on the machine again.

"Aren't there laws against kidnapping?" he asks seriously.

I pull off a shrug. "I'm hot and I have a shit ton of money, we're good. I've also got connections."

"Dude, that's kinda creepy," he says with a laugh.

"Yeah, I know," I say, and slow my rowing down.

"Ready for the bags? If we stay on this machine for too long, Dale is going to get suspicious."

"Yep!" he says as he jumps up to follow me over to the bags.

"Alright, we'll do fifty on each limb, then we'll see if we can find some sparring partners. I need Brett to work on takedowns with me," I say as I watch Dale heading straight for us with a face full of anger.

Thankfully we're both beet red and sweaty as fuck. We haven't been sitting idly by today.

"You two!" Dale growls as he stops in front of us. "What are you doing?"

"Bags, then sparring if I can get Brett to work on takedowns with me. He's the closest to Jamey's style of fighting," I say, and keep hustling Casey past Dale.

"Good, I better not see you two resting today! Too many fucking calories are running through this gym. I don't work in no fucking bakery!" Dale shouts at our backs.

Looking over at Casey as we reach the bags, I ask, "Did he just compare this place to a bakery?"

"Think we went too far?" he asks with a wince.

I shake my head. "Not yet. I want to order half a dozen pizzas around lunchtime under Bear's name."

His eyes go wide. "Oh god, please tell me we're heading home by then."

I slam my elbow into the bag. "Yeah, right when they're supposed to get here."

We go through a few repetitions before Casey stops and turns to face me. "Emmett?"

"Yeah?" I ask, wrapping my arms around the bag while I rest my sweaty forehead against it.

Without facing me, he asks, "How long will I be living with you?"

"College and beyond?" I answer immediately. I mean, who the fuck knows how long normal families have their kids living them? "You want to live with me?"

He doesn't respond at first. Refocusing on the bag, he begins to go through his left arm punches.

The silence is killing me, but I don't want to pressure him to say yes.

"Yeah, I do," he finally says while punching the bag.

"Even if I'm a dick that makes you go to school and do your homework? A dick who makes you do your chores and shit? You get to be a normal kid too, but our house will have rules, and I'll have to punish you if you break curfew or something," I say, and hope he gets what I'm trying to say.

Casey sounds almost hopeful as he asks, "You mean like a normal life and family?"

All of a sudden, I feel domestic. "Fuck yeah. Like you'll have dinners and we'll have homework schedules."

Casey starts to smile. "Yeah, I like the idea of that. I mean, I had that with grandma and grandpa, but..."

"You know I'll be a hardass on ya if you fuck around, right? And you can't just go back to them if you're mad at me. We're going to be a real family, Casey. Even if you don't like me, you'll be stuck with me."

"What the fuck are you two gabbing about!" Dale bellows out behind us.

We both turn to face Dale, but I speak first. "We're setting up house. He's moving in full-time with me."

"Oh," Dale mutters. "Good, don't slack off, dammit."

Turning away from us, he marches over to the front

desk. I swear I've never seen him do an about face that quick before…

Casey turns to me and says, "I love Grandma and Grandpa, but I need to do this for me. One thing though, and you have to swear on my dad to me."

Fuck, whatever he's about to ask me is serious.

"What's that?" I ask.

"You can't drink again, I mean it. Not a single drop. Not ever again."

From the look on his face, it's clear that he's dead serious.

Fuck.

How the hell do I swear to that? If I do that, I'm swearing I'll never slip up again. I'll never fuck up again.

I'll have to live life on the straight and narrow.

He's asking me to not do something that some nights every single fiber in my being wants to do. He's asking me to never again find the numbness in a bottle, to never again enter that state where my brain can quit thinking of all the bad shit.

"I promise on Tommy," I say.

"Okay, we need to call Grandma and get the rest of my stuff. Also, can we get Netflix?" he asks.

My head wants to spin with how fucking easy that shit just went down, but fuck it. I need this as much as he does.

"Sure, and Casey? I think your dad would be happy with what we're doing," I say.

"Me too, Mom," he says with a laugh before he starts kicking the bag again.

I'm going to kill the little shit, I swear to myself, and start kicking the bag too.

Two weeks.

It's been two long, hellish weeks since my father essentially kidnapped me and blackmailed me. True to his word, once I agreed to submit to his demands, my father immediately brought me back to his house. After confiscating my phone *for my own good*, I was locked inside my room like a prisoner.

Completely cut off from the outside world.

Less than an hour later, I was forced to face Tristan and his smug, punchable face across a dining room table. Without any input from me, all the details of our impending engagement and marriage were ironed out between our two families.

And tonight, during the biggest political fundraiser of the year, it will be announced to the world.

"You look beautiful, Aubrey," my stepmother, Valerie, says in her soft, throaty voice before she offers me a sweet smile.

She looks stunning herself in her shimmering white

gown. Seated beside my father, she practically glows like an angel.

Failing to live up to the evil stepmother trope, Valerie has always been kind to me, and I've always wondered how a woman like her could marry a man like my father.

Did he have to blackmail her too in order to get his hands on her money?

"Thank you," I murmur in response and manage to work up my own smile to offer in return.

Trapped once again in the back of my father's limo, everything inside me is screaming for me to find a way to escape. To get out before it's too late. My hand wants to reach for the door and my legs want to run for my life.

I want to run back into Emmett's arms.

But I can't. I can't save myself. I have to see this through, for Casey.

"Yes... you do look beautiful," my father agrees, glancing over at me.

My smile instantly tightens as his eyes meet my eyes.

"That little hunger strike of yours has done wonders for your figure. I'm sure Tristan will be relieved. You put on quite a bit of weight while you were away."

Valerie visibly stiffens at my father's little barb, but I keep smiling at him, not letting him get to me.

Over the past few days, locked up in isolation with nothing but my own thoughts to keep me company, I've finally come to terms with the fact that no matter what I do or how hard I try, I'll never be good enough for him.

I'll never live up to his expectations.

And I'm okay with that. I'm okay because he no longer lives up to *my* expectations.

In fact, he's fallen so far below them, there's absolutely nothing he could do to redeem himself in my eyes.

Nothing he could do except for having a change of heart and calling off this farce. But that would require him to have a heart in the first place. And even if he did call this off now, the damage he's already done...

Oh god, I can't even think about it right now.

If I do, I'll completely fucking break down.

After a couple of minutes, when I make no effort to respond, my father sniffs and glances away.

With his attention focused on his window, I force myself to relax and focus on getting through tonight.

Despite what he said, I haven't gone on a hunger strike. Yes, I probably haven't been eating as much as I should, and I have lost a little bit of weight, but it's not done out of protest or self-punishment. I simply have no appetite after enduring that dinner with Tristan and his family.

How can I eat after what I've done? How can I eat when I have a lifetime of being stuck with Tristan waiting for me?

Besides the little looks of pity Valerie keeps sending my way, the rest of the car ride to the event is quiet, uneventful, and goes by too quickly.

I'm still not ready or prepared to face what's to come when the limo slows then crawls to a stop.

My father's door is opened for him and he turns to look at me.

"Aubrey," he says ominously. Once he has my full attention, he gives me a hard, pointed look. "Do I need to remind you what's at stake if things don't go smoothly tonight?"

"No," I answer coldly.

He doesn't need to remind me that he'll ruin a little boy's life if I don't behave and comply.

"Good." He grins, showing his teeth.

After straightening his bowtie and jacket, he climbs out of the limo.

Once he's gone, Valerie looks to me with an expression that's somewhere between worry and compassion.

"Aubrey," she says, using my name like my father, but with a touch of urgency.

My father's hand appears as he reaches in for her.

Valerie glances quickly at my father's hand then looks back to me.

"Make time for me tonight, before the announcement," she says quietly then places her hand in my father's and slips gracefully out the door.

I get less than a minute to wonder why she would ask that of me before my door opens and my father reaches back in. It takes every ounce of willpower I have inside me to put my hand in his and follow his tug.

Lights flash as soon as I gain my feet and instinctively I pull my lips up into a smile for the cameras. Slipping my mask of false happiness firmly in place as we follow the red carpet and make our way to entrance of the gala.

Once inside, I go through the motions, stuck by my father's side as he makes his greetings. With no other option, I'm forced to play the role of his pretty doll. Meant to stay by his side to be seen and not heard.

After a while all the faces and names start to blend together, but no matter how much time passes I can't relax. The hotel has gone all out, providing all the glitz and glamour you'd expect from such an upscale event, but the sparkling chandeliers, flowing champagne, and endless gourmet hors d'oeuvres are wasted on me.

I'd rather be anywhere else but here… Hell, I'd even

take being locked in my room again if it meant I could avoid Tristan and what's about to happen.

As if just thinking his name has conjured him, Tristan appears in front of me with a small group of his friends.

"Ah, there you are, Tristan." My father grins. "I was wondering when you'd stop by and take Aubrey off my hands."

Tristan chuckles and looks me up and down as if he's inspecting me. Inspecting me like I'm something he wants to buy.

But that's exactly what he's done, isn't it? He's bought me from my father.

My skin starts to crawl before he even touches me. Moving to my side, his hand latches onto my elbow and he pulls me to him.

"I was a little delayed," he says, staring down at me, "but I'm here now."

Meeting his eyes, I feel all the hate I have for him rising to the surface, ready to boil over. Hating his touch, hating his skin against my skin, I jerk my elbow, no longer caring about appearances or what people will think.

He must have anticipated the move though. I almost free myself but his fingers sink down at the last second, digging through skin to find bone.

"You look stunning tonight, Aubrey," he says over my little gasp then his face lights up, eyes gleaming with pleasure. "I feel like the luckiest man in the world."

Spencer, the same jerk that was with Tristan when he came to the gym, starts to snicker.

Tristan shoots him a dark look and his grip on my elbow loosens just enough for me to pull myself free.

Tristan jerks his attention back to me, but I step back,

out of his reach, before he can grab me again without truly looking like an asshole.

"Excuse me, I need the powder room," I grit out between my teeth and turn on my heel, walking off before anyone can stop me.

With tears of anger burning in my eyes, I push through the crowd, my feet carrying me to the door.

I thought I could do this, I thought I was strong enough to survive this shit without breaking, but thirty seconds in Tristan's presence has proven that was a lie.

I can't marry Tristan. Not only because he's the biggest entitled jerkface to ever walk this earth, but because I'm in love with Emmett.

God help me, I love him and Casey both. And I want to protect them, I do, but there has to be another way out of this…

There has to be.

I just don't know what it is.

My thoughts consumed with despair, despair over what's going to happen to Casey now that I've failed him, I'm barely paying attention to where I'm going. I get turned around at least two times trying to fight the direction of the crowd.

Everyone is coming in when all I want to do is get out.

When I finally manage to get myself going in the right direction again, someone touches my arm and says my name.

"Bree."

After what I just went through with Tristan, my body's immediate reaction is to yank my arm back.

"Oh my god, what's wrong with you?" Ashley gasps at me in surprise. "God, you're such a basket case."

I blink at her, wondering if my luck has completely gone to shit and she's real.

She makes an exasperated noise and rolls her eyes. "I really don't see what Tristan sees in you."

Having neither the time or patience to suffer her right now, I agree and start moving forward again. "I don't either."

Momentarily stunned by my response, she just stares at me as I move away, but then she rushes to catch up and grabs my arm to stop me.

Fuck, I'm really sick of people grabbing me tonight.

I stop and look down at her hand then up to her face.

"What do you want, Ashley?" I ask impatiently.

Ashley blinks at me, exactly like I did at her, then she shakes her head, dark curls bouncing around her face.

Smokey eyes narrowing and sharpening as if she's trying to intimidate me, she says, "I just wanted to let you know that you marrying Tristan doesn't change anything. We're still going to be together."

I roll my eyes to the heavens, wondering what on earth I did to deserve this, and then sigh. "That's good to know."

Shaking off her hand, I start to walk off again.

I'm beyond caring about her and Tristan. A few weeks ago, what she said probably would have hurt me. It did hurt me to find the two of them in bed together. But it didn't hurt because I was in love and they betrayed me. No, it hurt because they showed me the truth.

The truth that I truly had no friends in this world.

Ashley gasps behind me, but before I make any significant progress toward the door, her damn hand is on me again.

I turn back, ready to tell her off for stopping me, when

she finally says something that actually surprises me. "He fucked me tonight. He fucked me in the limo on the way here."

Her eyes search my eyes, desperately seeking the reaction she wants. Its so clear, so out in the open, I feel the tiniest bit of pity for her.

Only the tiniest bit.

At my surprise, a smile starts to unfurl across her glossy, overly plump lips. "We've been fucking for the past three years."

I suspected as much. But I've been hurt by so many other things recently, learning this doesn't even register on my pain meter.

What I am curious about though is why they would do it. Why go through all the trouble?

"He loves me. He'll never love you," she goes on, a touch of desperation entering her voice. "You can get your daddy to make him marry you, but he'll always be mine."

"What?" I ask, truly confused now.

Eyes flashing with anger, she hisses, "Don't play stupid. You can try all you want to keep us apart, but he'll never be yours. Never. I'm not giving him up."

Oh my god. She truly believes I'm the one pushing for this marriage.

Tristan must have told her that…

Jesus.

He's a bigger bastard than I ever gave him credit for.

But Ashley's not completely innocent in this. She didn't have to carry on behind my back with him, she could have come clean sooner. And even if I give her the benefit of the doubt, even if she was afraid to tell me, she was still complicit in trying to hurt me.

This whole conversation is proof enough of that.

I can't even begin to understand what kind of sick, fucked up relationship they have, but I do understand one thing out of all of this.

The two of them totally deserve each other.

"Okay, Ashley," I say calmly as I try to extract my arm from her grip. "You can have him. He's all yours."

Ashley gives me a look of surprise that quickly turns into disbelief. "I don't believe you."

Dammit, I don't have time for this. I need to get out of here before the dinner starts or someone else comes looking for me.

"Look, I honestly don't care. I don't want him. If you want him, take him. Or leave him. Whatever."

Turning my attention away from her, I take in those around us. The crowd is finally getting thinner as people start to filter into the banquet area. It won't be long now before all the speeches start.

Ashley's fingers suddenly tighten around my arm and she starts to tug on me. "I still don't believe you. If you're not lying, prove it," she demands.

I take one stumbling step backward, damn these heels, then yank my arm back. "Prove it how?"

"Say it in front of him. Say it to his face."

I roll my eyes and make a sound of disgust. "I don't have time for this."

And I really don't. I've already wasted enough time talking to her. Why I even bothered, I don't know.

"See, I knew it. You're lying," she says accusingly and glares daggers at me.

I gasp at her audacity. She's calling me a liar when she's the one who was sleeping with my boyfriend behind my back? That takes some nerve.

Both angry and insulted, I almost give in to the urge to

storm away. To say fuck this and make my exit. I don't need this, I don't deserve this, and I shouldn't waste any more of my life on these people.

But there's something tempting about her request.

Originally, I planned on making my exit without saying a word to anyone. But isn't that what my father has trained me to do? Hasn't he trained me to be quiet and to keep our dirty laundry out of public?

To always protect his image…

If I walk out now, without a word, no one outside this mess will ever know what happened. He can spin it however he wants. He can spin it that I'm the one in the wrong.

I've already lost everything. What more do I have to lose?

"Okay, fine," I say, making my decision. I'll probably regret this, but I'll just add it to the pile with all the other regrets. "I'll prove it."

Turning around, I spot Tristan and my father still standing together where I left them. Only now a small crowd of people have gathered around them.

Perfect.

Without waiting to see if Ashley is following me or not, I make my way over to them.

"There you are," my father says with an irritated look as I walk up. "I was beginning to think you got lost and was about to send someone after you."

"Sorry," I say, but truly I'm not sorry in the least. "I ran into Ashley."

Talking to the man beside him, Tristan falters for a split second before he recovers.

I grin, turning toward him. "She was just telling me how she and Tristan fucked in the limo on the way here."

There are a few gasps, the loudest and most notable one coming from Ashley as she finally catches up to me.

My father's face turns beet red while all the color drains from Tristan's face.

"Aubrey," my father says sternly. "What is the—"

I cut him off, not letting him take control of the situation. "She also told me they've been fucking for the past three years behind my back."

"What the fuck, Ashley?" Tristan snarls, some of his color coming back.

"Well, it's true!" Ashley cries out in her defense and then real tears appear in her eyes.

Looking between Ashley and Tristan, my father seems to be at a loss for words. His mouth keeps opening and closing.

Knowing his speechlessness is only temporary, I push on, determined to get this all out.

"She was worried about us marrying, given what's been going on between her and Tristan, but I've assured her I have no desire to marry Tristan. Never have and never will."

"Now that's enough, Aubrey," my father says sharply, finally finding his voice.

Ignoring him, I step up to Tristan. He stiffens and a tendril of satisfaction curls through me to see him looking so uncomfortable and uneasy.

"She insisted I prove that I don't want to marry you. Prove it by saying it to your face."

Jaw tightening, Tristan looks down at me as I bore my eyes into his eyes.

"I don't want to marry you, Tristan. I wouldn't marry you if you were the last man on earth. I'd rather set myself on fire. I'd rather jump off a cliff. I'd rather eat shit and *die*.

You're a lying, cheating, despicable piece of shit who likes to hurt women and little boys!"

I slap Tristan so hard across the face he rears back.

"I said that's enough!" my father roars and grabs me by the arm, physically dragging me away from Tristan.

Face as red as my father's now and hands clenching into fists, Tristan tries to follow me only to have Ashley jump in front of him.

"Let her go, Tristan!" Ashley wails and pushes at his chest.

Satisfied now that I've spoken my piece, I try to jerk my arm free of my father's grip. "Let me go, I'm leaving."

"The hell you are," he growls, his fingers tightening as he drags me across the room.

A few heads turn our way, but he ignores them. After dragging me almost to the exit, he finds a secluded corner and finally releases me by giving me a little push.

I stumble, then find my balance and straighten.

"Do you have any idea what you've done?" he snarls at me. "Do you have any idea what you've cost me, you stupid little bitch?!"

Lifting my chin into the air, I meet his angry glare head-on as he steps into me, trying to intimidate me.

I refuse to feel bad, guilty, or even the least bit remorseful for what I did, and I sure as hell won't apologize for it.

He leans in close and jabs his finger at me. "If you think I'll let you get away with this, think again. We had a deal and you've broken it. I, however, will live up to my end. That little boy you care so much about… Well, I hope you're proud of yourself because you've just sealed his fate."

I shake my head in disbelief. Can he even hear himself?

"What did Casey ever do to you? It's over now. Hurting him gains you nothing," I try to reason.

My father's lip curls with contempt. "Hurting him will hurt *you*. Do you feel good about yourself now? I hope you do, because after this… After what you've done, I will make it my life's mission to make sure that's boy's life is a living hell."

Tears of anger and helplessness sting my eyes and it's everything I can do not to release them. To not give him that satisfaction.

"I hate you," I hiss.

And I do, my god, do I truly hate him at this moment.

"Oh, you will," my father says as he grins and straightens away from me. "You'll certainly hate me after I'm done with you and the boy. Perhaps I'll even go after that gym rat of yours. Yes, that's a good idea. I think I'll do that too."

Someone gasps behind my father. "Arthur…"

My father whirls around.

"Valerie," he says with surprise.

Her own eyes glistening with tears, Valerie's voice cracks with accusation. "How could you?"

All at once my father seems to deflate, his anger replaced by worry.

"It's not what you think," he says.

"Not what I think?" Valerie repeats incredulously. "Not what I think?! I heard every word you said."

"I didn't mean it," he claims after a couple of moments and begins to walk toward her. "I spoke in anger. I would never… *never* do those things."

Valerie shakes her head, clearly not buying his excuse. "I knew something was wrong, I just didn't know what."

"Valerie—" my father starts to say as he reaches for her, his hands going for her hands.

Valerie steps out of his reach and jerks her hands away from him. "No, don't you touch me, and don't you say anything more. I don't want to hear it."

"But—" my father tries to say, only to immediately stop when Valerie gives him a look full of contempt.

"We'll talk about *all* of this later, Arthur," she says, not even trying to keep the disdain out of her voice.

Then she turns her attention to me. "Aubrey, I'm leaving. You're more than welcome to join me."

I'm not sure I completely trust Valerie despite how kind she has treated me in the past, but I'd much rather leave with her than stay here and endure more of my father's threats and wrath.

Emotionally pulling myself together, I nod at her. "I'll join you, thank you."

Without looking in my father's direction, I follow her out, feeling his glare burning into my back.

Valerie doesn't speak, doesn't say a word until we're in the limo and pulling away from the hotel.

Then, her composure completely melting away, she grabs me by the hands and gives them a gentle squeeze.

There's so much emotion on her face and in her eyes, I finally crack, bursting open with the tears I've been holding back as she says, "Aubrey, I promise I won't let your father make good on any of his threats, but you must tell me what's going on. If I'm going to protect you, I need to know everything."

CHAPTER NINETEEN

EMMETT

Fight night. The time where fears, doubts, and hurts can be ignored. The time where I can be the monster I've always knew I was deep down.

The guy who likes to cause pain and take pain.

No more running away from my demons. No more hiding from the pain of loss and the pain of redemption. No, it's time to say fuck everything and be the one who claims his fucking life back.

A light rapping on the door snaps me out of focus. I've been focusing for the past thirty minutes on keeping my heart at a steady rhythm.

Who the fuck is interrupting me?

A quick glance at the clock shows me I have ten minutes until the fight.

Snapping my fingers at Casey, I point to the door. "Get rid of whoever the fuck that is."

"On it!" Casey says as he hops out of the chair he's been occupying since we got here.

Casey is as tightly wound as I am. He's been amped up on this shot of vengeance for both him and his dad.

Tommy never got the resolution he deserved for being cold-cocked inside the ring.

Fucking bitch ass Jamey and that cheap shot have been playing over and over in my head.

You just don't swing on a fucking trainer who didn't do shit. What a fucking pussy. I'm gonna whoop his fucking ass. I'm going to take a long time doing it too. I'm going to punish his ass. I'm going to make him my little bitch.

And when he thinks it's over, I'm going to hurt him some more.

"Bree?!" Casey gasps loudly. "Fuck off!"

Well fuck, there goes me keeping my heart rate at a good rhythm.

Turning toward the door to the little room I've been sequestered in since I entered the building, I see the love of my life standing in the doorway.

Casey glares at her then he slams the door in her face.

I start snorting with laughter, I can't help it. The look that was on Bree's face is priceless. She looked so crushed and defeated, like she had so many things she wanted to say to us.

"Dude," I mock whisper.

Casey starts snickering as he looks at me and shrugs. "Want me to let her in?"

I hop out of the chair I've been sitting in. "Yeah, let's see what the fuck she has to say."

Casey swings the door open but there's no one there. "Uh-oh."

"Ah, shit," I groan, and step up to the doorway.

After looking both ways, I see Bree walking away with her shoulders slumped.

"Hey, get your ass back here!" I shout at her.

She turns and her eyes widen at the sight of Casey and me laughing at her.

Shaking her head, she starts to walk back, and I look at Casey. "Be nice."

"Of course, I'm not a total jerk," he says before he gives me a smirk. "But I'm not calling her Dad."

"What?" I ask, confused. "Why the hell would you call her Dad?"

"Cause you're my mom," Casey laughs.

"You little fucking..." I trail off as Bree's eyes widen even more at the way I start to swing at Casey's head.

"Don't let him hurt me, Bree!" Casey cries out before he runs back into the room, acting like I beat him or something.

"What the hell?!" Bree asks, looking between Casey and me as if we're crazy.

Reaching out, I try to grab her hand, but she snatches it away before I can make contact.

What the fuck?

"Bree," I say, "What are you doing here?"

And why the fuck can't I touch you? I want to ask, but I keep my question silent. I need to know what the fuck is going on and looking desperate to feel that connection we shared is not going to help.

"You're hitting Casey?" she asks, staring at me with accusing eyes.

"What?" I blink

"He is!" Casey wails from the room behind me.

Ah, fuck.

"No, I'm not. Well, not with any real harm. He keeps calling me Mom..." I say, and feel like a fucking idiot.

But what the fuck? She doesn't need to know this shit. She doesn't have any say in what Casey and I do anymore.

"Why is he calling you Mom?" she asks, the anger in her voice slowly abating.

"Why the fuck are you here?" I ask, and fuck, now it looks like I slapped her across the face.

Those might not have been the best words to use. From the way tears instantly appear in her eyes, I can tell she's already hurting as much as I've been.

"I… I…" she stutters, and then looks around the room.

She looks like a scared rabbit ready to bolt at any second.

"You what?" Casey asks as he comes to stand beside me.

I want to gather her up in my arms. I want to sweep her up and kiss those plush lips with every ounce of my being. But I need to hear her words, I need to understand how she could leave us.

I have to restrain every single instinct to take her back because I saw what she did to Casey.

She looks at Casey and me. I know she can see that she fucked us both up and that she's gotta win us both back. If she's even here to do that. She could have come back just to tell us to fuck off and leave her alone…

We all just stare at each other, waiting for someone to make the first move.

Someone starts pounding on the door behind Bree, causing us all to jump.

"Five minutes, Angel!" Chase shouts through the door.

"Angel?" Bree shakes her head at the name. "Who's Angel?"

"Me," I say with a sigh.

I fucking hate the name, but it's stuck with me through the years, whether I wanted it to or not.

"Yeah, he called himself the Angel of Death one time

when he was doing a promo," Casey helpfully adds from my side.

Bree starts smirking. "Really? That's kind of… corny."

"I know, I know. As soon as I said it, I knew I fucked up. Now that's the ring name I've been given," I say, then try to get back on topic. "What's going on, Bree?"

"I… I had it all planned out on how I would explain what happened.." she says before biting her lip.

"But?" I ask.

"But it all sounds like excuses, like a pity party," she says.

"What's the real reason then?" I ask and cross my arms across my chest like I'm trying to protect my heart from the abuse it's already sustained.

She takes a deep breath, steeling herself, before saying, "That guy that pushed me outside the gym… Well, he was my ex-boyfriend… and my dad really wanted me to marry him. Wanted me to marry him so bad he tried to blackmail me into it…"

She launches into a story that sounds like something straight out of a soap opera, and the way she keeps glancing at Casey, I know I'm probably only getting half of it. And shit, I probably wouldn't believe it if it was coming out of anyone else's mouth.

But I do because it's coming out of hers.

When she finally finishes, my arms slide down to my sides on their own accord.

Well, *fuck*. That's not exactly what I was expecting.

"So why didn't you tell me all this?" I ask as I take a step forward, my hands reaching out this time to take both of hers.

"Because he has a lot of power and money, and he threatened you both. He told me he would ruin you with the pictures he had of you and get Casey sent to his mom," she says before she suddenly looks mortified, like she let out a secret.

Casey starts shaking his head. "No way, he can't do that."

"He can!" she insists with tears in her eyes. "He's the fucking governor. He has so many connections and so much money from my stepmother… he can hurt you both with a snap of his fucking fingers."

Shaking my head, I frown at her. "He couldn't do that, Bree."

Tears start falling from her eyes. "He can. He has all the pictures and he got a private investigator…"

Reaching up, I brush away her tears and pull her tightly to my chest. "Casey, is it okay if I tell her?"

Shrugging his shoulders, Casey looks from me to Bree. "I don't care, it's not even a thing in my life."

"Tell me what?" Bree asks as she clutches at my chest, her fingers wrapped tightly in my shirt.

"His mom overdosed on heroine three years back and died," I say, and hug her tightly to me.

"Yeah, the only mom I have is Emmett. He's my mommy dearest!" Casey says, but I can tell he's a little shaken from all this heavy shit going on.

Pulling Casey into our hug, I wrap my arms around them both tightly. "Your dad sounds like a douchebag, but he couldn't have done anything to me or Casey."

"But… But… he had pictures and he knew things… He had pictures of you passed out in your yard," she continues to argue but her voice is growing weaker.

"Seriously?" Casey asks from inside the hug.

He's squirming around but I'm not letting either of them go just yet.

"Shut up, it was a dark time for me," I say with a self-depreciating laugh.

"He said he was going to ruin you," Bree says with a sniffle.

"Not like I haven't already done that myself," I say. "Look... I looked into you and your family the moment you disappeared. I know who your dad is. He could try to ruin me, but I doubt it would work. I'm kinda rich, kinda good looking, and a sports celebrity."

"What?" Bree asks, pulling back to look at me.

"The world loves a good comeback story. Your dad would have fucked up royally if he tried to really fuck with me," I say confidently.

He would have too. I don't like shit getting out about how much money I have, but I'm not poor. Not by any means. I've made a shit ton of money fighting and investing, and money means I could write my own narrative.

He would have looked bad as fuck trying to smear the guy trying to piece his life back together. All I would have to do is call a sports broadcasting channel and offer them my story. They love putting together little documentaries about sports stars.

Fuck, I even know the music I would put to some of my scenes. Normally, I would never agree to be in one of those damn things, but if I was forced by Bree's father...

Fucker wouldn't know what hit him.

But she couldn't possibly know any of this, could she? I mean, she's even admitted to me that she's never really watched the sport. She doesn't even know about her own stepbrother's fame. She'd never even heard of me before she came to the gym that one day.

Fuck, I can see why she thought she had to do something to protect us. Fucking bastard of a father was using her ignorance to his benefit, trying and almost successfully scaring her into whatever Machiavellian schemes he has.

"Let's fucking go!" Chase yells as he slams open the door to the dressing room.

Seeing Bree crying in my arms, he stops dead in his tracks.

"What the fuck?" he asks before stomping over to us.

"Give me a minute," I say with a frown. "We're trying to work some shit out."

"I gave you a minute. They're getting ready to start your entrance without you," he growls at me. "Bree, why are you here? I mean, what happened?"

All at once everyone but me starts to talk. Then Dale sweeps into the room and starts screaming at us all.

The bastard even starts snarling at Bree's tears.

Fuck.

"Stop!" I bellow to everyone.

When silence finally falls, I say, "I have a fight, we'll talk this shit out when it's over."

Pulling Bree close, I kiss her as hard as I can, trying to push every single gut-wrenching emotion I have inside me into her.

I love this damn woman, and I'll never let her leave me again.

Her lips open to mine, and just like me she puts all the words she has for me in the kiss. It's scorching and searching, loving and binding.

She's not leaving again, I can feel it.

An arm starts to yank me away from the kiss and I hear Dale yelling at me to keep it in my pants.

Fucker.

Shaking my head, I nod at him then look to Bree. "I'll be back."

~

The pounding rhythm of my intro music starts as soon as I walk out of the curtained entrance. The hard beats of I Prevail's song "Bow Down" hit me straight in the chest.

Good fucking choice in music.

Whoever picked that song for me has it right because Jamey Silva is going to be bowing down to my ass.

Jogging quicker than Dale and the group following me, I get to the ring fast enough to see Jamey dancing around like some asshole. When Jamey finally gets a glimpse of me, he's not even phased, he just laughs at me and heads over to his corner of the ring.

Fucker doesn't think he has a thing to worry about. I'm going to enjoy wiping that fucking smirk off his face.

The ref outside of the ring starts checking my gloves over one last time and gives me a quick run through of the rules.

Dale pants a little when he finally catches up and pulls me to the side of the ring. "What the fuck? Couldn't wait for us all?"

"Nope," I say with a shrug. "I'm ready for this shit to start."

Motioning to the ring, Dale says, "Well, get the fuck in there."

Walking into the ring, I feel the mat beneath my feet, and it brings back memories of all the fights I've been through. At first, it's comforting to feel like I'm back home, but then it quickly becomes terrifying.

I look down at the mat and remember not so long ago I laid there with my shoulder in shambles. I can also see Tommy lying there on the mat, knocked out from the cheap shot he got from Jamey.

Each memory has my stomach churning with bile.

What the fuck am I getting myself into?

With all the shouting and yelling coming from all the people in the arena, it feels like I'm going deaf. Like I'm slowly drowning in noise and fear.

My fucking lungs are struggling to get a full breath of air.

"Emmett!" I hear a voice shouting at me, but I can't really figure out from where.

Hands grab my shoulder and all of a sudden I'm facing the referee for the fight, Jim Anders. "You okay?"

Nodding my head slowly has me feeling as if I'm suddenly back in my house, drunk and barely able to focus on what's in front of me.

Looking deep into my eyes, I can tell Jim's about the call the fight right here. He's about to wave his hands at the judges and say I can't competently compete in the match.

Fuck.

The last words I ever heard Tommy say to me ring through my head and I never even got to talk to him after he left that message.

I'll be there soon, brother.

Not soon enough. He's gone and I won't get to see him again for a very long time, if ever.

"Emmett, I gotta hear you say something, buddy. You okay? Can you fight?" Jim Anders asks me.

I'll be there soon, brother.

He's gone, he can't come back. There's no coming back from where he is.

"Fuck!" Anders whispers harshly and turns away from me.

He's about to walk over to the gate of the cage to end the match.

Shit. Fuck!

I gotta fucking do something.

"Jim!" I shout at him. "Come back here!"

Shaking my head, trying to get rid of the haziness that wants to swallow my brain, I give him a thumbs up.

"What the fuck, Emmett? You drugged?" he asks with worry in his eyes.

Jim could lose his job and get in real trouble if he let me fight while he thought I was under the influence.

"No man, sorry. My heads is just… I'm good, I swear," I say to him, and try to get back into the frame of mind I had before I stepped on the mat.

"If I think I need to, I'll stop this fight," he snaps at me before walking over to check on Jamey like none of this just happened.

I need my head in the game, but I can't seem to focus on anything. Words and scenes flood across my mind. And for the life of me I can't keep track of what I really am anymore. Am I going to be the man I want to be? Or should I slink back into my self-imposed exile?

Going through the motions, I walk to center of the cage and just stand here as Jim gives us a quick rundown of the fight. When he's done, I move back to my corner. I didn't even bother raising my gloves to touch with Jamey.

What's the point? I can't remember, all I can think about is these last six months.

Standing in the center of the cage, Jim makes a motion, asking me if I'm ready.

Am I?

Nodding my head, I raise my arm only high enough to acknowledge that I'm ready.

Then I hear Jim shout, "Let's do this. Fight!"

Advancing forward, I raise my hands up in a guard position and try to make myself feel the old routine of fighting.

Routine, fuck, that's a joke.

There is no routine to a fight. You go in and hope to kill your opponent because he sure as fuck wants to do the same to you. It's good to have a plan of attack, but the moment the bell rings, shit gets real and you have to make adjustments on the fly.

Fighting is anything but routine.

Jamey gives me my space, slowly circling the ring with me in the middle. He's hesitant because this isn't my normal. I used to come out with guns blazing, but I just don't know what to do right now.

I feel off-kilter, like the fucking mat is swaying beneath my feet.

Jamey darts in and his fists fly quickly at my face, a one-two combo meant to get at least one of the hits to connect. The right misses, but the damn left rocks my head back, and I feel it.

I feel the fucking pain of someone hitting me.

I feel the pain of all the loss I've been dealing with.

Darting back and away from him, I give my head a good shake. Slowly the world starts to sharpen with crystal clarity. It's like the hood has finally been yanked off my head and I can breathe again.

Taking a deep, soul-burning breath, I look at Jamey and grin at him with a smile that fills my whole fucking face.

Starting to close the distance between us, he says loudly over the crowd noise, "What the fuck are you smiling at, pussy?"

Laughing, I motion for his ass to come get some. "Thanks, man. I needed that."

That stops him for a moment. Stupid fuck has no clue what he woke up inside me.

"Well, you're about to get a lot more of it," he says and sprints the remaining distance to me, trying to do a flying knee to my face.

Stepping to the side, I push his body past me and grin. "My turn."

Squaring up against him, I fake a punch with my left before I snap my right hand at the side of his jaw.

It hits, not hard, but it's enough to snap his head to the side and force him to retreat.

Marching forward, I keep my hands up, snapping out a kick to his thigh. The kick lands and I catch just the smallest wince from him.

Good, I hope that fucking hurts, because it sure hurt my foot.

Fucking fuck, he's got thick ass leg muscles. I forgot that.

He sweeps into my midsection and I feel his shoulder as he tries to take me down. He wants this on the ground and I sure as fuck am in no way ready to do that. I might be fighting with crystal clarity, but I need to tenderize this fucker before I go to the ground.

Stepping wide with my legs, I let him push my ass up against the cage, then I clench up with him as he tries to get leverage to toss my ass onto the floor.

Unfortunately, that's all we do for the next three minutes. We trade maybe ten punches each while he keeps going for a takedown.

He wants to get this shit on the ground, where he can work on my shoulder.

Finally, at the one-minute-left mark, I get a big knee to his face as he tries once again to take me down.

Rushing in, I try to capitalize on the stunned expression on his face, but I don't get to his falling body quick enough to take advantage of him.

If was in better condition, I probably would have been able to get in some really heavy blows to his face. But despite all the working out I've done, I'm still not as fast as I could be.

Settling for getting top mount on his body, I sit down on his bucking hips and slam my fist down into his face as hard as I can. Hammerfist after hammerfist slams down on his arms, preventing me from doing too much damage.

But the times I do manage to connect slowly fuel that burning in my gut to hurt him.

When the bell sounds signaling the end of the first round, I slowly get up off his bitch ass and turn my back, walking away like he isn't even a concern.

I hear some muttering from Jamey about me being a pussy as he heads to his corner, but whatever. The first round is over, and I've already proved he isn't going to steam roll over my ass.

Didn't prove much besides that, but baby steps, I guess.

I sit down on the little chair Dale slides behind my legs.

He checks my face and eyes for a moment before muttering, "You gonna play pussyfoot out there or you gonna do something?"

"Well—" I start to say, and he snaps.

"That was a fucking rhetorical question, you jackass. Get the fuck out there and score some fucking points. If this dumpster fire of a beginning goes to the fucking judges, you're going to lose," he snarls out at me.

"Right," I say.

He's got a fucking point, if I don't do some fighting, this shit is going to drag on until the final bell and then it goes to the score cards. No one wants a match to ever go to the judges, it's too easy for them to say the other guy's the winner.

Dale gives my face a rough slap. "Wake the fuck up!"

Did he just hit me?

"Did you just hit me?" I growl out at him.

"No, I slapped you like a bitch. Now get out there and prove me wrong!" he screams in my face.

Standing up to get out of my way, he snatches up the stool out from under me. "You got a lot of people saying you ain't got the heart to win anymore."

Watching him march away from me has me seething fucking mad. That motherfucker called me a bitch.

Fuck that shit.

I'm not going to dig my own grave out there in the ring, I'm going to be the fucking avenging angel.

I'm going to kill someone.

The referee steps into the middle of the ring and looks at Jamey and me. "You ready?"

Nodding my head, I smile a little smile for Jamey.

I'm going to hurt this motherfucker.

"Let's get to it!" Jim yells and motions for us to start.

Time to shine.

My feet carry me across the ring faster than I thought possible as I go in for a flying knee. I miss Jamey's face, but my knee hits his shoulder.

Spinning him sideways gives me time to snap a kick to his ribs, and the kick sends him scurrying back and away from me.

Jamey's face may look set and pissed, but the look in

his eyes says that my attack freaked him the fuck out. He wasn't ready for me to use one of his signature moves against him—the flying knee. That's what knocked me down the last time we fought; it also gave him the chance to fuck my shoulder up.

Grinning at him again, I stalk over to him. He's got his elbow a little closer to his ribcage, as if he's protecting it. He probably doesn't know I've noticed, but I have.

I'm gonna use that.

Moving in, I swing for his face fully knowing he'll block it, but he can't block the knee I drive right into the side of him. It isn't hard enough to break him, but this fight is going to be about picking his ass apart.

Every time he gives me a piece to chew on, I'm going to make him regret it.

We end up in a clench up against the cage walls when I'm able to throw an elbow to his eyebrow that instantly splits the skin.

I can tell it dazes him too because his eyes go a little hazy.

Pulling back and away from him to give myself enough room, I start throwing punches as hard as I can. Each one connects with either his arms, the side of his head, or his face.

I'm doing damage to him now.

Doing damage is my specialty, that's another reason they called me the Angel. I used to fight with perfection. I was precise and efficient, and I would pick apart my opponent before they ever knew what happened.

It could also be because I'm kinda hot too.

My loss to Jamey was entirely my fault. I got sloppy, I grew a big head, and I got lazy. He took advantage of all my errors and made me pay dearly for taking the fight with him as a layup.

I took my fights as a joke toward the end. Not anymore. I know my ass still has a gut, and my abs need a lot of work.

My stomach definitely lets me know that its not ready for all the abuse its going to take when he gets in a solid foot to my side.

I hunch over and Jamey comes in charging for a knockout punch. Guarding my stomach with one arm, I'm able to get a hand up in time to deflect the blow and stop him from hitting my temple.

The instant flash of red though tells me he's cut me over the eyebrow.

"Fucker," I grunt as I push up against him to buy myself some time.

He keeps trying to slam an elbow up against the cut to make it bleed more. It's dirty but not exactly illegal. He wants to blind me with enough blood that there's either a stoppage or I can't see exactly what he's doing.

Pushing my shoulder into his, I wrap my arms up around his chest as I try to heave him up enough to knee him in the ribs.

Each time I get him right where I want him though, he squirms or drops a heavy elbow to my face.

"Fuck!" I shout out my frustration and then do the last thing either of us are expecting.

Sliding my arms down around his waist, I lift him up into the air.

Grunting mentally to myself, *what goes up, must come down*, I slam Jamey down to the mat on his back.

And all the air gets knocked out of him as I land right on top of his stomach.

"Gonna make you my bitch now!" I snarl at him as I sit up fully and start slamming my fists over and over into his face.

Jamey's trying to guard himself, but my arms are like fucking engine pistons. Each blow I rain down is connecting somewhere, his head, his chin, or his temples.

His face quickly becomes a bloody mess as I bust his lip and nose up.

I can tell it's over before the referee even gets between us. Jamey's eyes rolled back with the last punch, and fuck it, I'm not willing to kill the fucker as much as I would love to.

"Fuck!" I scream as I climb off him.

The ref didn't even have time to pull me off. Fuck no. I'm pissed as hell that I screwed up all my damn revenge.

This fucker's out.

"Goddammit!" I scream as I stomp over to my part of the cage and aim a massive doorbuster kick at the chain-link walls.

In floods everyone, all the training staff and doctors.

Dale and Chase rush in to calm me down, but I'm fucking pissed as can be.

It's not until I turn to stalk over to Jamey, who's now sitting up and looking fucking pissed he lost, that I feel the humor of it all.

Right now, as Dale and Chase are getting ready to literally hold me back, I remember Tommy.

He would have laughed his ass off at me for being mad that I won a fight.

It wasn't pretty, it wasn't the knock-down, drag-out fight I was looking for. But looking at Jamey's bloodied face, I can find some peace in knowing the fucker is going to need a lot work to fix the shit I did to his eyebrow and nose.

Looking up at Chase's big, hulking ass, I start smiling and point to my chest. "I put the donuts on your desk."

"I'll fucking kill you," he growls at me, and to the world I bet it looks like he's going to do just that

"Can't, bitch," I say with an even bigger laugh. "I'm going to be your brother-in-law."

Chase's wide, gaping mouth gives me all the happiness I need, and I charge over to the ringside and jump onto the rim.

Sitting with my legs on the fence, I raise my arms into the air and feel the thunderous cheers filling the arena.

This one was for Tommy.

It was short, ugly, and didn't go nearly as planned, but I won it for him and that means everything to me.

I glance over at Dale and Chase. They're pissed but forcing smiles.

And I gather from the way Dale keeps grinning at me that tomorrow I'm going to regret letting the cat out of the bag about the donuts. But if I've got Bree on my side, I don't think any punishment will take the smile off my face.

I can see her out there in the crowd, and right next to her is Casey and his grandparents.

Tommy would have made this whole thing complete, but I know I have to accept that he's gone, and those times are not coming back. The sadness doesn't have to engulf me.

I've got Tommy still looking over my shoulder.

He's watching over us all and laughing at the absurdity of me being pissed that I won.

Bree, I don't know what the fuck she's gone through to

get back to my side, but the fact is she's at my side now. She's here to stay, I can feel it.

Our fucking souls came together during our first kiss and this last one cemented that.

Hopping back down into the ring, I go over to the referee and stand beside him.

It's time for this shit to be official.

"By knockout in the second round, the new Welterweight Champion of the world! Emmett, The Angel, Bailey!" the announcer yells into the microphone.

Jim raises my right arm up in the air, and I can't believe just how recently the same damn arm was almost completely destroyed.

I do a quick interview where I agree that if Jamey wants a rematch, he's got one chance and that's it, then I head for the cage door.

Dale and Chase surround me so that everyone has to give me space as I walk out. They know exactly where I'm headed as I march my way to the front row of the arena, heading straight for Bree and Casey.

Helping first Bree and then Casey over the barricade, I wrap my bloody, sweaty arms around them as we make our way back to the private fighter areas.

Bree clings to my side, giving me a strange look as she looks up at my face.

"What's wrong, baby girl?" I ask her.

"I've just… I've never seen someone fight like that," she stammers and then I feel her arm tightening around me. "It was scary as hell."

"Ah, that was an easy one. I bet the rematch will be much worse," I say.

Looking up at me with wide eyes, she blurts out, "What? I barely survived watching that one!"

"Yeah, he's not going to be happy he lost his belt. I won't be giving it back to him, but it's probably going to be a war next time."

"Oh god, what did I get myself into…" she mutters with a laugh.

I lean down and whisper in her ear, "A family."

"Oh," she says and stares up into my eyes.

Finally able to stop and catch my breath, I pull her into the dressing room and quickly shut the door so that it's only her and me.

"Bree…" I say and for a moment my throat catches.

So many emotions have filled me today that I feel like I'm raw flesh being scraped by sandpaper.

"Emmett, I'm so sorry. I never meant to hurt you and Casey," she says quietly and motions at the door. "All of this is just so crazy and scary… But…"

My heart is breaking watching her voice those fears, but I have to hear them. I have to know where she stands. "But what, Bree?"

Eyes watery, her smile starts small and fearful, but grows into something more. "But I'm here. I'm here for the long haul. No more holding back, no more worrying about other people. All I want in this world, all I need, is you and Casey."

Gently butting my really gross forehead up against hers, I look into her eyes. "You were mine the moment I laid eyes on you, Bree. You just didn't know it."

"Did you really mean it when you said you love me?" she asks.

"With all my fucking heart," I say as I lean down to kiss the lips I've been dreaming about.

A t all the damn places I've shopped, and at all the different times of day, despite my best fucking efforts, I always end up with a squeaky cart. The one with the wheel that pulls the shopping cart one way or the other. I've tried everything, every-fucking-thing, to get one of those nice, smooth rides that lets me shop through the store without every single person looking over at the asshole.

But I always get stuck with the shit one like this one.

Sighing as quietly as I can, I pull my baseball hat down, hoping no one notices the dickhead with the cart. Not that me being incognito is going to help much, each screech of the wheel alerts everyone to my exact position.

Goddammit.

I keep pushing on, bypassing all the junk food aisles, my cart already heavy with meats and vegetables. Now that I've been working even harder at the gym, my gut is gone.

And Bree has been reaping all the rewards.

I've been spending long days at the gym and long blissful nights with her.

She enjoys my hard work, and she's slowly adapting to the fighter lifestyle.

I fucking love it.

After the fight, we spent the night in the hospital getting me checked out. And I think Bree was doubting her sanity a few times for sticking with me. She's never actually seen someone get stitches or endure a cracked rib.

I didn't notice it during the fight, but that fucker cracked a rib on me, so I had to go through an entire fucking ordeal before I could get her home.

It was worth it though to see the shocked look on her face when I started grinning like an asshole as the doc went through the list of my injuries.

I know it's probably fucked, but a lot of us fighters keep a tally of all the shit that's happened to our bodies over the years. When I started telling her about some of my more interesting injuries, like the time I broke two knuckles, she just groaned and turned away from me.

She didn't have any complaints though when I got her home and showed her that I wasn't going to let any of that shit slow me down.

Yeah, that was a good fucking night. She came home with me and I haven't let her out of my sight since.

Fuck, these past few months have been amazing. Casey has been working hard at the gym with me. He's also been working as hard as he can at school. He knows that he won't catch a break with me and Dale riding his ass.

Bree picked up her old job at the gym, and her father is no longer in the picture. Fucking prick has been going through some shit. From the reaction I got out of Chase and Bree's mom, nobody knew exactly how bad things were for her or what was happening to her. We threw around the idea of pressing charges against him but dropped it after all the shit about him started hitting the press.

His wife divorced his ass and he was forced to resign from his position as governor. According to Bree's step-mom, Valerie, the divorce was a long time in coming too. She was starting to catch on to all his shady crap. After talking about it with Bree, we figure that's why he pushed her so hard to marry Tristan. Dickhead knew he was going to lose all his money, so he was trying to use Bree to get more.

I don't think a day goes by that I don't see some new scandalous shit he was involved in printed in the paper.

Fucker deserves all the hell he's getting.

And he ever tries to mess with Bree again, I'll give him more.

I turn my cart into the alcohol and party supply aisle. I've been in this aisle so many damn times, I could probably find it in my sleep.

I'm just minding my own business when some jackass bumps their cart into mine. "Yo, what the fuck are doing in this aisle, man?"

I turn and hold up the happy birthday banner I picked out up to Brett. "Trying to get some stuff for Casey's birthday."

"Oh…" he frowns at me like he's trying to catch me in a lie.

I'd be suspicious of me too if I were him. I was a fucking bad drunk when he caught me in the store all those months ago.

"You, uh, need any help?" he asks as he peers into my cart.

Rolling my eyes, I shove his shoulder away. "Yeah, dickhead, you just volunteered to bring the soda."

"Wait, what?" he asks as he looks back at me.

"You and Mandy can bring the kids over and show us newlyweds how to throw a kid's birthday party," I say with a grin.

Brett starts to slowly back up. "Uh, we might be busy…"

Fucking pussy doesn't do kid parties… Well, we'll see about that.

Grabbing my phone out of my pocket, I make a show of pulling up my list of contacts of for him.

Before he can snatch the phone out of my hand, I push the call through.

"Hey Mandy, this is Emmett… Hey, did Brett remember to tell you about Casey's birthday party this weekend?" I say into the phone and smirk at his stupid ass.

"No, he must have forgot! What do you guys need us to bring?" Mandy asks cheerfully.

"If you could bring some soda, that would be great!" I say with a smile.

"Sounds good, we'll be there!" Mandy says before hanging up.

Brett's phone dings twice before he can even start to give me shit.

"See ya Saturday!" I say before I turn my cart away from him.

Even the fucking squeak of the wheel makes me smile.

"Fuckin' dick," Brett grumbles at me before he catches up to me.

He sticks by my side for a couple of minutes before he bumps his cart into my again.

"Dude, you got anymore college douchebags we need to fuck up?" he asks.

For fuck's sake! I can't believe he's bringing this shit up here.

Yeah, the guys and I may have paid Tristan a little visit. And I may have broken his nose and gave him a concussion for fucking with my kid and girl.

"Could you at least keep your fucking voice down when you talk about felonies?" I whisper harshly.

Shrugging his shoulders, Brett looks around the empty aisle we're standing in. "Ain't nobody around."

"You know what Dale will do to us if we get him busted for beating up college boys with us?" I point out, but I'm not truly worried about getting caught.

No, I'm pretty sure Tristan got the message, after I pounded it into him a little, that if he tries to retaliate or pull any new shit, the surveillance video of what he did will get out.

Eyes widening, Brett laughs. "I'm too pretty for jail."

"God help me," I groan and then wave at him. "See you Saturday, pretty boy."

I'm done looking at his ass, and I'm done being in this store. I need to get home to my swelling bride and boy.

It's been so long since I've hugged them, I think I'm starting go through withdrawal.

The End

Emmett's Playlist: https://spoti.fi/37ahEIF

The Jester - Badflower
Carry the Weight - We Came As Romans
Crooked Soul - Dayseeker
Low - Wage War
Public Service Announcement - Of Mice & Men
Hurricane - I Prevail
Hereafter - Architects
When Everything Means Nothing - Fit For A King
My Love (Justin Timberlake cover) - We Came As Romans
Wishing Wells - Parkway Drive
Bow Down - I Prevail

Bree's Playlist: https://spoti.fi/2TMJ7fA
Be Like You (feat. Broods) - Whethan, Broods
The Moments I'm Missing (Stripped Version) - Nina
Nesbitt
What's Left Inside - Conquer Divide
In Your Eyes - ASTR
Drift - So Below
You and I - PVRIS
Fade to Blue - Roniit
New Fears - Lights
Overgrown - machineheart
Wolves - Selena Gomez

STALK US

Seriously, stalk us and be our James.

Join our Facebook reader group where we talk about our books, give exclusive sneak peeks, offer random fan appreciation giveaways, access to ARCs, and live chats where you can ask us anything.

Facebook reader group: Izzy's Sweeties and Sean's Side Chicks: https://www.facebook.com/groups/IzzysSweeties

Our Instagram: https://www.instagram.com/seanandizzy/

Never miss our next release.
Follow us on Facebook: https://www.facebook.com/authorizzysweet/
https://www.facebook.com/authorseanmoriarty/

Follow us on Amazon: amazon.com/author/izzysweet
amazon.com/author/seanmoriarty

Follow us on Bookbub: https://www.bookbub.com/
authors/izzy-sweet

Join our no-spam mailing list. No spam ever, promise.
Only get emailed when we have a new release or sale:
https://dl.bookfunnel.com/bbfg23ehl8

Check out our website: www.dirtynothings.com

Izzy Sweet & Sara Page – The one and same brain.

Sean Moriarty — The real life alpha bad boy that Izzy tamed.

Residing in Cincinnati, Ohio, Izzy and Sean are high school sweethearts that have celebrated 14 wedding anniversaries, though they've been together since they were teenagers – over nineteen years.

Both avid and voracious readers, they share a great love and appreciation for a great story, and attribute their early role-playing days as the fledgling beginnings of their joint writing career.

You can see more of our works at our website - www.dirtynothings.com

ALSO BY IZZY AND SEAN

Disciples Crossover

Broken Wings: Royal Bastards MC

(Featuring Jude and Simon)

Disciples

Keeping Lily (Lucifer & Lily)

Stealing Amy (Andrew & Amy)

Buying Beth (Johnathan & Beth)

Breaking Meredith (Simon & Meredith)

Taking Meghan (Gabriel & Meghan)

Trapping Sophia (James & Sophia)

The Disciples: A Dark Romance Collection

The Pounding Hearts Series

Banging Reaper (Chase & Avery)

Slamming Demon (Brett & Mandy)

Bucking Bear (Max & Grace)

Breaking Beast (Alexander and Christy)

The Pounding Hearts Bundle

Pounding Angel (Emmett & Bree)

Propositioning Love (Zoe & Bryce)

By Sean Moriarty

Gettin' Lucky

Gettin' Dirty

Star Joined Series

Craving Maul

Taming Ryock

By Izzy Sweet

Letting Him In

Stepbrother Catfish